To Erwin,
with best wishes,
[illegible]

CRUMP'S TERMS

By the same author

POETRY
The Loss of India
Jets from Orange
The Violent West

AUTOBIOGRAPHY
Confessions of a Native-Alien

FICTION
Statement against Corpses
(*stories, with B. S. Johnson*)
The Contradictions
The Murder of Aziz Khan
The Incredible Brazilian: The Native
The Incredible Brazilian: The Beautiful Empire

Crump's Terms

a novel by

Zulfikar Ghose

M

SBN: 333 10744 6

First published 1975 by
MACMILLAN LONDON LTD
London and Basingstoke
Associated companies in New York
Dublin Melbourne Johannesburg and Madras

Printed in Great Britain by
The Barleyman Press
Bristol

HE WALKED in hushpuppied quiet as though the flagstones of the yard were consecrated ground. He stopped where the gym wall ended and leaned against it. Leaning, he remembered the buttresses of a cathedral; which one, he could not tell, could not immediately name; not a fault in his memory this, he said to himself, leaning, remembering: an indication really of the unimportance of the particular information. St Paul's, Wells, Cologne, Chartres, Canterbury, Rheims, Salamanca, Guildford, Orleans, Berlin – an incantation on his tongue this, he told himself, deciding there need not be any significance in the order in which he remembered the names, simply an incantation and not an attempt to summon a particular memory (To summon, the quotation, too, urged itself on his mind although the association was inevitably irrelevant, the spectre of a Rose), simply a pleasure he took in rolling words, the vast nouns, on his tongue: Crump, who had memories, incantating, reminded himself to observe precisely the procedures of the intellect – otherwise how else could thinking advance thought? he simultaneously asked himself while remembering, while rejecting the quotation, while silently muttering the monotonous but lovely incantation accompanied by the nodding of his head. The pebbledash wall he supported or was supported by had a texture which compelled attention, wanting a hand to pass over the rough, monstrously enlarged nail-filing surface, and it was there in the corner of his eye while he remarked, his hand playing a harp on the pebbledash, that he had never been able to bypass a cathedral city. Coventry, Munich, Burgos. The frilly spires in the air. Stone, smooth or weathered, but never pebbledash, never a bastardy, restored or black with the fires of air-raids, sandstone or granite or marble. But must entangle himself, never bypass, with the city traffic, sweat it out behind the plastic steering-wheel of his Volkswagen while his heels went sore with the constant shifting of feet, braking and changing gears. Leaning, he remembered, a plane coming down to land on Heathrow also in his eye, his ear having told him already that it was a Trident and therefore a B.E.A. flight and therefore very likely coming from Paris or Rome or Amsterdam or Frankfurt or Moscow or Copenhagen or fifty-nine other European cities, another chant, another insistence of information somehow acquired by simply having been alive and having lived in London pressing itself to be acknowledged by the intellect or by that part of the brain which delighted in observing peripheral trivia: as if publicity brochures were encyclopaedias, he remembered, leaning. God, he thought, compulsively looking up to see if the Trident had unlocked its wheels, Thou art holier than Thou. God, in Thy rubbersoled kingdom with Thy methods of a plainclothes policeman, creeping up on godless Crump. The Notre Dame, the Sacré Cœur. And at this moment the entire attention of Heathrow, from the Control Tower to the spectators on the Waving Base on Europa Building, is on the Trident hitting the asphalt with its rear wheels and easing its nose forward until the front wheels touch the ground, its engines reversing and six hundred miles an hour come to nothing, all the cities of Europe come to a stop in front of the man in blue, or is it yellow or white, overalls waving the ping-pong bats on the apron. The final revving, the final burning up of fuel eats up a hospital's supply of oxygen until the engines deflate themselves into a silence of exhaustion. All the world's a stage but the maker was such a master of acoustics that his own voice is never heard. Crump thought, having seen the passengers come down and one or two wave to a person recognized or half-recognized on the Waving Base on Europa Building. Thought Crump. Who was readylipped with the usual quotations; who would look up at the sky, as now, leaning against the gym wall, where the gym wall ended, and see a frowning Prospero there; sometimes, not always. For the sky could be mercilessly blue. And sensations, memories, expectations, apprehensions, or a cherry-red Aston Martin DB6 with black leather upholstery and smoked-glass windows, his gloved hands on the wood-rim steering-wheel, cruising at one hundred and twenty miles an hour between Bordeaux and Biarritz, that road through the fragrant pine, or questions he had not been able to resolve, recently especially why *Othello* was ultimately unsatisfactory, were there too, apart from the sky and the pebbledash and the thought that of course not *all* Heathrow turned its attention to the Trident landing, for the mechanics preparing planes for take-off, the drivers of fuel tankers, the chauffeurs of V.I.P. cars and the security men who could, if they wanted to, turn to look at the Trident landing would not inevitably do so, the event being ordinary and recurrent. Immediate sensation and thought were not the only reality, he told himself, thinking of the things he was thinking about and remembering that Aston Martin did not call their red cherry red but Dubonnet Rosso (there being worlds of difference between the subtle gradations of snobbery), it occurred to him, the green blazers and the green grass across the railway line as two, only two, of the things in his sight. It was a fundamental truth, hardly worth remarking upon, he remarked to himself, that vision saw more than it looked at. There were voices from the tuck-shop queue which had formed along the adjacent wall. Crump, the leather-bound lexicon among libraries of paperbacks, opened, readied himself to make an entry while two boys argued a fine point of language (within his hearing also was the Central Line train, aluminium coaches flashing the sun back at him from the distance, across the fence there, here in suburban Middlesex).

– What's a baby turd? asked the first boy.

– A shitette, said the second.

– No, arseface, that's a mummy turd.

– If a shitette's a mummy turd, what's a baby turd then?

– Why, a turdle!

The first boy laughed aloud and the second said, That's spastic! Crump smiled, leaning still, hands in pockets now, prepared to forget the pebbledash, as if he could forget anything! but the lexicon had printed, his unfailing memory would remember.

shitette, *n. fem,* excrescence of the feminine variety. [Deriv. vulg., attrib. to Peacock, 2A, Pinworth School.]

turdle, *n. neut.* presumed progeny of male and female types of excrescence. [Deriv. vulg., attrib. to Peacock, 2A, Pinworth School.]

turdle, *v. i.* to evacuate with difficulty during state of constipation. [Deriv. Crump.]

spastic, *n. neut. & a.* corrupt. Pinworth School slang for any thing or person odd, flabbergasting, surprising, brilliant, witty, poor, disgusting, broken, injured, beautiful, obscene, or in any way ordinary or extraordinary. Often abbr. to *spas* – pronounce spas to rhyme with *as.* [Deriv. vulg., attrib. to Pinworth School.]

But he did not laugh, only smiled, taking language seriously. He stood buttressing the gym wall, helpless as Harpo whom, too, he remembered in curly-headed detail, the big cop saying Whatta you doin' here, prohpin' up the wall? And when Harpo is scolded away by the cop the wall crashes down. Indeed, indeed, cathedrals, too, need their clowns, the poor fools to prop them up.

The cathedrals of Europe will fall and the building of new ones will be an exercise in architectural virtuosity, a solving of mechanical problems with modern materials, the severe aesthetics of functionalism.

He pondered the hypothesis he had formulated and looked for failures of precision. He remembered the dilapidated Dom in East Berlin. Fallen masonry and dust were heaped as little altars in the decaying shell of the cathedral; though there had been workers around and the sound of tools being lifted (*precision*, Crump!), implements, then, being lifted and dropped echoing in the mournful emptiness (Crump!), well, simply an emptiness, then, but an absolute one, an arena for tragic introspection, a silent breast-beating. He could not tell from the actions of the workers, when he had watched the actions, much of the time he had not watched the actions, he had not come to do so, whether they were demolishing or reconstructing, both procedures requiring slow and methodical labour, and one could not tell, Crump could not tell, not having been there before and never having gone there again, but having been there only at that time, that one time, on a rainy afternoon, whether demolition or reconstruction was in progress. At any rate, God had gone from the Dom, moved out with all his candles, holy water and incense to find an abode elsewhere, a reincarnation on some other ground, in some other stone. Crump could not tell what was heaped in the dark corners. And wondered if anyone attended to the dark corners or whether only a Berkeleyan God kept an eye there, proving existence of dust and decaying matter where proof was both unnecessary and irrelevant. God sulked in the dark corners, having been booted out of the centre, publicly disgraced, the decorations stripped from his breast. The mad old General, cracking his foul-tempered whip on the parade ground, had been overtaken by a *coup*, his autocratic mouth gagged. Crump had stood beside the heaped masonry and looked where the pews should have been. He had preached.

He had watched the burghers of Berlin listen to him. Oh, he could lift his hooded eyelids to stress a point, Archbishop Crump. He could look down his purpleveined nose and raise a chubby freckled hand. He could intone unintelligible Latin, make the burghers bow their heads in feigned understanding, patiently suffering the discomfort of their high stiff collars, fingering a gold chain, oh, he could make the bosomburdened ladies look up, eyes afire. The saliva could trickle down his chin while his lips intoned, while the weight of his voice became a millstone of guilt offering the burghers no escape from the diminution of their souls. Why such mockery, Crump? he could ask himself.

Until a worker removed the curtain of sacking from a window and the change in the intensity of the light showed him the dust he had been breathing for so long.

You who kneel, remember Saint Hilary who was once kind to the dust in East Berlin, who chanted a benediction in an emptiness. And who was profane with a vengeance.

Outside in the wet, workers were going home on bicycles and mopeds, and two old ladies left the museum where they worked, stepping into puddles as though circumnavigation were impossible, sharing an umbrella.

Old stone, old stone, Europe. Restoration, renovation, a face-lift when youth is irretrievably past. But not in East Berlin. Black, grey, drab old stone.

A few yards from him was the wire netting which fenced the playground. The green-blazered boys, the lion-and-unicorn-crested blazers, the gold-and-red embroidered crests, the boys in their unbuttoned green blazers appeared to his vision as a moving blur. White, red and black plastic balls, with their moulds imitating the leather panels of a football, were being kicked; so many of them, rising and falling in arcs, trajectories and parabolas; tennis balls being thrown up high into the sky; a constellation; the orbiting spheres; satellites; moonprobers; but to him splashings of colour, definitions and redefinitions of shapes, two-dimensional forms; so that he could look and shut his eyes quickly, look and shut his eyes again as though his eyelids were the shutter of a camera and he was taking pictures; for he could do that – oh, what could he not do to play tricks upon himself that he was there and not there? – look for an instant on the crazy activity around him, shut his eyes and hold the actions his vision had taken in during that instant. Instamatic Crump could click away the hours of boredom. Not boredom only. It was also a way of making pictures to himself or of teasing himself with the notion that it was possible – difficult, difficult, but possible – to put an end to the endless process of growth and decay, of presence and absence, of shift, change, alteration, even reversal of appearance, and to say that this picture is what it all is. Crump, a Wittgenstein among children's games, a mind defining words; what it all is. Which was one reason, he supposed, why he could enjoy being in Berlin, East or West, not knowing the words people spoke there; for one's ignorance of a language creates a silence and one sees pictures only. Supposed Crump. One looks for gestures. *Einbahnstrasse* he knew from the *A.A. Continental Handbook*, pronounced it cuddling the plastic steering-wheel, Volkscrump touring the deserts of civilization, but he did not need to know; the thick white arrow on the blue roadsign was all the information he needed. The voices continued around him, the shouting, the screaming, the calling of names and the swearing which he affected not to hear; but scribe Crump, the ancient wrinklebrowed grammarian of dry, academic wit who always laughed drily at Hamlet's answers to Polonius, whether at the theatre or reading the play or remembering the scene, worked away at the lexicon with a penholder which he dipped absentmindedly in a stone bottle of ink, flicking away, also without looking away from the writing in front of him, enough inkdrops to turn the spotlessly white dog – a cartoon he had seen in *Punch* (twenty years ago?) – who lay asleep on his right into a Dalmatian. The metamorphosis of inattention, or of shifting attention, changed perspective, gave to vision a startling revelation, for O my god, he could say, who had said it many, many times.

He walked towards the fence. This is what it all is. A fence. Criss-crossing wire. A partition. An obstacle. Positions for chessmen.

There had been barbed-wire when he drove into Berlin; the symbolic tank; the Wall. Buddha-eyed Crump walked with timetabled steps, asking himself, Why must I remember the desolation of Europe? while a line from some song insisted upon being hummed or uttered, and he added to his question – What is this city they call Mahagonny? – which brought to his mind the image of a canal in Amsterdam, the houses along it, the picture-frame windows and the prostitutes seated behind the glass: spit out your chewing-gum now, take a deep breath and enter, O groomed sensualist. And the rusted anchor discarded by the roadside on the edge of the canal; an old empire rotting.

There was a low wall at the foot of the fence; where he must stand, blow his referee's whistle, which he used also for taking football, and hope for the noise to come to an end and for the boys to fall into ordered lines, form by form. A fat hope. He looked up and kept his eyes open, deciding not to click the shutter of his eyelids, not, not now, not now, to compose pictures to himself. Rollei Crump, zoomlensed Hilary, the aperture kept open for too long an exposure of Europe.

What machinery was it within him, working at high speed, recorded in a succession of one-five-hundredth-of-a-second shots stills of a boy stooping to pick up a tennis-ball, another walking away from the tuck shop, eating crisps from a cellophane bag, two boys looking up at a plane, a Boeing, his ears informed him, a third standing next to them, Nash, he recognized, looking at the plane through a pair of opera glasses – could he have stolen them from the Aldwych when he took a party, which included Nash, to see *Henry V*? Very likely (An example of an eye-rhyme, Nash, he had told Nash in one lesson, would be Thomas Nash/Needs a wash) – one boy dribbling a dirty white plastic ball, yes it was a Boeing, he saw, Air India, come from Bombay, about to land at Heathrow, and, Crump knew, scheduled to take off for New York an hour and a half later, who knew nothing of Bombay nor of New York but saw the plane as on the apex of a triangle, reflecting the two cities on the two points of its base, bazaars and skyscrapers, heat and fur coats, now it is autumn and the falling fruit, but whose journey into oblivion, who's journeying?

Crump, a walking dictionary of the usual quotations, took another stride, ringing the bell on the period to another thought, succession of thoughts, the commonplace and inescapable futilities, which, he insisted, could be summed up by one word, shambles, or, if one preferred to be portentous, life, a capital L if you like, Life, the Meaning of, Life, the Purpose of, index entries for the vain. Shrug your shoulders, O bibliophile thumbing through a dusty tome, give it the V sign; turn away, turn away.

Now I ask you, he had demanded of a sixth-form group – he lifted a foot, decided to walk away from the two boys swinging satchels at each other (only the younger boys carried satchels, from the third year on they were already weighted with responsibility and carried heavy briefcases) – to whom he could talk freely, if we grant that the time-scale of the play is relative, a few of the boys, he noticed, clung on to their satchels and briefcases during break, already possessive, already conditioned to look after their petty property, is not, when you think of it finally, is not Othello wrong with *Othello*?

He had preferred to remain a spectator and an examiner whose business was the scrutiny of words. Leaving England annually for a visual feast of Europe, sensual satiation there made him hungry for the more wholesome diet of the language he knew, served and was succoured by. Why, then? he was beginning to wonder, ask, demand. You can repeat *Why* ten thousand times and all you get at the end is a question mark, he said to himself.

But that was not true, returning from Europe with his senses wreathed in the aroma of an Upmann cigar, that had never been true; observe, Crump, who demand precision, how an attempted neatness, a slight alliteration, how the old habits of language compel false utterances.

Strolling among schoolchildren, Crump paused, hanging his head in self-criticism. No, that had never been true at all, he admitted.

Grey worsted trousers on dark brown brushed pigskin, the

trousers falling neatly about the shoes; there was dignity in that; but he looked up again, taking another stride. Rose-bushes outside the prefab science lab, and, not incredibly, he had noticed it in other Novembers, a rose blooming as if it were June. June's twice June since she breathed it with me, also came to mind, inevitably; the burden of words. Frieda was tolerant even though he never wilfully wanted to be obscure. She could always look away or wonder to herself if her liquid eye make-up had not dried and begun to crumble. Or she could ask a question which was unrelated to what he had been saying.

He walked through the gate where the flagstones ended and the asphalt began, where the strollers and the idlers gave way to footballers, players of spontaneous ball-games which took the form of throwing a ball up and catching it or whamming it on someone's head, gave way also to the bullies. Though the morning was mild enough for cricket, no one brought a bat in the Christmas term, doing so perversely in the wettest May. His eyes scanned the playground and sought out Jim Sutton, an advance scouting for the enemy's position. Jim Sutton, an abandoned bastard from the Home, more blackheads tacked into his face than pins on the overcrowded staff notice-board, saw him, too, and laughed loudly and mockingly, shouting *El-ay-funt!* Other eyes turned merrily to look at Crump who wondered once again why Jim Sutton had given him that name. He pretended not to have heard or seen, but kept Jim Sutton in a corner of his eye, remembering a lesson during which he had made Jim Sutton stand facing the blackboard and when the class had been dismissed he had noticed, in that sweet relief of the room's emptiness, that Jim Sutton had unobtrusively created a wild action picture on the board by spitting all over it.

Wrapping-paper from dozens of Mars Bars, Toff-O-Lux, Toffee Crisp, McVitie & Price Chocolate Biscuits, Cadbury's Cream Flake and Chipmunk Potato Crisps littered the ground, while he saw too the thirty-second commercial of the dinner party (at which the hostess wore a white robe, pearls adorning her slender neck) turn its attention to coffee, brandy and cigars and the green box of After Eight – eyes and the ladies' diamonds glittering at the arrival of this supreme delicacy.

– Jacobs! he called to a boy near him, seeing him punch another boy in the back. You can stop molesting Jackson and pick up those bits of paper.

– Wha'? Those crumpled bits of pie-per?

– Cut out the cheek.

– Which one?

– All right. Go and stand on the wall. I'll deal with you later.

– Cor, he heard Jacobs say, jerking his offended head as he walked away towards the low wall on which the punished boys were made to stand facing the fence and where he himself must stand soon with his back to the fence and blow the whistle, bleedin' libbetees these danglin' pricks take nowadyes!

He saw the ball coming at him and knew at once that it came from Jim Sutton's direction. Deep square-leg Crump caught the ball next to his chest in the manner he had learned from a coaching book in which Jack Hobbs appeared in the illustrations. That, too, passed through his mind and he had time to say to himself: As long ago as *that*? Hobbs is dead now – his mind glanced at the obituary columns, clutching the ball next to his chest; and the nearest he had ever got to Hobbs was the shop in Fleet Street, flannelled fool Crump had always paused there whenever walking down Fleet Street, always, when looking at the shop-window, imagining himself going in to buy, say, a squash-ball, so that he could perhaps see Hobbs, perhaps even be served by him (and, imagining that, he had felt the old man's fingers touch his palm, giving him the change), but he had never done so, never entered the shop; all he had seen of Hobbs was the old motion picture, bony face, beady shifting eyes and the comic penguin walk from the cinema's jerky past; and, carelessly throwing the ball up and catching it again, he met Jim Sutton's disappointed eyes in the distance; serve the bastard right, he thought. He put the tennis-ball, whose worn canvasy texture gave him no pleasure to hold (and in that moment he thought of a new furry tennis-ball and of Lew Hoad serving at Wimbledon, showing new balls to his opponent before serving), into his pocket and heard a boy shout, Jim, I want me fuckin' ball back! You won't get it, mate, Crump said softly, not from bleedin' Crump. But just then Sutton came running up to him.

– 'Ere, that's my ball, Sutton said to Crump.

Crump pretended to take no notice and began to walk away.

– Just wait, you fat elephant, till the English lesson, Sutton threatened darkly while Crump looked at his watch and decided that he ought to be blowing the whistle in a moment, the long tunnel of the second half of the morning's teaching was approaching. He made his way through the jostling groups, the dribbling outside rights, the smart cover-points, his ears alert to oral graffiti picked up an item already in his book but he was glad to have the occasion to smile.

– Pete? I wouldn't piss on 'im if 'e was on fire.

And he heard, too, a word of recent currency, for one boy was saying to another: I'll spifflicate you. He asked the boy to define the word.

– Spifflicate? the small blond-haired boy willingly answered. To hit, knock out, mortify, stab, bash, wring, molest, throttle, plague, slap, pierce, victimize, decimate, thump, put to the rack, pinch, slam, immolate, pelt, asphyxiate, butcher, punch, slaughter, crucify, maltreat, strangle, kick, tweak, butt, wound, choke, slay, shoot, prick, massacre, assassinate, torment, torture, Vietnamize, murder, kill, suffocate, wipe out, destroy, obliterate, pin down, annihilate, liquidate, modernize.

Perhaps the boy stopped only to take breath, but Crump left him, satisfied that the word was adequately defined or, rather, that it was indefinable; it was itself a spifflication. He climbed up the wall and looked for a moment at the green blazer blobs splashing on the grey asphalt, the dull silver of the Central Line's aluminium coaches – had the sun gone up or had his perspective changed; there was no reflection, no streak of chrome as the train went by, only the tarnished silver – and again at his watch, two minutes after eleven, two minutes past break and, by the time they came to order and were sent up and were ready for lessons, ten minutes lost: work that out nationally, and what does it cost poor old weak-at-the-knees Britain? He blew quickly, sharply, as though an offensive foul had been committed in a football match. A few boys moved to their customary positions. He blew again, a full-time whistle. More assembled in their places. He envied Mr Williamson, who had only to blow a peep through his whistle and there would be immediate order. Just after two minutes past eleven, and ten minutes of his 3B lesson already gone, they'll have to start a new system, he thought, if teachers are going to put teaching before the frilly-frollies of administration. Mark the register, collect the dinner money, patrol the corridors, hang around on playground duty, line them outside the classroom, walk them down to assembly, walk them back from assembly, break up their fights, hound them out of the lavatories; and, if you're not killed to exhaustion by all this, teach them about the wonderful civilization and the exciting point in history in which they find themselves. He refused to shout in order to win their disciplined attention now that he had blown the whistle. He nodded to one of the groups of boys who had lined up, shutting his eyes for a moment, convincing himself that the entire school stood at attention, as at a parade, marvelling (and remembering Marvell, too) at his own capacity for making life equable by simple self-deceptions; though he wasn't to be fooled, for he knew what he must believe, balancing with this life of reiterated commands and the parallel facing mirrors between which reality danced, teasing the mind into expecting revelations, this other life beneath the eyelids, this serenity of the soul. They were dispersing at any rate, loitering towards the entrances to the school and, standing in the obscurity of a copse of trees, he could see across the wide plain the helmets of the cavalry troop bobbing up above the horizon, elsewhere, not here, not here. Some of the boys looked up, their eyes drawn by a sound that was not of a jet, and remarked upon the helicopter to one another. He saw it too, flying low, he saw it fly over tall blocks of flats on the roofs of which sexy girls sunbathed in bikinis, cut, the helicopter disappeared behind some flats, cut, its shadow ran up the road, but here, dissolve, it ran over the Central Line tracks and across over suburbia, that must have been elsewhere, but was here too, a Fellini film, or was it a Visconti, he ought to know, and indeed would know, the machine inside his brain would inform him if it was Fellini or Visconti if there was any importance in the matter, which there was not, and nor did he care for the film, now that he thought of it, and nor for the director, whether Fellini or Visconti.

And thinking of Fellini or Visconti, watching the helicopter disappear, he remembered taking a party of sixth formers to see a film at the Academy by a director who was neither Fellini nor Visconti, but one of similar pretensions similarly lauded by the critics. It had been an afternoon performance, and the cinema was largely empty, most of the audience consisting of lonely-looking men in late middle age. About half-way through the film there had been a very realistic sex scene, well, not realistic, but there was a great deal of grunting and groaning and suggestions of sexual savagery. At the end of this scene, the elderly men had all got up and walked out. An interesting comment on the *nouvelle vague*, he had thought later without cynicism.

A prefect came up to him just when most of the school had gone into the school and said: What are you going to do about them lot?

The prefects had lined up six or seven miscreants on the wall from which Crump had just alighted – he could have jumped or stepped off either on his right foot or his left foot, and just when he was about to execute one of those choices (not choices, alternatives) without thinking, Malone had come to his mind (or it could have been Molloy, it could even have been Watt) and, either paying respect to creation or being unable to escape the tyranny of what was in his mind, he had been compelled to give the action some thought and had decided he would alight in a dignified manner as befitted a schoolteacher who must set an example in all things, and so had alighted – and on which stood Jacobs whom he had himself commanded to stand there in expectation of punishment. The prefect looked at Crump, grinning, as though suggesting that he himself knew very well what he would do with them but doubted very much if Crump did.

– I suggest, said Crump, who could make such suggestions to Driver, the prefect, who had failed his 'O' Level English three times, and how many of Crump's ninepenny biros had been wasted in inserting apostrophes in his essays, you ask them to catch the bus to the tube station, to catch the train to Waterloo, they'll have to change at Oxford Circus, and from Waterloo to catch the first train to Aldershot and there to seek out the officer on duty and politely, if they're capable of politeness, a dying art that, Driver, to ask the officer if he would care to line them up against the wall and shoot them.

– Yes, but, said Driver.

– All right, then, I'll deal with them. You'd better go to your lesson.

The classes had already begun, Crump saw while Driver walked away, for the walls of glass looked out on to the playground, and it was interesting to see how the other teachers coped with the pampered generation of with-it teenagers; turning to the miscreants, he said, Right, get to your classes, thus weakly dismissing them, thus damaging what little reputation he had as a disciplinarian, bored with the alternatives of giving them lines, asking them to pick up litter from the playground, giving them a lecture (to what purpose the strict vocabulary of didacticism?), caning them, putting them in detention, referring them to the child welfare clinic (Dear Dr Mulheim, please acknowledge receipt of the seven kids, and if they arrive damaged it has not been for lack of care). Ah, forget it, it was easy to say to himself, though there were occasions when he could be scrupulously strict, could indeed be just; and whenever he had to mete out a punishment he remembered the first occasion he used the cane. It had been on the elephantine buttocks of a large, gross third-year boy called Hughes. He remembered the seat of the grey trousers, shiny and worn thin, as Hughes bent forward at the front of the class in the empty room. Crump had intended to give him two strokes. His first stroke, nervously executed (he was grateful that Hughes, bending over, could not see him) was weak and obviously ineffectual. But Hughes had sprung back and crying aloud. Oh, my balls, my balls, had gone trotting down the aisle to the back of the class and then run back to the front again crazily in the manner of a wounded animal. Crump dismissed him promptly, realizing later that, of course, it must have been a trick; for any boy suddenly crying aloud, Oh, my balls, my balls, must know that such an utterance must immediately petrify the teacher into a worried passivity. The boys he had weakly dismissed went off smartly, showing no gratitude. Crump slowly followed them, watching the naked blonde girl run up and down between the two rows of soldiers who whipped her as she ran, the *whish, whish, whish* of the canes and her soft helpless moaning the only sound in the camp where brutality pursued a perverted ethic, but not here, not here, elsewhere. He walked slowly towards the school, trying to look as serene and self-composed as a petty smuggler – one, say, who is bringing in fifty more cigarettes than are allowed and is worried to hell about it, who is just about to face the Customs officer.

In a suit of mohair and silk, twelve-guinea Bally shoes, a Swiss cotton purple shirt, a mauve tie with exquisite pink and green flowers on it, a black leather briefcase in his hand, Crump had walked through the airports of Europe, through the corridors of glass shepherded by high-heeled and heavily lipsticked stewardesses clutching their files of passenger lists, who could say he had not? he asked, remembering the fawn

Levi jeans, a nineteen-and-eleven black cotton poloneck from Millets and the hushpuppies he wore taking the crowded ferry from Dover or from Southampton each August, and sometimes in the spring, for his beetle's view of Europe. If anyone was really interested in knowing, he had even sailed to Byzantium.

Arriving from Lima or Los Angeles, Crump walked down the corridor and, approaching his classroom where 3B awaited him like a gang of press photographers for Frank Sinatra, heard more than the usual sounds from within that temple of his priesthood, for how else did he speak but with a sacredness of purpose, or from within that maniac's cell where he yelled the Truth before the bemused derision of thirty-one kids who had seen enough archbishops on television to have apprehended that the source of all knowledge was money and had therefore themselves begun on the treacherous path towards the kingdom of seven-figure fortunes by doing the paper round or the milk round in the mornings, grocery deliveries in the late afternoons, mini-cab cards in letter-boxes in the evenings and market barrowboying on Saturdays, and, hearing the more-than-usual sounds, Crump had to act urgently, deliberately and take them by surprise. So, he threw the door open, which he had locked at the beginning of break but which a colleague must have unlocked while Crump was on playground duty (the keys to the classrooms being identical), slackened his legs at the waist, making himself appear three or four inches shorter, and did the Groucho walk: knees bent, feet flatly skating just above the lino, the strides long, buttocks sticking out, ducklike man, his head turned like a soldier's in a march-past.

– All right, all right, all right, do you know what you remind me of, you remind me of women at the ladies' hairdressers, and indeed you may ask what other type of hairdresser can women be at than the ladies', sure, sure, they can be at the *coiffeur des dames*, but let's not introduce pseudo-refinements of language at this stage, and indeed you may ask who am I to have such an idea, I have never been a lady as far as you know and I have never been a ladies' hairdresser, also as far as you know, the incredible distances you have to go to know anything, poor little darlings of your mother's dreams, or shall I call you mum's fruitgum chums, sodding little sparrows chirruping in this secondary-modern nest, grinning your Mars Bars cavities at the sugary world, you sweet little pets in the adman's cage. . . .

Crump had to speak rapidly, audibly but totally incomprehensibly, and by now some of the boys had turned to look at the babbling phenomenon in front of them who had come to disturb what to them was a quiet natter, a fundamental democratic right; the ones in the two or three back rows who had vaguely seen him enter had been half-struck by his diminished stature and had been silent for a moment; Crump continued to speak faster and less intelligibly, for had the boys understood there would have been murmurs, cries and shouts of Bent, Off his rocker, Queer, 'E's bloody spas, Good old sir, Bleedin' fart. So that he went on:

– And, talking of hairdressers, how about this one? There was a young hairdresser from Shoreditch who couldn't tell a dog from a bitch; but must I go on, you unimaginative morons, there's one decent rhyme for Shore and she's a baggy old whore, but please, oh, please, don't ask me what goes into which, even though that would be a cock-eyed bloody way of constructing anything resembling a limerick, and I'll have you know that we must preserve, nay, cherish our respect for the forms, literary, artistic, musical.

But, of course, no one heard his rapid nonsensical improvisation although, realizing it was only 3B – hardly *only*, the maliciously impertinent noisy fourteen-year-olds, who would ask when he had managed a tolerable silence, Please, sir, what's the meaning of gossamer? who were probably themselves buying quantities of it under plain cover – he checked an inclination to be blatantly obscene, a Gulliver putting out the fire of Lilliputian voices. They continued as though at a cocktail party, and Crump, a late arrival, as if someone too unimportant even to be greeted passingly. He stood silently in front of them for a couple of minutes, and then announced clearly:

– The *Sunday Mirror* has just offered me twenty-five thousand pounds.

A decibel count might have recorded a slight lessening of the noise. He waited. The boys at the front had definitely heard him, for they turned round to shush the others. Crump repeated when more were listening: Yes, the *Sunday Mirror* has offered me twenty-five thousand pounds, and I suppose you'd like to know what for.

Now, at last, there was total silence. That's it, thought Crump, mention money and win the prize of attention, especially when there was a suggestion that someone was going to get a lot of money for no work, or not what one called work, like a T.V. quiz in which the money doubled from question to asinine question, hush, let's have shushquiet, a nation ogled at the box, the pretty girl smiling across her bunny-bosom holding out the question just below the cleavage, and so it goes, cash and pneumatic bliss go hand in hand. They really were silent, even Ashford with his idiotic grin had stopped looking out at the planes and Bennett next to him had switched off his V.H.F. on which he listened to the pilots contacting the Heathrow Control Tower.

– I'll tell you what for, said top journalist of the year Crump. It's an article they want me to write called 'How I Massacred Thirty-one Boys'. So, quietly and without panicking, please get up, line outside, walk silently down to the playground and stand against the wall. Think of yourselves as heroes, for this after all is an age of violence. I'll be there in a moment with my machine-gun.

The last sentence was lost, like a ball falling over the fence on to the tracks just when the Central Line came rushing down, in the booing, laughing, banging of desk-lids, clapping, stamping of feet, but Crump, feeling the worn canvas of the tennis-ball in his pocket, which reminded him of Jim Sutton's dark threat and of Lew Hoad serving at Wimbledon (which brought to mind the classy mini-skirted, flower-hatted, straw-berry-season women, suggesting the line, The breast's superb abundance where a man might base his head), took the ball out, juggled it in his hands, and said:

– You think this is just an ordinary tennis ball don't you? I wouldn't laugh if I were you . . .

– 'Cause you'd smell, mate!

– . . . for this is a disguised hand-grenade.

– Boo! Spas! Piss off!

– You don't believe me! I'd ask you to think of cigarette lighters in spy films which are cameras, pistols, bugging devices . . .

– Bugger you, mate!

– . . . all in one.

– All right, throw it then!

– No, I shan't waste it now, not on you. I'll keep it for myself, I'll toss it up . . .

– *Toss!* Toss it off, Crump! Jerk it! The wanking elephant!

– . . . when the four-minute warning comes and head it, a winner, a sure winner, bang, crash, at any rate an equalizer, throw up my own little bang in defiance of the big bang.

All right, let the bleeders scream, bang, crash, who cares, considered philosophical, meditative Crump, it's happened before, it'll happen again, take the long-term view and nothing matters, for there can be silences within one. Surely, there can be silences, a little silence, surely, when the breast has room for a Sahara? An easy defence, Crump, a wall of wool. During his first year as a teacher, he had shouted back at them and they had shouted with greater force and he had thought that his head would burst with the pain which would develop at his temples; and on occasion, while there was this pain of utter hatred at his temples, this throbbing anger, he had been uncontrollably violent, slapping some boys with so much strength that there would be a look of bloody murder on the boys' faces – and quite rightly, too, he thought now, Mahatma Crump, for his method now was of total silence, a kind of hunger-fast. He no longer suffered from the noise, simply pretended to be indifferent to it, took to sulking, refused to give them work when, at the end, they asked for it. So now he sat down at his desk, regarded the beech tree outside his window, dead leaves strewn below it, a pile of first-year composition books to be marked on his desk, text books, a B.B.C. pamphlet called *Listening and Writing*, prize entertainment that; he recalled the many attempts to use the broadcasts with this same 3B and how invariably there would be some phrase, there was one not long ago in Ted Hughes's nativity play – All night long you've been at it – or even something quite unremarkable like What are you doing? which would raise riots of laughter at presumed sexual ecstasies. The noise subsided while Crump paid it no attention. He took up an exercise book, opened it at the latest offering by Gold, 1C, a piece called 'My Breakfast', which, Gold declared, was uninstring, made up of cone flaks or rice kris piss. Crump gave that three out of ten – for what the mark was worth; he could have given it two out of ten or four out of ten without seriously damaging his own or Gold's or Gold's parents' or Her Majesty's Inspectors' or the rest of mankind's general outlook or moral standards – decided not to mark any more books, and took up instead his notebook of peculiar spellings and added Gold's contribution to his list, some of the words in which caught his eye: undisoblined characta, cariter, bad-manade, ill-manured, benefisherry, neuclia, blew a fews, bycicle inatube, proper-gander, siverlisation, prositcute, lives at steak, Portable Road, lenth and breath. Looking at these, his mind remembered, too, one or two classic misprints, soldier Aristotle in Yeats, President Eisenhowever from the *Guardian*'s Manchester days and, more recently from *The Times*, Prim Minister and for *return* the excellent coinage, *returd*. Well, Crump, that's how it is, what it's also about: errors of transcription; and that's what the whole bleeding mess is also about: errors of language. Define, define, well-educated infant.

There is our commission, from which we would not have you warp.

Ha! he laughed a short, bitter laugh to himself, remembering words from a printed page, saying to himself, But it's all warped, it's simple for uses to become abuses, and, like bamboo trees grown too tall to remain erect, man had become, yes, more words from a printed page, a giddy thing.

– Right, get your reading-books out, he commanded, and the class, which had been chatting away quite happily, now almost automatically obeyed him. With ten minutes left of the lesson which had never begun, they turned to the second chapter of John Buchan (of course, there was always the comment, Fuckan Buchan again)'s *Prester John*, decidedly a wrong book, Crump thought, now that the class contained eight African immigrants and Buchan used the word *black* in the sense in which it was no longer supposed to be used among civilized, racially integrated communities. Integration, as he saw it in American magazines in his doctor's waiting-room, was a matter of exercising a begrudging condescension by including black models in the advertisements, and thought What a fraudulent fucking civilization. He read the chapter aloud himself, finding they listened more readily to his voice, for he could dramatize, pause significantly, raise a pointing finger, be viciously sharp in accusation or softly meek in defence, mimic the accents of classes and races, give the adman's laughing confidence to his voice or the disc jockey's silly knowingness tinkling from his throat or the football commentator's speed, than to one another's faltering, dreary reading – though, to rest himself for a moment or in order to demonstrate his comparative virtuosity, he would sometimes ask a boy to read. No democracy from Crump, no universal participation in these matters, and if you think of it, he once said to some senior boys, all our organizations, from the big industrial corporations to the schools, are run as dictatorships. For a few minutes now they seemed absorbed in Buchan's naïve narrative while he thought that one of these days he must set fire to the English department's entire stock of Buchan, Scott, Twain, Haggard and Kipling and order some readable books. This thought was immediately confirmed by Buchan, for Crump found himself reading aloud: The natives round Blauwildebeestefontein were queer, and diamonds were suspected somewhere in the neighbourhood.

He saw the crash coming just as a driver who, approaching the traffic lights which are turning red, discovers that his brakes have gone, no sooner than he had begun the sentence. With a senior class – and there had been an occasion when they had come across the word 'bollocks' while reading *Lord of the Flies* aloud – he could maintain seriousness by pausing to stress the importance in writing of using a living language (not that, he pointed out with regard to *Lord of the Flies*, this is a good book and please don't get the impression that simply because a man uses a word like bollocks he's *therefore* to be thought of as a master of living language, Golding isn't that); but with 3B there was nothing he could do but let them scream their dirty little heads off, and would have been willing to join a chorus, had someone started one, chanting Fuckan Buchan Must Go, until the bell rang and they went, throwing chairs out of their way, banging on desks, stampeding out towards the slaughterhouse of ignorance.

There was a letter on his desk which had arrived in the morning; the headmaster's orderly had brought it up, and Crump had not yet opened it, for assembly had followed registration and 1C English had followed assembly, there hadn't been a moment. Now expecting eight 5A boys, who had to come from the drawing-office where they must just be packing away their latest technical drawing, and would take at least five minutes doing so, having noticeboards to glance at and lavatories to visit on the way along the corridors of indolence. It was postmarked Kent. He knew no one in Kent, he thought, the image of genial, chubby-faced Colin Cowdrey passing through his mind while he inserted the sharp point of a pencil into the envelope where the flap was sealed down, looking absently at the beech tree, the slate roofs of the semi-detached suburban houses whose gardens came to the bicycle shed and whose windows revealed nothing, no young maiden coquettishly beaming the headlights of her bosom through the darkness of the rooms, the misty blue sky, the inevitable jet, gone too far for the airline to be identified, and in that moment he saw the pilot's view of runway one, the dwarfed buildings, the Dinky-toy tankers and coaches and the insect men, remembered, too, having read somewhere that the pilot's heartbeat is at its fastest when making a landing, and tore open the envelope, extracted the letter from Kent. It was written on two sheets of ruled paper, the handwriting sloped backwards – perhaps the person was left-handed – and, without reading it, he could discern familiar spelling mistakes. On the top line of the right-hand corner was the name *R. J. Andrews*, a number, *759*, next to it. On the next line, immediately below the name, was *H.M. Borstal*. Below that was the name of the town and, on the fourth line, *Kent*. Leaving a line, Andrews had begun on the far left, and written:

Mr Crump
I hope this letter is not imposing on your most precious time, as I know that you are a busy man.

The reaseon for me writting is, that I thought I would let you know how I have got on since I last saw you, for I still rember way back, when I was a student under your supervision and they are the day's to rember.

Well, sir, the new's is bad for since I last saw you I have been in and out of trouble and now I have landed myself up in Borstal. I surpose you think I deserve it, well so do I but It is avery large problem to face up to for I have been in side now since I was fourteen.

I do not wish to bore you with this letter but there is one thing I would like to ask. When I sort my self out of this mess would it be possible for me to come and see you as a friend. For sir I do not wish to impose my self upon you but I need your prefesinly advise and I do not think no one else can give it to me except for you. For so far I have been to two approve schools, Wormwood scrub's prison and now Borstal and I would hate to think of carrying on like this for the rest of my life.

By the way sir the world has not been treating me that bad, for I am engauged and the girl is still willing to wait for me, so I am a lucky bloke realy.

Well sir I shall finish my boring letter now and thankyou sir for what you have tried to do for me in the past. Before I close, please give my regaurds to Mrs Whitaker if she is still working at the school.

Yours sincerely
Ronnie Andrews.

Crump was glad to observe that Andrews did not put a full-stop after the abbreviations *Mr* and *Mrs*, a point on which even *The Times* erred, but regretted that he had been unable to teach him the correct uses of the apostrophe. Once he had caned Andrews on the backside. Andrews was wearing jeans and his back pockets were tightly packed. Crump had brought the cane down with a severe thwack and there had been a small explosion, for Andrews carried a box of Swan Vesta matches in one of the pockets and the matches had ignited. Andrews had rolled on the floor, but had recovered from the incident soon enough to be telling his mates, Sir's burned a hole through me arse, and had had an affectionate regard for Sir ever since – much to Crump's disapproval, for he did not enjoy the notion of having a reputation for burning holes through people's arses.

5A were coming in while Crump sat thinking of Andrews, and he noticed that Barnes was in one of his moods, sitting grumpily, uncommunicative, for it had been possible to reach Andrews, he had talked with him, had tried to expound to him in simple terms the rationale of society. Andrews had always listened, he had always been apologetic about his recalcitrance, had sworn never to engage again in shoplifting, but, after a few days' attentive work, had been compelled to enter into one more quarrel with society which, on the one hand, told him that any life but the luxurious was not worth living and, on the other, denied him instant satisfaction, abused him, shouted at him, caned him, gave him sums to do and compositions to write which seemed to have nothing to do with finding money for fags and sweets and taking a girl to the pictures. 5A were all in place and were looking at him, the clerks, he thought, the petty civil servants, amiable young men, but possessing neither imagination nor ambition, the soulless plodders who will buy their clothes at sales and choose their wives from typists' pools, and husband and wife will together spend a lifetime accumulating h.p. debts; but still what a relief from 3 bloody B. The safe people, 5A, the don't-know column in a public-opinion poll. At least Andrews. Oh, forget it. Try that, Crumpmate.

He saw round-faced Stobbs leering at him from behind his thick-lensed glasses and said, looking at him but addressing the class in general: Don't talk to me today, I feel foul.

– What's it today, sir? asked the genial Stobbs, the mirthful roly-poly Stobbs who liked to ask Crump questions which would keep Crump talking for the entire lesson. Not cancer, I hope.

– Ooja ka pivi, muttered Barnes, pouting his lip, staring at his desk.

– I've sad news for you, chaps, announced Crump.

– Oh no! exclaimed Stobbs, playing Crump's game, laughing already.

– I hear from my scientific friends that the polar ice-cap has begun to melt. At the rate of two millimetres a day.

– Oh dear!

– By the summer, when you will have taken your 'O' Levels and exulted over your very mediocre result of three undistinguished passes and three abysmal failures, it will have melted sufficiently to drown the Hebrides.

– Oh how awful!

– By the time you've settled down at your jobs, begun to save money, gone so far with your giggling clueless girl-friends – no farther mind you, let us maintain a strict morality in these things – as to hold hands . . .

– Ooooh!

– . . . the flood will have submerged the counties of England north of Derbyshire.

– Woe is us!

– And then a sudden promotion enables you to put down deposits simultaneously on a car, a house and a wedding. Next, on your wedding-day, when you've taken delivery of the Mini in the morning and Molly in the afternoon and carried her across the threshold of your terraced, pebble-dashed, one-up-and-one-down-and-the-loo-in-the-backyard mansion, whoosh! You'll be five fathoms deep. If that's what you want to work for, right, let's start, get the bibles out.

– Ooja ka pivi! commented Barnes, and added as an afterthought: Spas!

There were mild boos from the rest of the class, Stobbs laughed, for nothing made life seem so comfortable to him than his teacher's obvious insanity, and Murray rose wearily and began to distribute copies of *G.C.E. Tests in English Language*, known to Crump's disciples as the bible.

– Choose an essay topic, any one, and write an essay, and remember that, though it will win you no favour with me, nothing will impress the examiner more than an appropriate quotation from Ralph Waldo Emerson, Benjamin Franklin, Abraham Lincoln, Winston Churchill, Samuel Johnson, John Lennon, Malcolm Muggeridge, Mary Whitehouse, Katharine Whitehorn, David Frost, Walter Lipmann, Liberace or Jesus Christ.

– You've got our exercise books.

– Murray, give them out.

– You haven't marked the last work.

– Nor the last.

– What do you expect, cried Crump, efficiency? Get on with the essay.

– Which one?

– I told you any one. Weren't you listening?

– When are you going to mark our work?

– Mark? Why should I mark your work? Your neat handwriting, your carefully chosen clichés, your beautifully expressed mundane thoughts, the measured indentation of your paragraphs ought not to be soiled by my ninepenny biro, it would be an insult to your dignity. You don't want to be reminded, do you, that you can't spell, that your prose is more polluted than the Thames, that you have no clue as to the uses of the apostrophe or the semi-colon, that your infinitives are always split?

– You never taught us them.

– Never taught us them! *Never*, Holroyd? Where were you on 12 October?

– In bed with a cold.

– Too bad, Holroyd, on 12 October, it was a fine day to walk in the park, I remember, I taught not only the apostrophe, the semi-colon, the split infinitive, but also analysis of compound sentences, neither nor, either or, further farther, its it's, the participial phrase, the elements of précis, and a guide to essay writing for backward students. Barnes was here; he'll tell you.

– Ooja ka pivi.

– Precisely. So get on with your essay.

– Which one, there's hundreds here.

– Ah, so it's difficult when the choice has to be your own and the alternatives are many? You'd rather that everything was like the two-party system and that you voted for one throughout your life? That you were spoon-fed at every stage of your miserable development? That every restaurant had a fixed menu? Don't you possess any sense of leadership or exploration? Can't you make decisions? I can just see you in ten years' time, Which one tonight, Molly love, B.B.C. or I.T.V.? Poor little undirected youths, my heart bleeds for you.

– Bleedin' Crump.

– Ah, a wit, a punster? Hurray for originality!

– Hurray, hurray, hurray!

– That'll do, Get on with the essay.

– There isn't enough time left.

– Time, White, I've told you a thousand times, is a relative concept, of no real significance to anyone except a pubkeeper.

– A time to live and a time to die.

– A good song that. I like the Doors too; but no, Stobbs, there is life, that's all. That's all you've got. That's all you'll ever have. Do something with it before the politicians, bankers, mortgages and the admen take it away.

– Why do we have to work, then?

– Because you'd die of boredom otherwise.

–Starvation, more likely.

– Starvation is also a quality of mental apathy, Murray. And who asked you to collect the books?

– You just proved there's no point in working.

– But certain things have to be done nevertheless. If only for your mother's sake. Remember, she loves you.

– Yeah, yeah, yeah.

– Right, if you agree so vociferously, Ringo and the rest, get down to that essay.

The reaseon for me writting is. It was two years since he had left school, Crump remarked to himself. Well if they were not going to begin an essay at least they are looking at the titles – What is so attractive about your hobby? Write a letter to a friend in the country telling him why you prefer living in a city and write the friend's reply giving reasons for living in the country. The pleasures of snow, Describe a camping holiday in bad weather, On mending my bicycle, The pleasures of gardening, the usual bloody list of absolute irrelevance – and why should he want to see Crump? What image had he projected of godhood that Andrews should make of him an idol fit for pilgrimage? What could Crump ever say to him which would not be insincere and false? Become like Stobbs and Murray, join the non-people, choose the middle way, Andrews, of the middle class, choose complacence, submission. The beech tree was in ruins, the planes were descending one by one, journeys were coming to an end. This is your captain speaking. Dearest Frieda, he had written, on fine days the planes take off through corridors of air they normally use for their descents. I suppose the wind is the other way on these days, the sunny ones. What power, what angry noise they make when leaving the earth, like embittered sons banging the door shut on their parents' house! Oh, Frieda, Frieda, my imagination goes with them, crosses the Sahara of your absence. How long will it be, how much longer? I am jealous of your Africa while it holds you in its embrace. Old adulterer, that continent of yours. That Whitsun, that mild morning in mid-May after the frost of late April had killed the cherry blossom, when they had driven to Dover, man and wife, coming over the hill into Canterbury, the cathedral appearing suddenly in the distance – rather silly that milky story about Wat Tyler he read to the first-years, who lapped it up – she had said, You wrote such good letters, it seemed a joy to live on in Johannesburg. I think we prefer ourselves as a piece of fiction, he had remarked.

– Sir, these essay topics are all spastic.

– They're all turdlified, if you ask me.

– Belt up; he ain't listening.

– Who?

– Crumpsteak. Who else?

– Spas!

He had seen her off on the ship, remarking that every South African's home was his Union Castle. They had stood on the clean deck beside the swimming-pool. He had imagined her coming from her cabin for a swim and a prolonged session of sunbathing once the ship was out of the English November grey. Standing with her on the chilly deck, he had imagined himself later imagining how, while he stood there with her, he had imagined her lying back in a deck-chair, sunbathing. Isn't that how it is, he had wondered, holding her hand and looking down on the murky Thames, thinking now that we might be thinking in the future of this moment now when we were thinking that we might think about it in the future, indeed that we will, for there is no choice in these matters, Crump, there's only an involuntary compulsion, isn't that how it is? The nuances of confusion. Impulses. The aggrieved mind. And yet this make-belief that there was a chronology to existence. Bits and pieces, that's all. Dear, dear Frieda, he had written, and she said, when they sat in the car at Dover, waiting for the ferry attendants to wave them on, It was like having a correspondence with a poet. She thought she ought to mention a name, and added: Like Keats.

– Don't talk to me of that wet poet, he said.

– Mike! she had been ready to scold, but had looked out towards France, wondering if the crossing would be rough.

By the end of February, certainly early in March, there will be blossoms somewhere to look at, there will be buds on the beech tree, those back gardens will begin to simmer and bubbles of flowers will appear. Spring will rise, frothy at the brim of England. He counted the bicycles, thinking they ought to paint the shed in pop colours, have a psychedelic cycle-shed, instead of leaving it stamped with the bureaucratic beige or dirty cream of mediocre conservatism, sixty-nine, and if England had changed, was changing, flinging its arms into the sky, then let it show its new gaudiness everywhere and not pretend that life was still the same, one hundred and thirty-nine. As well as three scooters and two motor-cycles. The second summer they had driven south, going through Rheims, scaffolding around the cathedral, God thou art on crutches, spastic God, appealing for pity now, for charity, and past Beaune into the murderous traffic of France in August, *C'est Shell que J'aime* on the yellow-and-orange hoardings, and it would have been meaningless to erase the *S*, as he had done in a moment's distortion of imagery, though the Renault with its nose crushed against the tree and the Citroëns hissing past him and a little later the ambulance trying to scream its way in the opposite direction, but just then Frieda had said, Remember when we went to Brittany last year and I said your letters were like a poet's? A pair of ragged claws, he remembered, beetle-scuttling across Europe.

And there was also the repetitive and insistent message *Total sur les Routes du Monde*, yes, in one way or another, in one language or another, the writing was on the wall, it was there on the horizon, and how much farther can we go than up to the horizon, the wall one must crash against in the end, the final and total surrender, for virginity, say, or innocence or freshness, once lost, can never be retrieved, penitence and prayer, policy and sanctions, medicine and surgery would never be of any use. The majority no doubt came by bus, he thought, looking at the bicycles, very few walked, some had parents foolish enough to bring them in a car.

– We can have a picnic lunch, Frieda had said, there's Camembert and some croissants, and we can pick up some wine.

O Heart: what was that from Kunitz?

They had swigged from the two-franc bottle of vin ordinaire under a pine tree in a forest, having left the route nationale to find a piece of land for themselves.

– I wish you wouldn't wear jeans, he said, his hand on her thigh. Especially not cords. I wouldn't mind stroking silk. But cords.

What she had wanted to tell him that mid-May morning when she had looked away towards France was something else, not that he wrote like a poet, nor that his letters had the old-fashioned flavour of an idealized romance, which they had not, for his words often possessed a frightening violence.

He was glad that he could appear to be utterly insane to 5A who would spend the rest of their lives surrounded by dull sanity; they respected him for it, and though they expected too much entertainment, a continuous variety show, when people are in groups, he thought, they too easily become spectators, they were prepared to listen seriously, too, to his teaching. They had little opportunity anyway to be anything but spectators, for their night out was at the pictures and day out at the football stadium and the rest of the time, of course, watching television.

– I'll change if you want me to, she had said, a half-eaten croissant in one hand.

– What *now*?

– We're alone, aren't we? And who cares if we're observed? This is France.

She threw the croissant away, rising.

– Christ, you give me the cockurge saying that.

She had smiled and walked to the Volkswagen, deliberately swaying her hips sexily. He swigged philosophically from the bottle.

Sitting there, they think they're a studio audience and Crump's here to compère a live show. Sometimes, when they asked him a question, he would sing back the answer, baritone Crump would thrill their Covent Garden ears, or he would assume a foreign accent, do an Italian or an Indian – Vhat is this qvestion you are asking me, Barruns, is it to show a many-festation of the inta-lect of your sharrup mind? – and because he gave them a sort of pleasure to be with which no other teacher gave they responded generously when he demanded work from them. If they protested, it was their contribution to the show. And that is one thing a teacher has to be, Crump thought, an entertainer. He has also to be a politician, a lawyer, a solicitor, a doctor, a nurse, a father, a friend, a sportsman, an expert at judo, an academic, an encyclopaedia, a judge, a jailor; he has to have one very good eye and one which can go blind, he has to have sharp ears and also be deaf, he needs the tongue of an orator, of a mob leader, and of a dictator.

In an orange skirt, stockingless in sandals, she came to him under the pine tree, took a long swig of the vin ordinaire and, the wine, not wholly swallowed, on her lips and tongue, kissed him.

And plain human flesh is better than silk, he was about to say when his hand, encountering no defence, discovered that she had nothing on under the skirt.

Ah well, this is France, who cares if we're observed?

– Did you hear this one? When the Germans invaded France, a German soldier took advantage of a French peasant girl in a barn. When they'd finished, he said, If something arrives in nine months' time, call it Fritz. She smiled at him, saying, Sank you very much for ze present, and added, If some spots appear in a few weeks' time, call it measles.

The boy who had been told the story looked baffled, frowned for a moment, and then asked, What do you mean, 'took advantage'?

– Christ, Jimmy, don't you *know* anything? said the first boy, annoyed that his story had provoked not even a smile from Jimmy.

For the rest of the lesson, Jimmy sat puzzling out the subtleties of language to himself, his own mind being obsessively concerned with computers, and when the class was dismissed, he stayed behind and came up to Crump and asked: Sir, if Murray were to copy my maths homework, would it be correct to say that he had taken advantage of me?

Crump agreed that it would, and Jimmy, thanking him, went out, laughing softly to himself.

The next morning, he moaned in the pre-waking reluctance ever again to emerge from sleep, while the words she uttered had entered into and been rejected by his consciousness, while, having his head against the pillow, he saw, only partly saw, for vision too rejected all but the vivid darkness of sleep, the profile of her face, a line of light running down from forehead to chin, a brightness in her eyes and perhaps she was saying, as she had said yesterday, It's a fine day. And then she said insistingly, appealingly, Is it going to be fine today? As if his affirmation would have the sanction of a decree and ensure that the day would be fine. He had to turn, rise a little, peer at the window. The sky was indeed blue, as it had been yesterday. His eyes brightened, too, and he was prepared to concede that there was some point in waking up, if only a selfish one of sensual indulgence, not a merit essentially, and certainly not a reason, a small, selfish point. Perhaps she saw the brightness in his eyes, or perhaps the moment had come for her to set an example, for she rose with a vigorous movement, her nightie being blown up so that he saw her buttocks for a moment before the garment floated down to settle at its proper and decent length just above the knees. She brushed her teeth at the basin in the corner of the room.

– Do you think it'll remain fine? she asked, washing out her mouth.

– It depends on the wind, he said, we might find a shelter against it.

She leaned out of the window, looked above her and said, I can't see a cloud. Withdrawing into the room, she asked, What time did we go to sleep last night?

– It was over eight hours ago, he said. In any case, we did it much earlier.

– That's all right, then, she said, putting on a gown and going to the bathroom, taking a little plastic bag with her.

He rose out of bed and walked to the window. Certainly a fine day, he remarked, at least certainly a fine morning; so it was yesterday until the wind blew clouds across the Atlantic just before noon. Before she returned from the bathroom, he had brushed his teeth and begun to shave. He saw her in the mirror, beginning to change. For a moment, he saw her standing naked before picking up a bra, and he looked at her without sexual interest, a moment merely of aesthetic appraisal, which, fulfilling certain theoretical speculations about the beauty of the female body, he found satisfying in a pure, unemotional sense.

– What shall we do today? she asked, putting on a blue corduroy skirt.

– What do you propose? he said, lathering himself again.

She put on a white sweater, chunky and long-sleeved. He declaimed:

When my love's on the seaside,
she's a sailor true;
she wears a white sweater
and her skirt is navy blue.

– Well, we could lie on the beach, he added.

– I suppose you're going to wear white flannel trousers, she remarked, for she could rebuke his quoting mind.

– That in our case we have not got, he said. I think it'll have to be shorts or Levis. Odd how some of the best bits of Eng. Lit. end up by becoming clichés. Yes, the Levis. And if the cheeks of heaven bulge with wind and the four-cornered earth blows like the devil, we could drive to Concarneau or Beg Meil or Quimper or Morgat. In fact, having successfully crossed the English Channel, there's nothing to stop us from driving to Singapore, all things, including man, being equal.

– Mike, do you mind being serious?

– Je m'appelle Hilary.

– Oui, Pierrot!

He washed his face, dried it, applied some after-shave lotion to it, and began to change. In Levis and black polo-neck, he thought of the hushpuppy and grey-worsted Crump who strolled through the corridors of a school in Middlesex. He heard a voice say: When I go past Mister Crump, my little heart goes thump, thump, thump.

They walked down to the bar of the little hotel where breakfast was served. Frieda ordered bread and butter and coffee, and inside Crump's mind, which had been wondering why breakfast had to be specifically ordered in France where it invariably consisted of bread and butter and coffee, Chico added: And two hard-boiled eggs. When the waitress had brought the order, Frieda said to her: Et de la confiture, s'il vous plaît, and when the waitress, smiling, was going away, Crump added: And two hard-boiled eggs.

– What? asked Frieda, pouring out the coffee.

– Nothing, said Crump.

– I thought you commented on her legs, Frieda said.

Crump's mouth was full of bread and butter and he was stirring his coffee. The waitress came and placed a bowl of apricot jam on the table and smiled, bowing now at Frieda and now at Crump; Crump, cheeks bulging with bread and butter, smiled back open-mouthed and thought he must look particularly idiotic smiling with his cheeks bulging out, showing his teeth which probably had bits of bread stuck among them.

– I hadn't noticed before, he said.

– What? asked Frieda.

– Her legs, said Crump.

She chewed gracefully in what he thought must be the approved manner prescribed by the finishing school she went to in Johannesburg, and swallowed some coffee, and just when he had taken another bite at his slice of bread and butter, again a large one, although, when thinking about his gargoyle grin a moment earlier, he had resolved to take smaller bites, she said: Oh, those. I thought you were talking of eggs.

He chewed slowly, ponderously. He took a sip of his coffee, and said: As a matter of fact, I was. Hard-boiled ones.

– Do you notice other women's legs? she demanded.

– It's a fine day, he said, paused to swallow some coffee, and added: I take a personal interest in any manifestation of the aesthetically laudable. You would receive no flattery else.

And she: Pills.

He lit a cigarette, puffed, inhaled deeply, thinking of cancer, exhaled, extolled the taste of the morning's first cigarette after a cup of coffee, and watched her brush away some crumbs from her lap.

– Shall we go to the beach this morning? she asked.

– Yes, he said, exhaling.

She poured out some more coffee. He added a little milk and sugar to his.

– Did you sleep well? she asked.

– Yes, he said. Did you?

– Yes. I think we must hurry. In case the wind comes up again.

– Of course, he agreed, but they sat there until he had finished his cigarette.

They walked up to the bedroom, he going to the W.C. on

the half-landing. The bloody French, he thought, sitting with his trousers down, will put a toilet where there's scarcely room for a broom-cupboard. His knees touched the door, which opened inwards, requiring one to be a contortionist to enter or to go out. He remembered a lavatory in a cheap roadside hotel in northern France where one had to sit over a hole in the floor; the flushing system was operated by a button beside which was a notice: POUSSEZ DOUCEMENT; and Crump, whose gentleness could be testified to by a hundred kids whom he had restrained himself time and again from knocking out with a clenched fist, had hardly touched the button when water from various obscure sources rushed into the toilet and out into the half-landing and down the stairs; he had quickly run down, walked calmly through the dining-room door, gone to his car, which was parked across the road, spent five minutes looking intensely at the engine, came back to the hotel through the door to the bar where he ordered a drink, a Berger, thus providing himself with what he hoped was, in the circumstances, a water-tight alibi. Perhaps it was different in the *grand luxe* hotels, he considered, but it seemed to him that the French, supposedly a race much attached to gracious living, had neglected an important fundamental in human existence: while they excelled in every detail in matters appertaining to ingestion, they had not realized that evacuation could be very enjoyable too. He was grateful to his own system which never failed him, provided he had access to a cup of coffee and a cigarette; he always imagined that the smoke which he inhaled of the first cigarette each morning was, apart from worsening the deterioration of his lungs, physically instrumental in stirring his bowels like a flushing system. He hoped, before he left the hotel, to write on the door which he now faced:

My intestines are made of copper,
I can shit as easily as dance;
but I can't do it nice and proper
in the lousy lavs in France.

He rose, not caring to make any comment on the deplorable quality of the paper, cleaned himself, worked the flush which sent a ringing sound in the plumbing throughout the hotel, read again while buttoning himself up the notice in French which begged ladies not to discard their used sanitary towels into the lavatory bowl, and squeezed himself out of the door.

In the bedroom, Frieda had changed into a bikini over which she was again putting on the blue corduroy skirt and the white sweater. He, too, changed into his swimming-trunks, wearing the Levis over them, before, towels in hand, they went to the beach. A straight road, no more than a hundred yards long, led to the beach. Beside the road on their right was one solitary villa, white-washed with blue window-frames. Crump took the last air-ferry on a Friday afternoon from Southampton to Cherbourg from where, putting on his black leather gloves, he cruised down to the south coast of Brittany at a lazy ninety miles an hour, the DB6 engine hardly humming under the cherry-red (or Dubonnet Rosso) bonnet, came to this villa where, with precise timing, his mistress Madeleine arrived two minutes later from Paris in her purple Lamborghini Miura, and they spent two days of enchantment in a manner which would be approved by any *nouvelle vague* director, and parted, making impossible and preposterous promises to each other, Crump driving back to Cherbourg to catch the first ferry on Monday morning and was back in his twelfth-floor office on Millbank in time for a board meeting. A hedge ran along on their left, enclosing a plot of land on which grew wild flowers and which, if they came here in a year's time, would have a villa on it.

She began to run, swinging the towel above her head.

He walked, assuming the gait of a pompous dignitary.

She stopped, stooped to pick up something.

He ran and went past her.

She stood up, throwing away whatever she had found on the ground, a sea-shell, a pebble, but imperfect, not possessing the perfection she looked for; or perhaps she had been deceived by the appearance, for the thing was not what she had thought it to be when it attracted her eye, and ran, again swinging the towel in the manner of a cowboy lassoing cattle.

– There isn't a cloud in the sky, she said when they were placing their towels on the sand, having reached the sheltered spot among some rocks where they had come on the previous day.

– The jolly heaven above, he said.

– Do you think it'll get windy later? she asked. It's only a gentle breeze now. Will it get windy later?

– We're protected anyhow, he said.

They stripped off their outer garments and lay on the towels.

– My mother, she said, is an amazing woman. At least was, though I suppose she's still alive.

– This is your story, he said.

– I ought to have told you a long time ago, she went on. It was amazing what she did. Though I feel sorry for father sometimes; poor old father. Embarrassment and shame hurt him more than personal loss. At least so it seemed, for one can see how embarrassment and shame work on a person; one can't always see the inner grief. Her first name was Sybil. She was quite a beauty, I believe. There goes Sybil Lowes, people would point her out when she and my father did the social rounds. Sybil Lowes, that's before father changed the name to Lewis. He never told the full story. I'd love to know where they met. I'd love to know about their courtship and marriage. Their days in Germany. He was a Berliner. She came from Munich. An odd couple, in many ways. He is tall and thin in the old photographs, rather severe-looking. It may be the impression of the sunken cheeks and the thin lips. She smiles in all the old photographs. He was a wine merchant, had been born into the business. In some of the photographs it seems there is a mouthful of wine behind the tightly shut thin lips and that he's tasting the wine and will presently be spitting it out. So, I don't know how they met. Maybe she was in some academy in Berlin, maybe he was travelling south. They met as people meet, I suppose; what accident is not possible in life? They left Berlin soon after the wedding, left Germany; well, not soon after, but about fifteen months after. They left not with the ugly haste with which refugees leave, they were not refugees, although it was the thirties and Hitler was, well, you know, but they left with dignity, with ostentation, there are the pictures on the ocean liner. And both my brother and I were born in Johannesburg. They called him Johann at first, of course, and then simply John. I don't know what happened to the wine business in Berlin. Maybe he sold it, maybe he went bankrupt, what with the war coming, I don't know. One thinks one knows a lot about one's parents, hearing their stories, reminiscences, but one doesn't. One knows more about Napoleon or Stalin than about one's father. Anyway, by all accounts, they were happily married. Father did well in business and for a time they must have had a very busy social life. Mother kept a scrapbook full of gossip titbits from newspapers in which their names were mentioned. Sometimes their pictures appeared. Then it stopped altogether. I must have been eight or ten. I don't know what I noticed. I couldn't have noticed much at that age. But I suppose I noticed intuitively, like looking at something without knowing one is looking at it and yet taking it in and later one is surprised by one's own memory of something one thought one had not noticed. Mother kept to her bedroom much of the time. We thought she was ill. At first everyone was convinced that she was ill. Doctors came to the house. And father, still continuing the social rounds, explained that his wife was indisposed. But then the doctors stopped coming. And still she would not leave the house. John and I didn't talk about her, about what could be wrong with her. John was two years older and I suppose he didn't think it appropriate, talking to his kid sister about something important. Father, too, stopped going to the parties and preferred to spend his evenings alone at his club. There was a horrible silence in the house. But you would hear mother. She would walk through the house like

Lady Macbeth without looking at anyone. Then one day, when father was in his office and John and I were at school, she disappeared altogether.

A few minutes later, he rose, saying: I think I'll go and take a dip. He ran into the sea and at first it seemed that the cold water was tying chains to his ankles, halting his desire to submerge himself in the sea, but he broke loose, bounded forward in three leaps until he was thigh-deep in water. He flung himself at a breaker, dived deep into the swelling water, stood up after swimming a few strokes and found himself chest-deep in the stinging cold sea. He let a breaker knock him shorewards, swam with it for two or three lengths, reached a shallow point and began to run out. He picked up his towel and dried himself.

– What's it like? she asked.

– Delicious, he said. Wonderfully warm. Go and try it.

– That's what you said yesterday. I froze.

But she rose and ran to the sea, halting no sooner than she was ankle-deep, and screamed.

– Go in, he called. It's warm once you're in.

But, essaying to take two or three steps forward, she abandoned the sea and came running back, saying, It's bloody freezing. Let's go for a walk.

They left their clothes beside their towels. The beach was half a mile long, and they slowly walked down it. She paused to turn up with her toes shells and pebbles embedded in the sand, but rarely picked one up. He drew cartoons in the sand.

– Perhaps we shouldn't compromise, he said, taking up another conversation from another time. For we're surrounded by extremes.

– In Europe? she asked, glancing at the sea and at the sky in a swivelling movement of the head.

– In Europe, he said.

– We're the losers, she said, picking up and immediately throwing away a piece of plastic which had looked like a shell.

– I talk of this to my boys, he said. I worry them with my

worries. Or perhaps merely entertain them. Pass the time.

– Doubts! she said, and added, looking at the breakers crashing against some rocks on a point in the distance: The sea is chewing up the land.

– Definitions, he said. Once you understand the abstract words, then there's nothing.

– Another abstract word!

– Once you, he began, but ran away, sprinted to the end of the beach and sat on a rock, waiting for her. She took her time, searching the sand for what it might contain. It became perceptibly windy before she reached where he was, and when they turned to walk back they saw that clouds had gathered on the horizon.

– It's going to be the same as yesterday, she said.

The wind increased in force by the time they were again in their sheltered spot. They lay on their towels, their backs to the sun.

– What time is it? she asked.

He took out his watch from a pocket in his trousers.

– Eleven thirty, he said, just gone.

– We must have slept, she said.

– Perhaps, he said. Or it is possible that all the watches and clocks in the world were advanced by two hours in the last few minutes.

– My back seems to have got burned, she said. And yours is red as a crab's!

– I used to teach a boy called Jim Sutton, he said.

– This is your story, she said.

– Not mine, he said. But it's a story.

– There's time before lunch, she said.

– Well, teach is perhaps the wrong word. I had to endure him for a number of lessons; that would be a more accurate description of the teacher–pupil relationship between Jim Sutton and me. He drew attention to himself the first time I took him. In no spectacular way, simply by talking a lot. I asked him his name and thought I heard him say Stern. Well, Stern – I was about to crack some joke or abuse him, but the whole class burst out laughing when I said Stern, and that just about ended the lesson. He was something of a conjuror. He had a way of leaning back in the last row, his chair tilted against the wall, quietly lighting match after match. You could smell the matches igniting. But whenever I called him out he wouldn't have a match on him. That's what he wanted, of course, to be called out and given the chance to make a scene, to act in front of the class and to make me look a fool. Once, I'm sure, he lit a cigarette, took a puff and stubbed it out right in front of me and all I saw was a puff of smoke in the air. Once he spat out chewing-gum, trying to get it to stick to the ceiling. If I sent him out, commanding him to stand outside the room in punishment, he'd spend the time carving initials on the door or, if it was the last lesson of the day, simply go home. The only way to get some work out of the class while he was there was to stand next to his desk, allow him to read a comic, and ask the class to write a composition. Another of Sutton's tricks was deliberately to damage things. He would write obscenities in books, tear out pages from textbooks, spill ink on his companions' exercise books so that I had to give them new ones. Sometimes, when I was taking another class, he'd burst in, shout something to some mate of his and go away, banging the door shut. I tried to suppress all the vicious and murderous impulses which his behaviour aroused in me. I tried to reason with him. Whenever I talked to him alone, he would hang his head down as though in shame and not answer or simply keep saying *I don't know* to all my whys and hows. It was useless to offer him friendship, for he would abuse it in the very next lesson. I thought of punishment, but hesitated. Also he was a difficult boy to punish. Most boys will accept punishment, for most boys caning *is* a deterrent, and there are some boys who'll try a teacher's patience deliberately and see how far they can go, and these if you cane them once they become model pupils ever after. But not Sutton's type. I caned him once, and that, too, ineffectually, for he wouldn't stand still. It would have had no effect anyway, but I had to make the gesture for the rest of the class. The only thing that had an effect on him was calling him a bastard once in class. He left school when he was fifteen. A week later, he was caught by the police for breaking and entering. He broke into a warehouse through the skylight. As soon as he entered, the skylight shut upon him and there was something about the mechanism which he couldn't figure out. He was trapped there for the night. The next morning he was handed over to the police and he got two years since he already had a criminal record.

– If we walked back to the hotel now, she said, we could have a shower before lunch.

They rose and put on their clothes and, flinging their towels over their shoulders, walked back towards the hotel. A hedge ran along the road on their right, enclosing a plot of land on which grew wild flowers. Crump stood on the plot of land, observing the builders put the finishing touches to the most handsome villa in Brittany which he had commissioned Oscar Niemeyer to design for him. On their left was a solitary villa, at present unoccupied, whose owners would probably come and spend August there.

– What shall we do if it rains this afternoon? she asked.

– What shall we do, what shall we ever do? he mocked, but perhaps the mockery was directed only at himself, for he hated the facility with which the obvious quotations came to his mind and insisted on being repeated.

They went into the bathroom together, and stood in an embrace under the shower. He faced the window, which was open, which he liked to keep open, for he could see the Atlantic through it.

– We're only having a shower. Why does that excite you? she asked.

– Christ, he said, if pressing against your fanny and milk-white tits didn't excite me, you'd be bloody worried.

– Here, scrub my back.

He rubbed the cake of soap on her back, continuing the action round her body, so that, throwing the soap away, he could massage lather on to her breasts, and that was an interesting sensation, slippery breasts in his hands. He held her under the shower and watched the water wipe away the smears of soap from her body.

– That's fine, she said, withdrawing. You'd better cool off. You can't go to lunch so obviously advertising your virility.

They dried themselves and powdered, deodorized, anointed and variously pampered their bodies, he with Old Spice, she with Max Factor and Elizabeth Arden. She chose a scarlet-and-orange dress, he wore a suede jacket over his Levis and black poloneck. There was still time before lunch began, however, and he poured out some whisky into two tumblers, diluting it with a generous quantity of water.

– You were talking of your mother, he said.

– Compromise, she said. And, of course, we're the losers.

– In Europe? he asked.

– In Europe, she said. For look, it's an extreme situation, demanding commitment. But we live with compromise, which is a corrosive element. European life has become rusted with cosiness.

– I sometimes wonder if we'll ever have the courage to make a choice.

– If it comes to that, she said, if it ever.

– The way things are going.

The lunch began with oysters.

– We can drive to Beg Meil after lunch, she said.

A mayonnaise salad consisting of potatoes, green beans, peas and shrimps followed the oysters. He ordered a bottle of claret, Château Boutisse, to go with the main course, a steak.

– The clouds might blow away, she said.

– As long as it doesn't rain, he said.

For cheese, he chose a Boursin, she a Brie. They finished the wine with the cheese. They were offered a bowl of fruit. She took some grapes, he an apple.

– I think, he said, when the coffee was being served, you'd better go and prepare yourself.

– Let me finish my coffee, she said, adding: It's a pity the pill makes me sick; it would be so much easier.

He had fantasies of spontaneous sexual assaults upon her without prior notice when they left the dining-room together.

– You go ahead, he said, going into the W.C. on the half-landing. He peed to the last drop he could urge from his bladder. What difference a urine-free penis would make to his performance, he did not know to any degree of scientific satisfaction, but he told himself that it must help for the very reason that he thought it helped, such being Crumpsychology, quoting to himself, The force that through the green fuse, saying aloud, Etcetera, while zipping himself up, determined not to allow quotations to rule his tongue, but just when he had freed his tongue it became enslaved to another line from somewhere else and he said, Hell, I might as well say it, and said it, By our own spirits are we deified, adding, Amen, at last leaving the W.C. She had drawn the curtains and was already in bed, naked. He removed his clothes slowly and methodically, considering haste an unnecessary concession to lust: sexual intercourse had to be an act of diplomacy, one's mind negotiating a difficult peace with one's body. And don't give me that nonsense either, Crump said to himself when lying with her, that it's a distillation of two into one. Sex, mate, is the most selfish one-sided act two people can commit together.

– Oh but no, said the learned voice of some manual on Married Love while Crump went on with what he had to do to placate the oysters and the Château Boutisse inside him, not at all. Sex, because it is the highest manifestation of the attraction of two bodies to each other . . .

– What about prostitutes? Crump yelled.

– . . . its climax is that rare moment when a simultaneous orgasm is reached by the two bodies. So much for your prostitutes, Mr Crump, when the experience is uniquely that of oneness . . .

– What, with a Dutch cap and half a pound of Orthocreme? questioned aporetic Crump from immediate personal experience.

– . . . and the ecstasy is, one might say, essentially a spiritual one.

– Oh balls, Professor! Crump cried, exhausted.

When they dressed again, she wore light-blue bell-bottomed trousers, a white sweater and a navy-blue reefer jacket, he his Levis, black poloneck and a suede jacket. They drove towards Beg Meil. Green-and-yellow foliage on the roadside to their right, the blue sea to their left; their perceptions generalized into abstractions of form as they drove.

– And so we accept, he said. A drive in the afternoon.

– Through the Forêt de Fouesnant.

– The garden beside the river in Pont Aven, a path leading to a poet's bust.

– Looking for a choice.

– Making do with alternatives.

– A drive in the afternoon.

– Europe!

– It was a fashion, leaving South Africa, coming to Europe.

– You were talking of your mother, he said.

At Beg Meil they parked the car under some trees, pine trees, he noted in case a precise observation would be of some consequence in the future, and walked down the beach, a long white beach. The wind blew into the bay as if the bay were the mouth of a wind-tunnel. The sea had spewed back the litter of plastic cartons which it had probably swallowed at high tide. They walked back to the car and drove to another beach, a smaller, less sandy crescent. By jumping from rock to rock, they could be on dry land and yet in the middle of the sea – though the novelty of this experience was, of course, of no great consequence. The wind was louder here.

– Does it ever stop blowing? she asked.

– Perhaps it does in June or July, he said, accepting the cocktail which a servant had brought to him on his yacht moored on the still, blue waters of the Mediterranean while he lay sunbathing on the deck after a morning of skin-diving.

They walked back to their car and drove away from Beg

Meil. He drove at an erratic speed, being neither in a hurry nor wanting to kill time, now slow and now fast. Still enough of forest in spite of property developments and camping-sites, he thought, still somewhere to disappear into if you wanted to get the hell out, but he said, But, suggesting in answer to what she was saying that there could be a doubt about one's doubts.

He parked the car on the quayside in Concarneau. They went and walked down the main street, looking at the shops. The clothes boutiques would look provincial in an English provincial city, she remarked, surprised that the French peasant girl remained very much a peasant girl in spite of the universal availability of *Elle*. They passed a shop which sold pistols, rifles, guns and fishing-rods. They went into the Prisunic.

– I want to buy an oyster-knife, he said.

– But we never have oysters in London, she protested. And besides.

But he bought the oyster-knife, saying, We'll have some reason to now, and I could always use it for scraping off mud from my shoes after taking football at school.

– As with the admen, she said. Give us a product and we'll give you a good reason for selling it.

– There, he said, you've touched the very heart of capitalism.

They walked out of the Prisunic. They passed a shop which sold sailors' caps.

– As for other commitments, he said, but changed the subject, saying, Let's have a drink.

They went into a bar at the corner of the street, facing the old walled city. He had a beer; she had a coffee.

– What could we sell apart from the house? he asked. After paying what we owe the building society, we could probably have a clear two thousand.

– I shan't need anything except the clothes I wear.

– There's the car. My books. The furniture, of course.

– Let's not worry about it. Let's not even talk about it.

He had another beer; she had another coffee.

– That would be best, he said, almost heroic. For what heroism is worth today. Not to talk. Not to anticipate. You make your own arrangements, I'll make mine. A tidiness in all things. Just tell me, when you know, how much money you'll need.

– It won't be much, she said. But let's not.

– Let's not. Just let it happen. Don't even tell me when the time comes that it has come.

They walked across the street into the old walled city which they had seen before. The fishing-boats in the harbour exposed themselves to tourist Kodachromes. The shops in the old city offered souvenirs of Brittany. They did not want souvenirs, the purchasing of which suggests that one is already looking forward to the time when one will be looking back to what is now the present. They stood on the ramparts. They loitered amidst visual sensations: water, boats, fishermen – an amateur photographer's clichés. They walked back to the car on the quayside. They drove back to the hotel.

– It's only five o'clock, she said.

– We can rest a while and have a drink.

Curtains drawn back, they lay in bed, watching the heavy clouds trudge across the horizon. He rose and poured two drinks from the bottle of whisky they had bought on the ferry across the Channel. He saw her sitting in a long white brocade gown on a black leather sofa under a chandelier, and himself in black dinner-jacket and bow-tie, offering her a Scotch in a crystal glass, music, probably Brahms, playing from the rosewood stereo unit in the background. What a crummy ad, he thought. As if that's what makes people buy this brand, a phoney feeling of splendour.

She removed her bell-bottomed trousers and white sweater to change for dinner. He embraced her, saying, The frequency with which you change one would think you were on a bloody ocean-liner, and prevented her from reaching for the orange-and-scarlet dress which she was going to wear. He unhooked her bra, momentarily grasping the fullness thereof and quoting For still temptation follows where thou art, and began to push down her black nylon pantie.

– Not again, Mike. We can't, she said.

– It's all right, he said, I'll use a rubber.

– Oh, all right.

He poured out some more whisky which they gulped before going to bed. His mind between two lines, he was obliged to utter As high as we have mounted in delight, there's some joy in this, thought Crumpoet, who soon was whispering silently: In our dejection do we sink as low.

– Maniac Mike, she mocked.

He lit a cigarette, remembering the Spanish émigré in Paris and the girl in Hiroshima.

– At school, he said, I keep remembering the places we've been to, I keep remembering images, bits of our experience together, and if I ask what's so special about the particular images there's no reason, no answer.

– Which experiences?

– That we're here now, for example.

She wore her orange-and-scarlet dress and made up her face. He put on the suede jacket again over his black polo-neck and Levis. They went down to dinner. They ate potato soup with burnt garlic in it, a grilled fish, salad, apple pie, and cheese, and drank a bottle of Muscadet. After dinner, they went out to walk on the beach.

– It's funny how the wind drops after sunset, she said. That's when you wouldn't mind it.

There was some light on the horizon; the sea was dark grey. They walked the length of the beach. Turning round, he said, It's lovely and peaceful now. It must be terrible in the season. The usual chaos.

For something to say.

But went on: The annual breakdown. Europe needs towing in one direction or the other. The slow disintegration we live in. I spend so much time warning my students. We're a little Europe, our school. Muddling on. I once told them that that was the best thing old England could do, just muddle on. I wouldn't now. I'm clear in my own mind now. But, to tell you the truth, I wouldn't know what to tell them, I wouldn't know how to explain. How can I stand up and say, Look, chaps, we can't go on like this, pretending week after week when what I should tell them is We must either learn to play an elaborate game and we must know when we play it that we are in fact playing it, and this too will be a pretence, a more sophisticated one perhaps, but still a pretence, or we must give up pretending altogether, and that would mean giving up full-stop, there's nothing else.

– It's marvellous to have a hotel to ourselves, she said when they had reached the hotel and were entering the bar.

For something to say.

They sat in the bar for twenty minutes, drinking coffee and cognac. There were a few locals in the bar, talking to the *patron*.

– You were talking of your mother, he said.

– That time in Berlin we decided we wanted warmer weather, we drove south, remember?

– There was snow in Bavaria.

– Rain pursued us.

– Until we reached the snow in Bavaria.

– We could have gone to Cadiz, I suppose, had we had the money.

– And no ferry to catch after reaching Bavaria.

– When was that?

– The year after the year before.

– Time!

– There was the rusted anchor, he said, beside the canal in Amsterdam, an abandoned scrap of iron. Opposite the pleasure houses.

– And in Berlin two old ladies left the museum where they worked, stepping into puddles as though circumnavigation were impossible, sharing an umbrella.

– In East Berlin.

– It had been a cold Easter.

– You were looking for something, someone. You did not

say it. You were not obviously searching for something, someone. But when I saw you look over my shoulder when we sat in the café on Friedrichstrasse there was apprehension in your eyes. I talked to you of the heart of things. You listened, but your eyes would not rest on my words. As on the beach in the mornings when the sky is blue, you look for the clouds which are not there. As when you look for shells, listening to what I have to say, but not looking, seeing the shape you're looking for in the shell but not finding it. The heart of things. Did I read that somewhere, like so much that I mutter? I sometimes think I'm reading about my own life.

– Even this conversation of the past and the future.

– Words, that's all, read or remembered, printed or uttered; images shored against ruin.

– That time in Berlin, it gave one an odd sense of security to be able to drive between East and West, something the Berliners could not do.

– It was Easter, remember, and West Berliners could visit their relatives for the holiday.

– Old people wept on Friedrichstrasse station, saying good-bye to their Western children.

– You were talking of your mother, he said.

– We drove south, remember?

He yawned.

– Tired? she asked.

– No, it must be the fresh air, he said.

They went up to their room, he pausing to make use of the facilities on the half-landing. They went to bed, deciding to go to sleep early, the decision being hardly necessary since their consciousness had conceded most of its territory to the kingdom of sleep by the time they changed into their night clothes.

Outside in the mid-afternoon heat, the road white from the print's over-exposure, the silent track suddenly loud with a tank on its conveyor-belt motion; the menace of pre-thunder-storm heat in East European midsummer and the tank with its invisible driver who himself saw everything, knowing his target precisely; the uniformed officers who uttered commands and oaths in a foreign language, gods of the rules they themselves had decreed. What images return, Crump was about to ask when his memory added, O my daughter, making a quotation out of his question. And if there was fornication among the empty stalls, dark-haired Anna in a meaningless plot, what vivid flickerings on the screen could possess an absorbing fascination and what could the projectionist know who, invisible in his room, concerned merely with a mechanism, was supposed to start, continue and end whatever necessarily had to begin, having presumably seen it all before, what images? Isn't there more than this? he had wondered walking in some European city. And it was distortion, surely, he remembered that his memory had not remembered accurately, though he did not pretend to infallibility, for it had not been afternoon, but evening, the tank had devoured the long evening shadows; not a cinema, but a stage on which dwarfs – *dwarfs!* is that it? – performed. All right, then, that's what you are, a dwarf performing, not the stalls but the empty corner of a church where Anna had lain, soiling her white dress. What does it all mean, poet? some poet's question echoed in Crump's mind as he rose to leave his room, wondering from where the memory had come, for there was only the blue sky outside, the mist dispersing, there were houses, roads, cars, bicycles, scooters, gardens, flowers, weeds, boys going home for lunch, people, but really only the blue sky with the jets descending in a line as if they were coming down on a track. But he could not remember the name of the fair-haired one, locking his door, carrying the keys like a jailor – the keys dangling from a crooked finger; he had never seen a jailor but that was how he imagined jailors carried keys; the fair-haired one who lay in the hotel room as if in a hospital, picking up a few words of the foreign language, teaching them to the boy, but he remembered, Ester, the dying one, the note she left – *Dear Johann*, to whom she had to explain, for he had asked *What does this mean?*, pointing to some foreign word in a train compartment, and she had said

I don't know and could not let him go with *I don't know*; she had to show him something she did know before she died. We're all translators, Crump thought, walking down the corridor, almost expecting dwarfs to come round the corner. That's all there is to it, a translation. Shut the phrase-book and there's nothing.

– Hi, King Mod, a voice said behind him, a hand slapping his back.

– You're late leaving your class, he told the boy. That's how they behave, he told himself, as if you're an uncle or a cousin.

– I got the stick, sir.

– Good for you, Robbins, that's the way. Stand out from the crowd, be an individual, make sure your voice is heard. Play the fool and you'll be noticed. Some of you kids are no better than show people who'll try any trick to attract publicity.

– Come off it, Robbins protested. It wasn't my fault.

– Never is. What's for lunch, do you know?

– Pilchards and salad.

– A pity. I was hoping for oysters.

He entered the staff-room. Two or three members of staff sitting there looked up to see who had entered, and he remembered how in his first year he had once knocked on the door of the staff-room before being about to enter, had realized what he had done, had walked away and returned a little later wondering when his mind would accept the fact that he was a teacher and not a student. He hung his keys on the board, noticed a pile of papers on the top of a locker, left there by Mr Davies two years ago when he changed jobs, sat down in an arm-chair and lit a cigarette. No one spoke. Time had to pass. She was in Johannesburg that winter, flirting with idleness or cleaning away the encrusted earth that bound her roots; a banal notion, roots; the casuistry with which we either flatter ourselves or suggest a complexity of character in a life essentially simple has its source in vanity; or waiting for tea to be served on the lawn beside the camellia bushes while Crump knocked on doors to rooms to which he had free admittance. Bid farewell to the New World, Frieda. More of his colleagues entered the room. He inhaled cigarette smoke, shutting his eyes, thinking of lung cancer, recalling some statistics which proved that his chances of dying of lung cancer were greater than being run over on the road or being killed in a car or a plane crash. For to have created industry and leisure, to have fulfilled the conditions for a sybaritic existence, is not necessarily to have created civilization; how can I explain this, Frieda? The greatest happiness of the greatest number is a futile conception now that we seem to have achieved it, and how much worse must the concept of the greatest happiness of a selected minority be? How shall I explain and what shall I say? I shall, I shall try when thou hast bound bones and veins in me, fastened me flesh, I whose sleep is a voyage in the *Deutschland*, navigating the gale-whipped seas of your absence and waking up shipwrecked.

O Heart: Kunitz said more.

He stubbed out the cigarette and rose from the chair, wondering whether Hindu gods with eight or ten arms had specially built chairs with eight or ten arm-rests, glad that he at least was not averse to pilchards like many of the boys and since they did not care for salad either, give them bangers and chips and they'd eat like pigs, he ought therefore to have a substantial meal, and, walking out of the room and passing the staff cloakroom, decided that he would defer the pee till after lunch when he would also wash his hands with the soap called Buttermilk. Two boys stood outside the headmaster's room, Mockler and his constant companion Golding; the latter he remembered addressing an Indian teacher who spent the previous term at the school – Where are you going for your holiday, sir, Southall? – and both Mockler and Golding had gone to Ireland for a fortnight one term, truanting, and no one knew until Mockler's mother rang up to ask when the geography field-trip to East Anglia would end. Crump entered the dining-hall which was also the assembly hall, the examination hall, the ping-pong room and badminton court, the theatre and the concert hall. Sounds of cutlery being knocked against the tables, and chairs being scraped, the voices of three hundred boys filled the air with a barbarism peculiar to children just before a meal; red curtain across the stage on which dust enacted a universal rite with the solemnity of a melodrama, an empty stage, that's all you need; he sat at his table where the other five seats were taken by fifth-formers who took no notice of his arrival but continued to chat. The teacher on duty blew the whistle, and said, Bow your heads for grace, and while grace was being muttered tight-lipped Crump, trying to suppress the relevant bit of Eng. Lit. which he remembered at this point every day, could not do so and remembered again: Grace is grace, despite of all controversy: noticing that a good proportion of the boys did not say grace at all but continued to chat. The appointed boy from Crump's table dashed for the tray of food. Sinclair, sitting next to Crump, said: My prayers have been answered. Crump looked at him and Sinclair explained: I prayed last night that I get into the football team.

– If the Almighty is so kind to you, Sinclair, I suggest you pray devoutly and intensely during the next week that we are served oysters next Friday. If your prayer is answered, I promise you I'll believe in God and immediately embark on a combined pilgrimage to Jerusalem, Mecca and Benares.

– But how can we have oysters when we pay only a bob for our dinner?

– God's ways are mysterious as you well know, Sinclair, and who are you to doubt the possibility of miracles?

– You've got to be reasonable.

– Is God reasonable?

– I hate pilchards.

Crump served the pilchards to those who wanted them, three didn't, so he served four portions for himself, decided that that was too much and put back one portion, each boy helped himself to a little salad, some taking a little grated cheese, some a tiny helping of grated carrots, some a quarter section of a tomato, and everyone had a large helping of boiled potatoes. In the hall three hundred knives and forks scraped the white plates, but he quietened the noise, raising his eyes from the white table-cloth, the silver cutlery and the two wine glasses, to look at the duck which the waiter had brought for his approval, and a nod was sufficient for the waiter to go away and to put the duck in the silver press, wringing its blood out, while another waiter brought a bottle of Montrachet (Baron Thénard, 1964) to go with the first course. Or, beside the river in Pont Aven, O demon memory, sick of an old passion, these things happen, Crump, there were the belons to scoop out with the tiny oyster-fork and the oyster-shell to tilt in front of one's mouth, neck thrown back. Gastronome Crump could give a colour supplement's spicy odours to pilchards in tomato sauce, making a delicacy out of coarseness, spread freshly laundered cloth over the formica, the conversation around him softly whispered French.

Turning away, what had she seen but the bluey misty sea, not France? I should like, he remarked, to give her attention a geographical distraction, if not focus, thick this tomato sauce, the potatoes overboiled as usual, what abominable cuisine, to drive across Holland and Germany. Perhaps her eyesight was sharper than his – who knows what anyone else sees? – and saw France from the Dover quayside, or some point she could regard with more than a vacant interest, for she hardly turned round, weakly demanding: Why?

– Oh, just to see what it's all about.

He munched the grated carrots with some gratitude to the school meals service, decidedly the best thing, grated carrots, without the repulsive off-white salad cream.

– Is there anything wrong in wanting to look? Germany should stir some emotion in you. At least.

– Even if all I know of it are those awful calendar pictures of Bavaria my father insisted on framing!

At least some emotion had returned to her, at least some animation, saying that, not the abstraction of gazing away, sadly.

And driving on to the M.V. *Compiègne*, he had said, pleased that it was a French boat and thinking that it was always more reassuring to return on a British vessel, one experienced a feeling of instant security, Oh hell, let's see France anyway, noticing that her abstraction, or could it have been distraction merely, had now quite gone, and locking the car and walking up to the bar deck was slightly moved by the spontaneity with which she said, I'm excited. Buying two hundred cigarettes, a bottle of whisky, and, for immediate consumption, two glasses of whisky, he remembered the line he had quoted to himself when he had seen her off on the Union Castle, and repeated it now to himself, My heart, but you were dove-winged, I can tell, and then had written to her as though there had been an entire history to recount between the ship's edging away from the dockside and his returning to his flat when, before writing, he had sat and looked at the poem to see what his memory had remembered and why, and he had used the word, without having clearly determined why, but it seemed vaguely appropriate, he had called her dovewinged Frieda, for she could be so light-spirited, as he realized now seeing her spontaneity, taking the whisky and the cigarettes to where she sat, the white cliffs receding behind her, he saw through the porthole.

Ground-rice for pudding, slimy and insubstantial after the pilchards and salad which most boys detested, and therefore ate little of, can be guaranteed to create chaos in the classrooms this afternoon, he thought, pouring out a ladleful for each boy on his table, why don't they give them rich generous meals and render them soporific and submissive to learning, though he thought of other things, remembering that he was fortunate in having a double lesson with an 'A' Level literature group, but the third lesson, the final one of the week, was 4B whose reigning monarch was Jim Sutton, a kind of destructive conqueror like Tamurlaine.

As in the second dovewinged summer, when she had come to him in the forest, under the pine tree, stockingless in sandals. Ah, this is France, who cares if we're observed? Pine-cones in the damp earth. It's simpler to fulfil one's lust. Were you happy? Yes. And are you still as happy? Yes, and you? Then more kisses. He knew all about it then, the passionate Victorian, rediscovering and recreating the Renaissance, in nineteenth-century Italy. And Crump in Renault-fumed France saying, We plagiarize each other's emotions. The dampness in his thighs.

He decided, after two spoonfuls, that ground-rice was of service neither to his taste nor to his appetite, thought regretfully of the peasants in Bihar, said, Remember, Sinclair, to pray for oysters, rose from the table, walked down the hall as through a wind-tunnel of noise, tapped a fifth-former called Fairhall, fatty Fairhall, on the shoulder just when Fairhall was about to swallow a spoonful of ground-rice, said, Watch the weight, Fairhall, remember that fat men, though beloved of Caesar, can die with the sheer pressure of over-eating, remember what happened to King Farouk, and before Fairhall, swallowing hastily, could say, which he did a moment later, I'm 'appy, ain't I? Crump walked on and was out of the hall. Mockler and Golding still stood outside the headmaster's room, the latter remarking, Cor, ain't I bleedin' 'ungry, to which, more distance between them and Crump, Mockler commented, Whose bleedin' idea was it to set fire to the toilet paper? Crump entered the staff cloakroom, stood hands on hips at the urinal, raised his head, shut his eyes, allowed the bladder to drain out, remembered the aquarium-type cisterns in the public lavatory in Holborn, the polished copper pipes in the Gentlemen at Shepherd's Bush, shook himself, zipped up his trouser-front, washed his hands with the creamy soap called Buttermilk, dried them on Cresco paper towels, remarked for the *n*th time on *Worthing* on the Cresco container, wondered how many people Cresco employed, thought of the schoolteachers instructing young boys and girls in the beginnings of civilization, Mesopotamia and Egypt and China and Greece and Rome, attempting revelations into centuries of poetry, informing them of the importance of coal in the Ruhr, of iron in Minas Gerais, taking them to the theatre, what assumptions did teachers not make into the desirability of inculcating the elementary truths upon the tender, oh the willing, credulous minds of children even when they would leave school at fourteen and live in Worthing all their lives, making paper towels and affixing the instruction on the container: Use Towel Double. He applauded Cresco, saying to himself in a mood of surrender, If each one of us, attempting to build his own palace of Knossos, must die, then why not prefer the disposable culture made possible by technology? Indeed, why leave legacies of woodworm and outdated plumbing? he added, rolling up the Cresco sheets and throwing them into a bin, thinking that it was doubtful if the youths of Worthing, any more than their contemporaries in London, were willing to commit themselves to a life-long career at a factory. When he had taken a party of fourth-formers on a factory visit, the supervisor from the welding section had proudly informed them that he had been working at the factory for forty-one years; they had felt no admiration for him, only pity and contempt. Leaving his thoughts in the cloakroom to continue whatever debate they had begun, he entered the staff-room where one of his colleagues had just made tea and was pouring it into red, green, blue and yellow Melaware mugs. He took a red one, put two spoonfuls of sugar into it, tried not to think, while stirring the tea, why he had chosen a red mug when he could have taken a blue, a yellow or a green one, for he did not drink from a red mug every day or during three successive breaks on the same day, therefore there must be an unconscious choice and an unconscious reason, but he tried not to interpret the smaller choices which were probably made, and had to be made, because at any given moment in his life there was a host of alternatives demanding a selection to be made; that's how it is. He sat down in an arm-chair, a particular one out of ten, another choice, and, thinking about choices, wondered again about the Hindu god with eight arms who surely must have had a problem when making love to a woman with only two breasts and she surely must have felt an eerie sensation when he mounted her and pressed into her and there were, when she shut her eyes and surrendered herself to the ultimate ecstasy, eight hands and forty nails digging into her back. Torn by passion, indeed. He sipped his tea, remarked to a colleague, We are to the boys what flies are to the gods: they kill us for their sport; a remark which was wasted upon the particular colleague who did not see the peculiarly literary nature of the joke. More teachers returned from the lunch, each one, as he entered, made some gesture, verbal or physical, a jerking of the head, a raising of eyebrows, a grimace, complaining about the appalling quality of the meal, but Crump eased himself in the arm-chair, lit a cigarette, sipped his tea, and though there was conversation around him, one long wall of staff notices, one wall of plate glass showing a lawn outside and a sky which was still blue, he was tired with participating in the repetitive routine of supposedly serious or blatantly frivolous discourse. The same old anger about the political situation. The same old abuse at garages which overcharged for a service which they did not adequately perform. The same old reminiscences of days in the Army and days in the sun. The same old frustration with the teaching profession. What shall we talk about today, Stobbs? he had asked, what interests you, Barnes, apart from scooters and girls? Are you at all worried about what's happening to the world? Do you ever talk about it? But it had been the Nigerian boy, Kola, whom everyone inevitably called Coke, who had said, There's nothing we can do.

– You're fortunate, Crump said, in not having that illusion, for, at your age, we believed that what we thought and said was important, we spoke at debates as if it was an assembly of the world's heads of state. I suppose the seriousness of our enthusiasm was as foolish, why foolish, let's say irrelevant, pointless, futile, misdirected as is your total disinterest.

– But what's the point, insisted Kola, No one's going to listen to us, whatever we have to say. I don't think students have the power which newspapers flatter us into thinking we do. It's a trick to make us feel good. They just want us to keep buying the papers, that's all.

– What do you have to say? What is it that worries you?

– Everything, said Kola bitterly, and he did not have to elaborate since he had worn a C.N.D. badge for two years now and had shrugged his shoulders to anyone who had remarked that C.N.D. was no longer fashionable.

– But girls mainly, interpolated Chapman who had been trying all term to provoke Crump into a frank statement about sex; but Crump had always abused him with Shut your trap, man, Chapman.

– Unfortunately: Crump embarked upon a lecture, glancing at his watch, deciding there was insufficient time to set a précis, noticing Stobbs clasp his hands in front of him on the desk – how well Stobbs knew his mind! – unfortunately, man's situation at this time in his history is futile. It used to be important, even noble and glorious. He was second only to God, being especially gifted with an intelligence and with a language – a language at times of Miltonic loftiness (look that up, Murray, and take down one more brick from the great wall of ignorance which surrounds you). The more man has developed, however, the smaller he has become. Until recently, his situation was seen to be an absurd one – as evidenced in the works of some of our ninth-rate dramatists. Every act of emancipation which was necessary to his development had led to his becoming more and more isolated; the freer he was of, say, poverty, the more dependent he became on himself alone; losing his belief in God, he had to believe in himself alone. His actions became meaningless, then absurd. But even when his actions were absurd at least they had that quality. Absurd. Now, however, there is nothing he can do which is not futile. Whether he's creative or destructive, it's all the same. In Europe we have achieved a utopia beyond the dreams of nineteenth-century thinkers, and that is the great irony, for all we feel in this utopia is a sensation of nausea inside us. Soon, inevitably and necessarily, for we cannot leave half the world hungry, the whole world will be a universal welfare state.

– Why should that make you think it's all futile? asked Kola.

– Yeah, said Stobbs, shaking his head to emphasize Kola's question, afraid that Crump might have come to the end of his speech and might be about to set work.

– We make things, said Crump, inventions which are aimed at advancing our condition. But whatever makes life easier also imposes a limitation on the human body, subtracting from its physical functioning by rendering some of its capacities redundant.

Damn Chapman, he thought, I'll tell them about sex.

– Take, for example, the pill, one of the most marvellous of inventions aimed at making the world bearable by containing its numbers. There's no need to start giggling, Chapman, I'm not about to tell you a dirty story.

– What a pity! said Chapman.

– You don't have to listen if you'd rather be looking at *Playboy*. So, consider the pill, or, indeed, any of the several ways in which women, or men, can be rendered temporarily sterile. An advance certainly. But, for a start, each one of the ways diminishes to some degree the pleasure of the sexual act.

– How do you know, sir?

– I'm surprised at the level of your wit, Chapman; I'd have given you a C minus had you said that that was a pregnant thought, but, alas, you're quite retarded.

– Sorry, sir, I'll try harder next time, said Chapman.

– Technological change leads to, or ought to lead to, moral change. And this is where we fail, for we're slow to respond, our history is against us, some of us still go by Elizabethan notions of degree – anyone who doesn't know what that elementary notion is is unworthy of my teaching. All right, Murray, you don't have to slide out at the slightest hint of your incompetence. Sit down. Look it up later. But what I mean is this. Every now and then, technology makes mockery of what we think are enduring values. To continue with the example of the pill, women are, for the first time in their history, for the first time in thousands, perhaps millions of years, equal to men. Neither votes nor equal pay makes them as equal as when they can enjoy sexual relationships on the same terms as men have been at liberty to do for thousands of years. So, what happens to the idea of marriage? Technology has catapulted us much farther than we can immediately reach; but, instead of thinking about it, responding, all we do is continue to pretend that things haven't changed, that the young men and women who live together are obscenely immoral, and keep remarking upon the fact that the bride, all lachrymose virginity, who was given away by her father, wore a full-length white gown, with bodice and sleeves of guipure lace, and white slipper satin base with an overlayer of organza, falling into a train at the back and edged with lace, and carried a bouquet of red roses and white freesia. And that, frankly, thinking as I do about the futility of man's situation, makes me wonder at the stubbornness of people who do not even try to look at what's happening around them. But take another aspect. In practising birth-control, in doing what is obvious to most of us is the right and sane thing, are we not denying ourselves a basic human fulfilment; or, when people have children by error in spite of birth-control, is that not worse than having children simply because you want them? Nature is haphazard, nature is a wanton, nature is a computer gone crazy; man, on the other hand, calls the natural aspects and inclinations of himself barbaric, and attempts to impose controls. Nature is vicious, and murderous, nature is a sniper on the top of a building, shooting for the insane pleasure of killing; man tries hard not to be a killer and when he does kill his justification is usually in terms of a political rationality or a psychological disturbance and not that he felt naturally inclined to do so. Nature breeds and nature destroys. Man plans, organizes, forecasts; and he needs to do so. But it's only a delaying tactic; because the more subtle, the more sophisticated his planning the more it is against nature; and if he doesn't plan he'd only kill himself the sooner. It's not God and nature that are at strife, to use a line from the pompous old Victorian – Tennyson, Murray, if you want to look it up – but man and nature. Futile, I say; utterly futile. Think of these matters, Barnes, when you take Molly to the pictures on Saturday night and sit in the back row, not knowing later even the title of the picture you'd gone to see. Take another example. We create industries which are calculated to make life easier, more comfortable, which, and this is the least they can do, provide employment to idiots like you.

– Speak for yourself!

– I'm speaking for all of us. We produce the goods and, in doing so, turn the air we breathe into poison and turn the fresh water of the sweet Thames into some nasty chemical. No, don't mistake me. I live in a centrally heated house where two years ago I had to light fires; it's marvellous, though I used to enjoy building up a pile of sticks above balled-up pages of the *Times Literary Supplement*, for which there is no better use, and watching the fire slowly build up; it's great to have uniform warmth in the house, to know that it'll be warm before I get there tonight. It takes me ten to fifteen minutes to drive to school when it used to take three-quarters of an hour by train. And everything else. In all this, I am a supreme hypocrite, for I enjoy those pleasures and comforts most which I know are destroying me. My condition, too, is futile. My only compensation is that I know of the futility of my existence. The only thing I can do with any real meaning is, from time to time, to scream out as loudly as I can. I am not allowed to change my condition, for if I were to reject what the general mankind calls progress, then I would have to exclude myself from society. It's true, in this sense, that to be a dropout is the only heroic choice open to Western man now. But I do not wish to opt out, for I do not think that a singular personal example is going to alter the world. I do not think anything is going to change the direction in which we're going, that of becoming smaller and smaller. I am a hypocrite then, in many of my actions, for they are the ones which my mind is passionately critical of. But I don't have a choice. When the Concorde's built, I'll be obliged to travel by it if I need to go where it's going and have the money it'll cost. But I ask myself, and I'd like you to ask yourselves, Why? Civilization is a process by which we commit ourselves to comfort; and then to ultra-comfort. But that is not necessarily progress, it's simply a drift of events. There are two sorts of progress. One can be summed up by the idea of Liberty, for which all Europe fought at one time or another in one way or another, during the last two hundred years; and what this progress has given us is a kind of justice, what it has established is a principle of humanitarianism, which makes it easier for us to live with one another, and what this progress has to offer to us is a useful, purposeful, creative expression of our energies. Clichés, Crump, vague gestures, words, but he went on: This progress is an intellectual one, its workshops lie in the moral consciousness. The other sort of progress, the drift of events, is the one which substitutes a Boeing 707 with a Boeing 747 and a Boeing 747 with a Concorde, which gives a new heart to a dying man, which, in other words, attempts, through a proliferation of technical inventions, to appeal not to man's mind but his body; in short, his vanity. I'm not belittling this sort of progress; I find it marvellous, breathtaking; I applaud the inventive, dedicated brains who make it possible. But what I am saying is that by keeping us alive longer in more and more comfortable circumstances, this sort of progress is in effect killing us. Not you and me individually, but the whole bleeding lot of us. And what I insist upon saying is that this progress is really quite secondary, we could survive, even live happily without it, we could still be human beings; whereas to think that we can do without the first sort is to recede to a form of barbarism. And *this*, allow me to conclude, is precisely what's happening to us today; man has turned from ideas to things, from language to artifacts. Any questions? Yes, Chapman.

– You mentioned the pill, sir, What are the other ways?

– Goss'ma, muttered Barnes to Chapman's delight.

– We all know *that*, Chapman said.

– So? Barnes retorted. It's mod, ain't it?

Chapman shrugged his shoulders and remarked, Well, a bit surgical, if you ask me.

– Perhaps I should have qualified my question and asked, Any sensible questions? Yes, Kola.

– What do you expect us to *do*?

– Think, Kola, think. That's all.

He lit another cigarette, sitting in the arm-chair, having finished his tea. The conversation around him was about cars, and two of his colleagues were playing a game of chess. Crump smiled, his thoughts leading him to say to himself that he was a John Stuart at the mill with slaves. Though he enjoyed talking of cars himself, for the image of black-gloved Crump at the wood-rim steering-wheel of the cherry-red Aston Martin DB6 would often take him drifting through the Pyrenees. The first term, when Frieda was wintering in discontented South Africa, tearing up or tying into little bundles, he supposed, letters and mementoes, or clearing out bits and pieces accumulated in the obscure corners of drawers, twenty-three years to be reviewed, sorted out and appraised before returning to London to marry him, he supposed, rightly or wrongly, it did not matter, he had entered into debates that term, sitting here in the same arm-chair, but not now, not now. He knew what he was now, at least up to a point, at least as far as self-knowledge could go. Past the forest, it had taken them all the afternoon beetle-cruising down the Rhône valley, the quarter-lights angled to let the airstream form a continuous towel wiping the sweat on their foreheads, fields of sunflowers in Montélimar, to go past Orange, whence the Mistrals, flying low, cutting the baby-blue sky in the falling light, scissor-jets, making a sound of satin being ripped, had been coming.

She read: 'L'arc d'Orange fut élevé après la victoire de César.'

But after such ecstasy, pine-cones trampled into the earth,

after the more than silken texture of sensation, what triumphs brings Caesar to those whose victories are not martial feats? Gone, Rome, gone the marching legions, he thought, whose own feelings were more poignant than the streaks of vermilion in the western sky. He drove on although she was reading:

'Le théâtre d'Orange est le plus beau, le mieux conservé, non seulement de Provence, mais de tout le monde antique.'

He drove on past *des débris lapidaires*, that's what it all is, although Rome pretended to power still, and he, in another mood, would have wanted meanings from stony rubbish. On the flat plain outside Orange, taking the road to Carpentras, Provence stretched out with its vineyards. We must go, she said, looking at the map, for a drive along the Gorges de la Nesque, there should be interesting walks into the hills there. And he, agreeing to proposals with the inevitability of a monarch giving a royal assent to a bill already passed by parliament, found the little road to Venasque, changed down to third gear to negotiate a slope, woodlands around them, a cool watery valley, oaks.

– I've seen photographs, he said, of your South Africa, answering at last something she had asked before they drove into Orange, and it was too late for her to retrieve a conversation she had thought had been taken away by the wind like a pink scarf she had lost when they were driving to Brittany and it was hot enough to have the windows down, and she said, Oh that, but this is lovely.

– We carry countries within us, he said, when we've been given the world. I'm not going to.

But there were the agency's instructions to follow, the street and house to identify.

– I shall pick thyme and rosemary in the fields, she said. I shall lie under an almond tree.

He could smile at that, laugh even.

– And another thing, he said. To gaze at the stars, to read palms, to construe arrangements of tea leaves, to consult the horoscope in the evening papers, to interpret statistics, to invest on the stock market, to lower or to raise the bank rate, to undertake market research to predict consumer demand, to see the bank manager about an overdraft, to book the ferry in January for an August crossing. The future!

There was time for another cigarette, which he lit, noticing that conversation had ceased in the staff-room, two of the teachers were asleep, and he himself was no more awake if human intercourse is the condition of being awake. With freedom, however, and this is the inescapable and despairing conclusion, with equality and justice, has come diminution, he had told the four sixth-formers whom he taught literature, wondering whether he had said this to another class at another time or whether he had heard someone speak to him what he was speaking now, but went on nevertheless: We've become smaller in stature, living in maisonettes, cooking in kitchenettes, dining in dinettes, serviettes in our lap to protect our leatherette and suedette clothes, washing clothes in launderettes, we're becoming petty, the range of our vision has narrowed and we don't see beyond the small print of the small ads which offer us better jobs and second-hand bargains. No, Frieda, you mistake your wide plains for areas of freedom, I will not come, I should say cannot if one thinks of paying fares, but I say I will not, for to say I cannot is to suggest the decision has not been mine but forced upon me by circumstances; and you, going with a return ticket, are the one who has to make a decision. Come. I look at spaces which should contain your substantial form. All I see is a poet's image: Some lovely glorious nothing.

– You're a pessimist, she said, opening the windows of the cottage. The plumbing should be all right. We can always get the agency's local man to come and look at it. And, in any case, the view should be gorgeous when the sun rises.

He stubbed out the cigarette, for the bell was about to go, and was ringing when he rose from the chair, kicking away the flecks of cigarette-ash on his jacket, remembering Ash on an old man's sleeve is all, but enough, he said. He walked to pick up his keys from where he had hung them, thought of Mr Davies, seeing again the pile of papers on the locker, and just before leaving the room he said to his colleagues who had not yet bestirred themselves:

– Gentlemen, we ought to give our work the same professional attention as the Beatles give to theirs.

Smiling, he left the staff-room. He walked past the boys' notice-board, saw some prefects standing there looking at the notices, told one: I am a kind of burr; I shall stick. Look that up, Matthews, it's in the Works.

– What the hell are you on about now? asked Matthews whose pimpled face was like oxtail soup coming to the boil.

– You will know, Matthews. Look. He pointed to a chart of Francis Chichester's course which had been pinned up on the board several terms ago and had curled up at the corners. Ask yourself why he bothered.

– What's it got to do with me?

– Everything, Matthews, everything.

He walked past a succession of classrooms, observing how patches of plaster showed on the walls, until he reached the staircase where, shaking himself out of an hour's inaction, he climbed the steps energetically, and, reaching the top, marched down the corridor as he had seen Nazi soldiers do in films. Goose-stepping, jack-booted Crump halted, unlocked his room, entered, wondering whether Andrews expected a reply and what Jim Sutton had been plotting for the last lesson. Stop chewing in class, he had once commanded Sutton, and Sutton, paying no attention to him, looked up at the ceiling, contracted his mouth, spat out the rolled chewing-gum with such force that it bounced off the ceiling, and cried aloud: It didn't *stick*! He ought to mark a book or two before the sixth-formers came, in fact he ought to have marked several books in the lunch hour, how quickly they accumulated, like rubbish. He looked at a fifth-year literature essay, discovered the interesting remark: One can say that Viola and Cesario is the working of the Jaqueline Hyde complex – and was relieved of any immediate obligation to read the rest, for the sixth-formers were arriving.

Somewhere in the Gorges de la Nesque, the precise point

located by an almond tree to which he could again find his way, sitting under the tree, the river knocking its way through the rocks in front of them, he had said, Remember Brittany? She had turned from the bowl of the half-melon, the other half in his hand though he did not eat from it yet, only held it like a begging-bowl, to look at him, and perhaps she implied a nod, for she did not in fact nod, a look then, a certain look expressing that she did remember before she turned back to the melon, her half of it, for at least that was something tangible. She could have remembered, he had realized, although he had already taken her look to mean that she had remembered what he meant she remembered, one of the million fractions of moments which constituted her experience of Brittany, which was all there was, and he realized too that he had been on the point of thinking of the experience as *their* experience, but that would be a total falsity, and as soon as she had turned again to the melon he had said, Well, why should this be any different? And that would have been a perfectly valid question, he reflected; there would have been some truth in what he was saying, even if it was something else that she had remembered.

– What are you waiting for? he asked the four sixth-formers who were now seated and were looking at him.

– For your pearls of wisdom, sir, said Burnett.

– I think it's you I see, Burnett, but never mind, what I see is another matter. Well, answer me this, Burnett, why do you read literature?

– Because I hope to take an exam at the end of the year which I hope to pass.

– What, the exam or the year? Careful now with your word order.

– Censure accepted, apology tendered. The exam.

– Is that your only motive for reading literature?

– I hope to teach it, like you're supposed to be doing now.

– Your censure is ill-timed, Burnett. You can hardly qualify to be a teacher of literature when you do not care to pause to consider whether the subject is worth pursuing in the first place. So far, the only reason for reading literature you've given is that it offers a cushy career.

– I didn't say cushy, but looking at your example I'd agree that it entails very little work.

– Remind me to praise your wit in your end-of-term report. And you, Cave, have you any other reason to give to excuse what the tax-payer probably thinks is a waste of public money? After all, all we're doing is reading novels, plays and poems which is not too unpleasant a pastime.

– I agree, said Cave, that you're wasting the tax-payer's money by taking up our literature lesson with trivial talk.

– I suppose you want a commendation for your wit, too. All right, then, if an attempt at rationalizing what it is all about is of no interest to you, take down quote It can be said that to some degree Iago is motivated by racial prejudice unquote discuss. Get on with it.

– What are *your* reasons? asked Franklin.

– A poor straw to clutch at, Franklin; the essay's already been set.

– You've aroused our curiosity, said Hellard.

– I doubt it. All I've probably aroused in you, Hellard, is an inertia, an apathy, an utter reluctance to work.

– He's hurt now, said Franklin to Hellard.

– Your bloody fault, said Hellard to Cave.

– You can borrow my notes if you like, said Cave to Hellard.

– We can write essays at home, said Burnett to Crump.

– All right, then, take down for homework, Discuss the importance of Roderigo in *Othello*, Crump said to all of them.

– Christ, Brunette, what are you trying to do? said Hellard to Burnett. You're ruining my social life.

– I never know what you mean, Frieda had said, having finished her half of the melon and wondering whether she should discreetly place the rind in some obscure corner among the rocks or throw it into the river or take it back to the house in Venasque, but the bin there was a small bucket, not a bin at all, and that had to be tipped on to a hillside and the accumulation of litter there already looked vile, nobody ever collected it, only dogs poked their noses there, not when you talk like that, she added – to make sure that at least he understood what she meant. He watched her throw it towards the river. She did not throw it hard enough and the shell landed on a rock.

– Well, do you remember Gordes, then?

– How can I forget it, we saw it only yesterday, she said with some impatience; not that she thought him inscrutable, for had he said, You know what I mean, she would have agreed that she did.

Houses emptied by wind, Gordes, a hilltop culture surrendered to the wind. While down in the valley, the soil held together by pines and oaks, cultivation, subsistence still, down in the valley. Call at Gordes, stranger, knock on doors which the wind opens, howling its cynical welcome.

There was a knock on the door, a boy's head appeared as the door opened, the boy saw Crump, said, Sorry, sir, and withdrew, shutting the door.

– That's all right, Crump said to the shut door, and to the class: Notice that. Boys come all the way simply to apologize to me.

Franklin was glancing at his copy of *Othello*, no doubt hoping to find a clear statement of Iago's racialism in Dover Wilson's splendid introduction – that was something, scholarship, like Dover Wilson's, a lifetime spent looking at words, deciding which were the right ones, that was all, words to be thought about, considered, weighed, and the final conclusion, not always the ultimate conclusion, but final for him, final as far as he could tell, that these were the words which were the right ones. Hellard was looking out of the window, Cave and Burnett were writing. Crump picked up the first of a pile of 3B exercise books in which the latest comprehension work had to be marked; he opened the text-book, glanced at the appropriate passage which described an old man trying to cross a road, saw that the first question asked, Where is the old man standing? cursed the writer of the text-book for his pathetic notion of teaching English, and began to mark the first book in which the answer to the first question was, The old man is standing on a zebra. Having put a query next to that and deciding not to put an exclamation mark after the query, he looked up at his audience of educational theorists in the conference inevitably called The Teaching of English in the Modern World and continued: Two types of text-books are current today. The writer of the first type invariably considers children to be innocent, delicate and clean-faced. He will include sentimental stories in which the heroes are kind, tender children who love animals and who are more intelligent than adults. He will set questions giving the answers to which will in no sense advance the pupil's thinking or his ability to write. He will include mainly those poems which can be relied upon to give poetry a reputation of being fit only for pansies and set such irrelevant questions as At what time of the year do daffodils grow? At best, such a book is harmless; but more often than not it acts as an irritant, making the subject seem dull, making the pupils impatient with its seemingly pointless demands, say, to turn nouns into adjectives. The other type tries to project the image of being with it, of knowing teenagers' obsessions. From the carefully planned smart typography and layout to its use of dramatic photographs, it will give the impression of being urgent, important. Instead of using sentimental stories, it will use sociological documentary stuff. It will go out of its way to find passages with a coarse language as if coarseness equals toughness and toughness equals reality. The poems in it will be about boxers and motor-cyclists. It will contain articles about slum dwellings, the downtrodden Negro and Asian poverty, suggesting that only that is to be considered reality which happens to be a contemporary social problem. It will invite pupils to write creatively, but will insist as a kind of democratic dogma that the pupils need learn nothing about form. Frankly, I find neither type satisfactory. The first is too naïve to be taken seriously; the second is sickeningly vulgar in its tone, and reminds me of the aggressive kind of salesmanship which insists that the customer is always right. The first is a kind of misguided paternalism, the second an invitation to participate in a phoney democracy. Marking the books mechanically, he pondered the truth of a generalization he had arrived at early in his teaching: set easy, dull work which assumes that the children are mentally subnormal, then they will lose interest in the work, descend to a level of mental subnormality and their attentiveness and general discipline will deteriorate. And a corollary to this theorem: the behaviour of children in a class is a measure of the teacher's quality. But there are exceptions, Crump thought, knowing he was looking for an excuse, saying like any boy immediately does when accused of a misdemeanour, Wasn't my fault! as when a class contained a Jim Sutton whose nature had absorbed a violent vindictiveness long before he was of school age. Though Crump thought that he ought to add that, of course, a teacher could only maintain quality if he were not overwhelmed by a succession of large classes (although he himself was fortunate in this respect with his small fifth- and sixth-year groups) and if the teacher were allocated enough free periods in which not only to revise the lessons he had prepared, mark books and deal with the various administrative matters which came up from time to time, but also to recover his physical energy. No one who determined teachers' working loads ever made an allowance for the expenditure of physical and emotional energy. Too often, however, society expected a school to be little more than a zoo for the monsters it had created; certainly, for many parents teachers were little more than baby-sitters whose job was to give the children enough homework to allow the parents to watch television in peace. The blue had gone out of the November sky, the light failing rapidly and the western horizon beginning to crimson, look how the belly of the descending jet reflects it, the dove descending, he quoted unconsciously, breaks the air, and his own mind, he knew, was air broken into fragments of images, in flames of incandescent terror; he remembered that every time there was a red sunset and there was a plane descending, a flame, an incandescence, a terror. Franklin and Hellard had given up attempting to understand Iago, and even Burnett and Cave seemed to be finding the effort wearying; so Crump said to them:

– The week-end approaches. I shall go to the pictures tonight. Tomorrow morning will be spent in shopping, the afternoon in cleaning windows, hoovering the carpets, and the evening probably in going to a pub. Sunday morning I shall wash my car and look at the colour supplements to see which gold watch I ought to buy, which leather-bound works of Dickens or Tolstoy at a cut-price offer ought to decorate my shelves – that's one thing literature is about, Burnett, profit for certain types of publishers who do luxury editions long after the writers are dead and cannot be owed any royalties and when they run out of the acknowledged masters they'll raise any old writer to the stature of a classic to keep the profits going, and, another thing, their advertising usually suggests that these are not books which you must read if you wish to be considered civilized but books which make a good impression on your visitors – which Caribbean island to choose for my holiday, which exotic recipe to use for the preparation of my dinner (which will be attended by the six most brilliant conversationalists in London), which luxury-length cigarette to smoke, what a life, is that what you're working for, too?

– At least you've got a car.

– And if you're so critical of it all why don't you do something else?

– I'm trying to point to a moral, Cave. I'm trying to demonstrate to you what sort of people we're being made into. I'm trying to get you to ask a question or two (or three, as Groucho would add: Mister, let me tell you a thing or two or three); why, for instance, this unremitting pursuit of pleasure.

– Why shouldn't one have the best of everything?

– We can have the best of literature without having the phoney, decorative luxury editions.

– But you might enjoy the same book more in a luxury edition than as a paperback.

– You've a point there.

– Thank you.

– Though my point is that people who buy luxury editions very probably don't read them. Look at it this way, then. Are we working for anything other than to be consumers of things which are really inessential?

– You seem to be enjoying it. You go to the Continent every year. And teachers are supposed to be poorly paid!

– The point is this. Are you going to inherit complacently the kind of life I am leading, or I am being compelled to lead by a variety of forces, for the concept of free will has in many respects been discredited, or are you going to think out a new mode of existence for yourselves? And, if you do, are you going to avoid the danger of equating better and new with hedonistically more refined and technologically more complex? The artificial manipulation of society, the creation, say, of industries in depressed areas, is always well meant, but how are you going to avoid the danger of turning people into artificial beings? And, if you are not aware of these dangers or cannot avoid them, are you not, not you particularly, but your generation, going to die of sheer boredom with luxury and with loss of imaginative inventiveness?

– I suppose we could try crossing the Atlantic on skis.

– Or climbing up the north face of the Eiger on roller-skates.

– Frivolity, that's all you have to offer.

– Is your example a serious one, not you particularly, but your generation?

– You're becoming very sharp, Cave. I suppose frivolity is the current fashion. Seriousness has gone out of life. Virtue is measured by its sales potential. Our hearts beat faster when we see the colour ads and no longer, alas, when we read a line of verse. In a sense I suppose it's a good thing. The air has been cleared of unnecessary stuffiness. Only, however, to make way for a new pretentiousness. All I'm trying to do is to warn you.

– All we're trying to do is to study for an exam.

– Have you finished the essay on Iago? Your wit is very wearying. Get on with it.

– The essay or the wit?

The next morning, he moaned in the pre-waking reluctance ever again to emerge from sleep, while the words she had uttered had bounced back from the defensive wall around his consciousness, while, having his head against the pillow, he saw, only partly saw, for vision too rejected any other colour but that of sleep, the profile of her face, a line of light running down from forehead to chin, a brightness in her eyes and perhaps she was saying as she had said yesterday, It's a fine day. And then she said loudly and demandingly, Is it going to be fine today? As if his saying that it was going to be a fine day would be a guarantee of excellent weather. He had to turn, rise a little, for the loud voice had shattered the wall, and to peer at the window. The sky was indeed blue, as it had been yesterday. His eyes brightened, too, and he was willing to get out of bed, for he felt like a guest at a dinner party who is nervous on his arrival but becomes convivial on seeing a banquet spread before him. Seeing him about to rise, she rose with a determined air, her nightie being blown up so that he saw her buttocks for a moment before the soft uncrushable material of the nightie floated down to the prescribed hemline just above the knees. She brushed her teeth at the basin in the corner of the room.

– Do you think it'll remain fine? she asked, washing out her mouth.

– It depends on the wind, he said. Our usual shelter against it among the rocks might suffice.

She leaned out of the window to look at as much of the sky as she could and said, I can't see a cloud. Withdrawing into the room she asked, What time did we go to sleep last night?

– Sleep sleep or sleep screw? he asked.

– You know what I mean.

– It's all right, he said. We went straight to sleep. That must have been the night before or some other night.

– That's fine, then, she said. It's difficult to tell sometimes, one day's so like another, and, putting on a gown, she went to the bathroom, taking a little plastic bag with her.

He rose out of bed, saying This is all we do, and walked to the window. Certainly a fine day, he remarked, at least certainly a fine morning; so it was yesterday until the wind blew clouds across the Atlantic driving them to an early lunch. Before she returned from the bathroom, he had brushed his teeth and begun to shave. He saw her in the mirror, beginning to change. For a moment, he saw her standing naked before picking up a bra, and he observed her with objective detachment, as he might a painting, enjoying the particular disposition of form and colour during the second or two in which her body seemed still, stooping in the pose of being just about to pick up the bra.

– What shall we do today? she asked, putting on a grey herring-bone-patterned tweed skirt.

– What do you suggest? he said, lathering himself again.

She put on a white sweater, and he recited:

My love's bound up with cable-stitch
in a sweater that sailors wear;
her bosom swells like the ocean,
like sea-weed floats her hair.

– Well, we could lie on the beach, he said.

– And listen to the mermaids singing each to each? she taunted before the quotation could come from him.

– Luckily, it's not yet the tourist season and the mermaids are in the deep waters of typists' pools.

– And what if it blows, what if it rains?

– We could drive to Quimper or Morgat, Florence, Istanbul, anywhere, what about Johannesburg, Frieda, why don't we start a business running arms to South Africa?

– Mike, do you mind being serious?

– Je m'appelle Hilary.

– Oui, Pierrot!

He washed his face, dried it, applied some after-shave lotion to it, and began to change. In Levis and black polo-neck, he thought of the hushpuppy and grey-worsted Crump strolling through the corridors of a school in Middlesex, worrying whether the Boeing he could hear descending was VARIG from Rio or EL AL from Tel Aviv. He heard a voice say: He walks like a camel, does Mister Crump, he has droopy eyes and a bloody great hump.

They walked down to the bar of the little hotel where breakfast was served. Frieda ordered the Continental breakfast, specifying bread and butter and coffee, and Crump again wondered why the items had to be specifically ordered when they never varied from one day to the next. He was certain that if they were suddenly to order orange juice, bacon and eggs and toast and marmalade, the waitress would say, I'm sorry, madam, today we have only bread and butter and coffee.

– Et de la confiture? the waitress asked before going away with the order.

– S'il vous plaît, Frieda said.

– How would you like your eggs? Frieda asked Crump in the silence of the waitress's going.

– What eggs?

– You wanted them hard-boiled yesterday, she reminded him.

– Oh those!

The waitress came and placed the breakfast on the table. Frieda poured out the coffee. He hastily ate a slice of bread and butter, not caring for the apricot jam. Frieda ate slowly and self-consciously as, he supposed, she must have done in front of her parents. He lit a cigarette and imagined the smoke enter his bowels like a piston-rod, setting a complex of cog-wheels in motion.

– Let's not waste the glorious morning, she said, pouring out some more coffee.

He added a little milk and sugar to his; he sipped and inhaled alternately, a kind of dual supplication to the gods who ruled his bowels.

– Did you sleep well? she asked.

– Like a log, he said, if the cliché is all right with you. Though I had a dream in which I floated in space and observed the earth spinning, now the Americas and now Asia and Africa came in view, and human preoccupations and predicaments seemed pretty ridiculous, if not absolutely futile, from that point of view. The oceans were dripping, by the way, the seas were gradually draining out in the hourglass of the universe. I suppose it's an omen, though it's no news to me. And you, did you sleep well?

– Yes, she said, like one of those artificial logs in an electric fire when it's not switched on. I think we must hurry. In case the wind comes up again.

– Of course, he said, swallowing the coffee and stubbing out his cigarette, after one final puff, saying to the god who randomly bestowed the gift of lung cancer on mortals that he had not smoked more than half of this particular cigarette and, therefore, this one ought not to count in the final reckoning.

They walked up to their room, he going to the W.C. on the half-landing. The bloody French, he thought, sitting with his trousers down, will put a toilet where there's scarcely room for a broom-cupboard. Sitting, he saw the door, which opened inwards, a foot away from him. It was painted a dirty cream colour so as never to show the dirt and deserved, he considered, a dirty rhyme to go with it. He tried to compose one, glad that he did not need to strain at his bowels, and came up with:

My bowels are hard as iron,
I can shit like a bloody lion.
But French lavs are for the birds
and not the evacuation of turds.

He remembered a lavatory in a cheap roadside hotel south of Bordeaux situated, like this one, on a half-landing. He could never tell whether the people going and coming up and down the stairs did not want to use the lavatory; that always had the effect of obstructing his passage, the feeling or thought that he was preventing or delaying someone else's need to use the toilet; knowing for certain that someone waited outside always slowed the natural procedures within him; and whenever he was conscious that someone waited outside he remembered a hotel near Tours where, coming out of the lavatory after one such disturbed attempt at evacuation, he had seen a young girl waiting to use the toilet, a slight, night-gowned creature, apparently suffering from some urgency. She suddenly appeared outside each lavatory he used on a half-landing in a French hotel. He rose, detesting the very cheap quality of the paper with which he was obliged to clean himself, thinking, bloody brown paper, what do they expect you to do here, clean your arse or tie up parcels? worked the flush which sent a ringing sound in the plumbing throughout the hotel, read again the notice in French which begged ladies not to discard their used sanitary towels into the lavatory bowl, upon reading which he saw a crowd of summer-tanned young ladies remove their sanitary towels and put them down the drain, the hotel proprietor go out of his mind at the clogged situation and the plumber roll up his Breton sleeves and get down to business, and squeezed himself out of the door, relieved both that he was out of the suffocating little room and that his system had functioned unimpeded.

In the bedroom, Frieda had changed into a bikini over which she was again putting on the grey skirt and the white sweater. He, too, changed into his swimming-trunks, wearing the Levis over them, before, towels in hand, they went out and began to walk to the beach. A straight tarmac road, no more than a hundred yards long, led to the beach. Crump looked at the villa on his right, decided he should grow a hedge at the end of its garden so that there would be a barrier against the wind which came up from the sea when they lay there to sunbathe beside the swimming-pool. There was a hedge along the road to their left, enclosing a plot of land on which grew blue and yellow wild flowers, and, Were I Kubla Khan, Crump thought, I'd have a decree or two to proclaim.

She began to run, swinging the towel above her head.

He walked, thinking of a university procession in which crimson-and-black-gowned Crumprofessor walked slowly, conscious of his bushy grey eyebrows, on his way to receive an honorary D.Litt.

She stopped, turned to call out to him: I don't think there's any wind today. And ran on again, swinging the towel with more zest.

Sprinter Crump bounded forward, hearing the gun fire, and for fifty yards the crowds at Melbourne, Rome, Tokyo and Mexico City cried Crump-Crump-Crump/Crump-Crump-Crump, clapping their hands to the beat of the cry.

– There isn't a cloud in the sky, she said when they were placing their towels on the sand, having reached the sheltered spot among the rocks where they had come on the previous day.

– Do you think it'll get windy later? she asked. It's a very gentle breeze now.

– We're protected anyhow, he said.

They stripped off their outer garments and lay on the towels.

– What do you mean disappear? he asked. A mother can't simply walk out of her house and never come back.

– She did disappear, that's the amazing thing. Father became terribly silent, philosophical. He really didn't understand it, mother going away like that. He became withdrawn. When he was with us, he was edgy, irritable. At dinner, he would be sarcastic about little things, or angry. If I had a report from school, he'd never be satisfied with it even when it was fairly good. I'm glad to see you're doing well at hockey, he'd say, a fine discipline, don't you agree, John, hockey? Especially for a growing girl, eh, John? Teach her to dribble her way through life. I kept silent, knowing he wasn't attacking me or anything, just feeling bitter, just feeling bloody rotten. He'd criticize John's clothes. The world's run out of starch, he'd say, they need buttons to hold your collars down. Or he'd be finicky, or he would shout at the coloured woman who worked as cook and served the dinner. But then he got over these moods; he seemed to take control over himself if remaining more or less permanently silent means taking control over oneself. It became business and nothing else. That probably saved him, business. I don't think he'd have gone mad or anything. He could never respond that way to any situation. He could have become aggressive as he seemed to be becoming when he was edgy and irritable at the start. A stricter authoritarianism than he'd hitherto practised would have been characteristic, but he channelled that into business, did not direct it at us. John hated him after that. I think John would have preferred it if father had abused everyone in the house and had openly expressed his maximum vehemence against his absent wife. Because for John that would have meant that father was still father; that mother had gone because of some quirk, some eccentricity, that she had fallen out of the pattern into which she had been born, into which she had married. Not understanding his mother, John now couldn't understand his father either. He hated it at school, too, where some of the boys had heard about mother's disappearance and had begun to tease him. For a while his answer was to develop illnesses and not go to school for long stretches at a time. Then he took to cricket, made it his sole preoccupation and became so good at it that the other boys had to respect him. It didn't affect me like it did John or father. Maybe I was still too young. I missed mother, of course, I'd miss her badly at times and want her to come back. But I felt she was right in going away wherever she had gone to. I don't know why I felt that. Somehow, I felt that I was in sympathy with her, and wished I could go to where she was and tell her not to worry. I didn't accuse her of disloyalty. Yes, of course, father went to the police. But not for a while. Maybe a week passed before he did. He was embarrassed, you see. It's the worst thing, to be publicly embarrassed, especially when you have a social position. But he did eventually. I know it was humiliating for him. I imagined the scene, father going to the police station and asking to speak to a senior officer. He couldn't very well have told the first constable he met. I wondered how he phrased his disclosure, his problem. It must have been terrible to say, My wife has disappeared, if he did say it. He must have said something like that at some stage to the police officer. And surely there must have been unpleasant questions, like Would you describe your relations with her as satisfactory? Or, You have two grown-up children, you say? There must have been a lot of polite coughing. They made enquiries. I don't know the nature of the enquiries. It wasn't like when a child is missing and whole areas are thoroughly combed. I suppose they had to be discreet. They were dealing with a woman of forty who had deliberately chosen to disappear and not merely with a child who was lost. But they came up with nothing. They checked at the frontiers, at the ports and airports. As far as they could find out, no one by the name of Sybil Lowes, or anyone resembling her description, had left the country. There was a rumour, probably with a malicious beginning in the social circles, that mother had gone to live among coloured people. They must have had a few laughs over that. Oh, by the way, you know that Sybil Lowes, she's reported to be living with a black man, ha, ha. But I knew mother wouldn't do that; it was too silly and too obviously romantic a gesture for her. It was a cliché. Then the rumour developed into a wild fantasy, that she'd gone and joined some African tribe. I didn't believe that either, though I suppose it's possible that she could have done that. I think now that it's possible, I didn't think so then. For I can understand now that one can be so sickened by the set-up around one as to want to defect to another, apparently alien one. But it remains only a possibility. I don't know what my mother's intellectual preoccupations were. Looking at those pictures, you'd think she's happy with the set-up. No. There was nothing then –

and there's only a vague conjecture now – in what I knew of my mother to suggest that any of the rumours could have been true. Perhaps, looking at the beauty of Sybil Lowes, they'd never seen the person she was. And I, I had only looked at my mother. It was only when she had been gone for over a year, maybe much longer, that I began to see the person; at least I began to look at the person to see what there was for me to see. But still I could not find in my memory any feature, any characteristic belonging to that person, any action, any statement, which would, which might have revealed her psychology to me and answered the question: why had she gone? Without the answer, she had become an incomplete person. She lives in my mind now like a character in a book which I didn't finish reading. She need not have had the reality I think she had. That's what it is, I suppose, that's what we are in the end, fictions in other people's minds. My mother is a story you need not have heard. For all I know, you may not have heard it. You've been lying there with your eyes shut. When you opened your eyes, you looked at the sea, and perhaps you saw, too, as I did, while I was speaking, three boats, their sails like the breasts of doves, slowly moving west. And then you shut your eyes and turned your back to the sun. I've been telling you a story, that's all. We think we understand each other just as literary critics think they can understand Hamlet. What is your story?

A few minutes later, he rose, saying, I think I'll take a dip. He ran into the sea, building up the security of body warmth against the cold depression he would soon plunge into, which he was plunging into now, clenching his teeth, spending his energy in diving into a breaker, diving deep into the swelling water. He swam a few strokes and found himself chest-deep in the stinging cold sea. He flung himself forward, his chest slapping against the sea, cried, Hero, here I come, swam shorewards till the sea was too shallow. He walked out of the water, running on the sand to where she lay. He picked up his towel and dried himself, feeling the sun warm on his back.

– What's it like? she asked.

– Marvellous, he said, warm as butter on a hot bun. Go and try it.

–That's what you said yesterday. I froze.

But she rose and ran to the sea, halting no sooner than she was ankle-deep, screaming.

– Go in, he called. It's warm once you're in.

But essaying to take two or three steps forward, stooping to plunge an arm in the water, she abandoned the sea and came running back, saying, It's bloody freezing. Let's go for a walk instead.

– All right, he agreed.

They left their clothes beside their towels. The beach was half a mile long, and they slowly walked down it. As she walked, she kicked up shells and pebbles which were embedded in the sand, stooping sometimes to look at them closely, but rarely picking one up. Whenever she paused, he drew cartoons on the sand with his big toe.

– I doubt if I could live here, he said, though I love France. It's part of the disintegration.

– Europe? she asked, bending down to massage her toes, for kicking at what seemed to be a pebble she had kicked at a rock most of which had been buried under the sand.

– Europe, he said.

– We're the victims, she said, walking on. Still, I shall miss this, she added, waving an arm which indicated the sea and the sky.

– You're decided?

– Yes. As firmly as you are. Otherwise, it's all a fiction, and we might as well pick parts in a suburban saga.

– Even that, he began, but ran away, sprinted to the end of the beach and sat on a rock, waiting for her. She took her time, loitering to the sea's edge to look at the shells the tide had left behind. By the time she reached him, the gentle breeze became a slight wind, and when they turned to walk back they saw that clouds had gathered on the horizon.

– It's going to be the same as yesterday, she said.

The wind was audible, at least the sea was louder, by the

time they were again in their sheltered spot. They lay on their towels, their backs to the sun.

– What time is it? she asked.

He took out his watch from a pocket in his trousers.

– Twenty to twelve, he said.

– We must have slept.

– Perhaps, he said, or it's possible I forgot to wind my watch last night and it stopped at twenty to twelve.

– How can that be? she said, taking the watch from him and seeing the second hand go round.

– Then it must be twenty to twelve, and we must have slept.

– Time passes!

– Nor can you long be, what you are now, called fair, he quoted.

She surprised him with: Do what you may do. Rubbing some Johnson's Baby Oil on her legs, she said: My back seems to have got burned. We must have slept for at least an hour. And yours, yours is like a crab's!

– Must we have that cliché again?

– Sorry. Yours is like a setting sun in the tropics.

– I'll accept that with the qualification that I may comment on its accuracy when I see a setting sun in the tropics.

She turned to lie on her stomach, giving him the bottle of oil so that he could massage some on her back.

– There was a boy at school whose name was Yeo Wren and whom everyone naturally called Pisspot. One of the teachers wrote a short story about him, so old Pisspot is already a fiction. Sometimes, when I catch this teacher looking at me, I wonder whether he's making a fiction of me, too. But that's by the way, though that's what it is, as you were saying, that's what we are. Pisspot was tall, handsome and sixteen when he left school, having learned nothing. He had a ruddy, chubby face, a full, sensuous mouth, dark hair – if these trite short cuts to description mean anything. All he ever did in my lessons was to ask silly questions which were phrased as a pun with obvious sexual overtones. But he was harmless really. The worst he could do was to ask unambiguously, as he dared to do only once, What's the meaning of copulation, sir? Without giving it much thought, I said in the absolute silence of the class's expectation of a witty answer: Fucking. Not only Pisspot, but the entire class was shocked into a silence of disbelief at what I had said. Had I said something long-winded like The performance of a biological function, they would have sniggered or booed, but the sheer audacity of *fucking* simply stunned them. Anyway. So Pisspot left school, equipped for nothing but aimlessness. One more of the many who leave school at that stage and one never thinks of them again, except that I thought of Pisspot from time to time, for you can't forget a queer name like Yeo Wren. One day, late in the evening, he unexpectedly turned up at the house of one of the teachers. Well, Yeo, what can I do for you? the teacher asked when he had overcome the surprise of finding one of his former pupils at his door. Can I see you? Pisspot asked. Yes, of course, the teacher said, inviting him in. Sit down, would you like a drink? No, thank you, said Pisspot, sitting down, I want two pounds. You want *what*? the teacher asked. Two pounds, said Pisspot. The teacher grew a little angry at this and said: You have a damn cheek, haven't you? You leave school without having learned anything but having spent mine and other teachers' lessons in endless frivolity, you turn up suddenly after two years, you don't even ask how I am or how the school is, you say nothing about what you've been doing all this time, you suddenly turn up at midnight, taking it for granted that you can call on anybody at this hour, and have the impudence on the top of all this to ask if you can borrow two pounds. Pisspot replied: I didn't say borrow. I want to *earn* two pounds. The teacher, getting angrier, said: That's great, that's just wonderful. You want to earn two pounds. Let me see now, what can we do at midnight. Clean the windows perhaps? Hoover the carpets? Pisspot interrupted his tirade with: Come off it, you know very well what I mean by earning two pounds. The teacher, realizing what Pisspot meant, said: No, I *don't* know what you mean, and I shall be grateful if you'd kindly leave my house. But Pisspot didn't move. He just sat there, smiling, coolly watching his former teacher's defences break down. He said: I promise you, you'll enjoy it. Why pretend you don't know what I'm talking about? You know that I know what you are, why you live alone. It'll be two pounds you'll never regret. The teacher began to shake, a kind of convulsion which could only be remedied by his accepting what Pisspot had to offer.

He finished massaging her back, having gently coaxed the oil to enter into her skin.

– Why don't we walk back to the hotel and have a shower before lunch? she asked, rising.

He held out his hand to her and pulled himself up. They put on their clothes, and, flinging their towels over their shoulders, walked in the direction of the hotel. The blue and yellow wild flowers behind the hedge on their right grew close to the ground, he remarked, and were not disturbed by the wind which prevailed so persistently in these parts. Crump sat cross-legged on a slab of marble, a ruby on his turban, two maidens belly-danced in front of him while he threw golden coins at them; a black slave, wearing nothing but a turban and pantaloons, came running up to him, threw himself prostrate at his feet and said: Kubla sahib, there is a poet come from England, U.K., it is your pleasure dome he is wanting to see. On their left was a white villa with its blue window-frames. Crump saw a short, plump, balding middle-aged man drive up in a Peugeot 404, his wife and three daughters aged probably between six and ten and each one of them flabby-fleshed and white as chalk rush out, spend all August in the villa, shut the windows, lock the door and drive away.

– What shall we do if it rains this afternoon? she asked. Look, how dark those clouds are.

– We could drive to Paris and catch a plane to Florida, he said. It's bound to be sunny in Miami.

– Mike, can't you ever be serious?

They went into the bathroom together, and stood in an embrace under the shower. He faced the window, which he had opened, which he liked to keep open while using the bathroom, so that he could look out on the sea while he had a shower.

– You've got the urge again, she said.

– It must be your curly fanny-hair, he said. Let's do it standing up.

– *No*, Mike.

– Come on, co-operate.

– What, with nothing?

– Why not, it would please His Holiness for a change.

– *Mike!*

– Mais je m'appelle Hilary.

– Oui, Pierrot!

– First let me lather your back and breasts with this soap of the stars. It'll give the embrace a slippery kink.

– Careful.

– Careful? It's bloody difficult unless you bend a little. Christ, there must be a way. Ooooops. That's better.

– Don't forget to come out.

– I feel giddy, he said, coming out of the shower in his bathrobe, adding: Man is a giddy thing. You know what I wished then, he went on as they entered their room, I wished you were wearing Kurt Geiger boots which came up to your thighs.

– Kinky Crump, she said.

He collapsed on the bed while she went through her Max Factor and Elizabeth Arden routine. She wore a mustard-coloured trouser-suit. He rose, sprinkled some Old Spice hair tonic on his head, massaged his scalp, brushed his hair, and wore his Levis and black poloneck, having to brush his hair again. There was still time before lunch began, however, and he poured out two small whiskies, weakening them with three times as much water.

– You were talking of your mother, he said.

She said: Being neither one nor the other, we're the losers.

– In Europe? he asked.

– Yes, she said. There's Gaullism here, and student revolt. A referendum is only a public-relations trick.

– We're all right, up to a point, he said, in Shepherd's Bush. I suppose you're right. That's not all.

– In a sense, she said, welfare-state cosiness is the last thing people want. They've always enjoyed hardship.

– Or the other extreme, he said. Power to exploit.

– So we compromise, she said, and we're the losers.

– It's coming to that, he said.

– Rapidly, she said. Bloody rapidly.

– You're right, he said. You must tell me more about your mother.

–You will know, she said. I'll give you the title of a book.

Lunch began with grapefruit, which they thought was rather thoughtless of the chef. A tomato and onion salad followed, seeming to confirm that the chef was either in a lazy mood or was going out of his Breton mind. But crab came next with a vinegar and olive-oil sauce, partly reinstating the chef's sanity. The fourth, main course, a fowl dish, was quite a masterpiece. They finished with cheese and were about to order coffee when a bowl of strawberries was brought to them. They drank a bottle of Sancerre.

– It's something new every day, she said. I love the balance between sea-food and game which he manages to create.

– Can you remember all the dishes we've had? he said.

– I remember the little dishes, she said. Courgettes with minced meat and garlic, omelette *aux fines herbes*, although an ordinary thing – but is there anything ordinary in French cuisine? – was exquisitely done, whole shrimps *à la vinaigrette*.

– I wonder, he said, how long he can go on inventing new dishes.

– This is France, she said as though it were a matter of patriotism for her.

– The last time you said that, we had a screw under a pine tree in a forest.

– Don't get ideas, she said.

– Shall we go? he asked, finishing his coffee.

– Where? she said. What are we going to do now?

– Upstairs, he said.

– It's cloudy outside, she said.

– I said upstairs, he said.

– But you've had your little do, she said.

– I like that, he said, laughing, my little do. And sang softly:

If I ever do
fall in love with you
then let me also do
a little do with you.

– Why don't we drive out now?

– It's cloudy, he said.

– Precisely, she said. The clouds are in the east. We could drive west.

– Where shall we go? he asked, driving away.

– How far west can we go? she asked.

– All British atlases assume that California is as far west as we can go. Though I suppose the Japanese consider San Francisco to be in the east.

– Be serious, Mike.

– That was a perfectly serious unoriginal statement, he said. Morgat, I suppose, he added.

They drove through Concarneau and Quimper.

– You were talking of your mother, he said.

They crossed a bridge in Quimper.

– Notice, he said, there are sweet-chestnut trees in the square.

The road went through little villages, farms on either side of the road when they left the villages, sometimes the sea in the distance. The road cut through some of the farms, entered woodland and emerged into the open again, presenting rapidly changing sensations, even of smell. The road had short straight stretches and many blind bends, hedges and branches of trees seeming to narrow the road. The road sloped gently up hillsides or curved for the satisfaction of sports-car enthusiasts. There was little traffic. A few Citroëns glided past on their sensitive suspension. The only danger was from the slow tractors, pulling trucks laden with compost or hay or mud, he never looked to see exactly what they carried, appearing in unexpected places. Two lorries held them up for a time, it being difficult to pass them on the narrow road. And once Crump had to brake hard when approaching a corner, for a crazily driven green Morgan suddenly appeared from the other side doing a four-wheel drift, a grinning bearded face at the wheel. Otherwise, it was a pleasant drive during which he did not drive at more than sixty miles an hour and to which he attached no ponderous symbolism.

Coming down into Morgat, they parked the car beside the beach.

They walked to where the fishing-boats were moored, dark greens and blues.

They climbed up some steps on to a pine-forested hill and went up a path to the top of the hill.

They agreed there that the view from the top was one of the best in Brittany.

The Atlantic was still and silvery.

The murderous Atlantic, dimpled, gong-tormented, he recalled, a silver cymbal.

Waiting for the sky to come down with a crash.

Yes, they agreed, a fine view.

He lit a cigarette, thinking of the television commercial in which couples lit cigarettes when they paused beside spots of natural beauty, panoramic views, waterfalls, the mighty ocean and remembering, too, that cigarette advertising had been banned on television and consequently it was all the more magnificently produced in the cinemas.

They sat on a rock, looking down on the semi-circular bay and the houses on the waterfront, while he smoked.

They walked down the hill and when they reached sea-level the clouds from the east overtook the sun.

They went to a bar from where they could look out on the sea.

She had a Pernod; he had a coffee.

Silence. An afternoon to kill. So he told a story.

– There was a boy at the school, he said, called Macaulay Westwood. With that name, you'd think he was born an aristocrat, but he was in fact a Jamaican, black as coal, with bright happy eyes, white, white teeth and a smile so sweet you couldn't help liking him. Straight from Jamaica he came to our 3B. Unfortunately, the boys who befriended him were the worst types who, a year later, made their début at the local magistrate's court. They were Maucaulay's only friends at the school, and since they must also have been the only English boys he knew he must have had a pretty confused picture of the English way of life. And naturally enough he fell into their ways. But he was such a clueless little fuzzy-wuzzy of a boy that instead of settling for a modest beginning, say, with lifting the odd pen from Woolworth's or the occasional copy of a nude magazine from Smith's, which is what boys of that nature usually do and grow out of as soon as they're caught, instead of that, Macaulay walks into an electrical shop, and not when it's busy either but when there's no one but the assistant looking after the shop during the lunch hour, makes a stupid attempt to divert the assistant's attention, picks up a radio and tries to walk out. Now, he doesn't pick up a little transistor which he can hide under a coat or something. He picks up a damn big receiver in a walnut cabinet and tries to stagger out. The assistant, who's only turned away to look at a shelf and hasn't even left the room, looks at him in stunned amazement. Now, the next thing, Macaulay, our outrageously daring broad-daylight-gangster who you'd think would have an E-Type Jag waiting outside for a quick getaway, considering the unperturbed manner in which he's still trying to stagger out, hasn't worked out his next problem. How to open the damn door. And what do you think he does, the damn coon? Trying to open the door, he *drops* the bloody radio, cracking the walnut shell and shattering its vital parts. But, worse, he drops it in such a way as to make the opening of the door difficult, for the cracked-up radio is obstructing the door. And before he can do anything about running out, the assistant has collected himself and overpowered him. Helpless little bastard, one of these days he'll get twenty years for some daft exploit for which he himself will have no reason and he'll wonder where the hell he is and what it's all about.

When they drove away, it was beginning to rain.

– What's worse, he asked, a rainy afternoon, free roads, or the height of summer, blue skies, not a whiff of wind and an endless traffic jam?

She said: Still, it's nice experiencing it at this time.

– You should get those Kurt Geiger boots, he said.

– What's that got to do with being here?

– It just struck me, silver Kurt Geiger boots up to your thighs and nothing else on.

– You're becoming perverted, she said, and, besides, silver is no longer in.

– Late spring is a fine time of the year, he said, adding: These are not perversions but propositions for a higher ecstasy. What about doing it in the mud on a rain-sodden field, getting really filthy?

– Sex used to be filthy, she said, until they invented paper tissues.

– *That*'s it, he said, that's what's been bothering me.

– What?

– In films, he said, and you might well ask if the *nouvelle vague* cinema would have got anywhere without great helpings of sex; they show you degrees of realism, but I've yet to see lovers, all grunts, rolling eyes, twisting entangled arms, finger-nails in backs, unlock themselves in the end and turn to a box of Kleenex. If the men use rubbers, what do they do with them, keep them on until they next go to the toilet? That, in fact, is the only situation in which they could do without a paper tissue. Even that I doubt. Whenever I use a rubber, the first thing I want to do when it's over is to take the damn thing off. Ah, the cinema has made sex clean when the post-coital minutes are dirty in a very literal sense.

– I think I saw a tractor round the bend, she said.

– Dearest love, I'm round the bend too. Don't worry, I'm watching the road. I haven't forgotten that crazy Morgan which may well be on its way back. An American poet rhymes France with pants.

– So what? she asked.

– For there's forsythia on the roads and an erection in my pants, and here I go cruising on the hilly roads of France.

– Even talking of sex makes you randy, she said.

– You should interpret my randiness as a compliment to you.

– This part is called Finistère, she said.

– Time for a drink, he said when they arrived at the hotel in heavy rain.

He half-filled two tumblers with Scotch when they were in their room.

– I don't think I want to change for dinner, she said.

They sat on the edge of the bed, drinking.

– I wonder if it'll stop raining by dinner, she said.

He rose to pour himself another drink. He saw a white horse walk into a pub. He looked at the label on the bottle. It was not White Horse. That's cheating, he told the ad.

– Oh, I think I'll change after all, she said. I feel like wearing a dress. Something to cheer me up in this depressing weather.

He watched her remove her clothes and, when she was in her underclothes, he went and embraced her, unhooking her bra and pushing down her pink nylon pantie.

– Not again, Mike! I'm not going to prepare myself and I'm certainly not going to dinner dripping between my legs. After what you said about the cinema, she added.

– It's all right, he said, I'll don an electronically tested, pre-lubricated Gossamer, make a magnificent entrance, say my lines and limp out gracefully.

– Oh, all right.

– Ah, he said, but quoted: A chaos of deep passion . . . but present exhaustion made him lose the line.

– Maniac Mike, she mocked when getting out of bed and beginning to dress, hairy Hilary, crackpot Crump.

He lit a cigarette, remembering the Spanish émigré in Paris and the bored wife in the Italian city, and said softly: How dull it is to pause, to make an end.

She wore a dark-blue dress and made up her face.

He put on the suede jacket over his black poloneck and Levis.

They went down to dinner. They ate soup, artichokes *à la vinaigrette*, fried sole with boiled potatoes in butter sauce, Camembert, Breton cake, and drank a bottle of Muscadet. It was still raining when they finished the meal; so they ordered coffee and cognac immediately.

– You were talking of your mother, he said.

– That time we drove through the rain across Normandy and Brittany, south, south, and did not find the sun until we had crossed the Loire. Where were we going? What had we come to see?

– We went on. Past Bordeaux, past Biarritz. We entered villages which were nothing but petrol stations. We drove on. It was a bad summer.

– We kept driving south, I remember.

– It was a foul crossing.

– They sold honey and peaches on the road to Biarritz. And you said, What's left of Europe? This, I said, when we had oysters in Bordeaux, knowing that was not what you meant, this, I said, when we cut a melon in two sitting by the river in the Gorges de la Nesque, knowing it wasn't that either, you meant something else. That was last year or the year before.

– That was another time.

– Time!

– It was after Berlin or before Berlin.

– We're coming to that! Not now.

– Soon.

– What's left of Europe? you said again and again. There

were cities and villages, farms and forests. That was all. How could I tell you, how could I show you what was behind the windows of stone houses? How could I interpret the gossip of the coffee bars? And the woman who sat in the courtyard of the Spanish hotel, in the narrow street in Valdepeñas, in the corner of the tiled courtyard with its fishpond and potted palms, what did she think, watching us, asking ourselves these questions? And others? How could you know what went on elsewhere, you who asked What's left of Europe? As if I could have picked up a handful of dust from the square in Mazan, where old men played *boules* under the pollarded trees, and said this, *this*!

– That was not all. I expected more. That was not there.

– How could you know, living in London and speaking only English? A tourist can't know. He can only look and make a generalized response. He goes back, develops his films, sticks the pictures in an album and looks at them from time to time. That's all. How can he know? Oh Mike, you have strange ideas sometimes!

– You were talking of your mother, he said.

– We drove south, remember?

He yawned.

– Tired? she asked.

– No, it must be this idle life, he said.

They took twenty minutes over their coffee and cognac.

– What shall we do? she asked. It's still raining.

– Why don't we retire early, he said. It's been a long day really, considering the four hours spent driving to Morgat and back.

They went up to their room, he pausing to make use of the facilities on the half-landing. They fell asleep almost as soon as they went to bed.

Crump did not answer, but resumed marking the 3B books. The old man is stepping on the zebra. A few minutes to go to the mid-afternoon break and already there were sounds in the corridor of boys having left their classes; some of the teachers habitually dismissed their classes in order to time their arrival in the staff-room to coincide with the ringing of the bell; they did not leave the staff-room until after the bell had rung for the end of break, and then, and often only then, made use of the lavatory, so that by the time they were again in their classrooms the ten-minute break had effectively been extended to twenty minutes. Maintaining such a deplorable level of productivity, many teachers did not deserve the higher salaries they felt justified in demanding: apparently, they did not work hard enough because they thought they were underpaid and the employers probably did not pay them salaries comparable to other professions because they did not work hard enough. Another ulcer to keep grey-at-the-temples, doddering old Britain bed-ridden. The old man is on the road and will be run over if he is not careful. Crump wondered when the music master would begin rehearsals for the Christmas Carol Concert, for the rehearsals were traditionally held in the last lesson and since six to ten boys from each class were in the choir, and two or three were usually absent as well, it meant that the last lesson was effectively deleted from the time-table; and Crump, knowing that in many things he was as wasteful as the worst teachers, could wish for no greater relief, for his last lessons were invariably of an epic nature, Hollywood widescreen vistavision extravaganzas featuring black-headed, pimple-faced Jim Sutton, Oscar-winning star of juvenile violence. Thinking of the choir rehearsals, he thought of last year's Carol Concert and the one in the previous year and the one in the year before that, parallel mirrors again, for the similarity of incident in each was enough to confound the most sensitive and precise memory – though, of course, there would have been certain senior boys in the Concert three years ago who had not participated a year later, and in its specificity his memory would need to focus again to be at all truthful, but this did not matter, a quibble did not matter in the generality of repetitive experience – and after the event, when images recur it is only a conceit of the mind which presumes that they are accurate representations of what was observed for a moment once or twice or many times, successively or separately, recently or a long time ago, everything, after all, is metaphor, including language, the mind a phrase-book. And out of this seemingly uncouth material, this rough mixture of gentle and coarse youths, the music master made divine music annually, gifted or crafty as Prospero, the music master, an enchanter, standing at the rostrum, slim and tall, magic wand in hand, flaxen hair fluttering on his head; nor were the words, the same old hymns and carols, any better than the general academic standard of the boys. Such banal rhyming, such syntactical contortion by eighteenth- and nineteenth-century adorers of Christ who possessed no virtue but that they were virtuous. And although the event bestowed a transient, albeit spurious, aura of beatitude on the assembled choir for an hour or two and a halo momentarily glowed above the school, nobody really placed any credence in what was being enacted. God had become a compulsive habit with the community, that was all, an event in the time-table of a school. For a day later the boys were the same as they had been the day before just as after the bonhomie of the office party in which the managing director and a junior trainee may share a joke a solemn hierarchy again asserts its cold rigidity on the Monday morning. And so, too, with the daily morning assembly, piously ritualistic, but making no difference: only one more item in the time-table had been fulfilled; and the boys who had gone in pulling at one another's blazers, emerged from the hall pulling at one another's blazers even though the same boys had rolled their eyes up to heaven in a devout recitation of the Lord's Prayer. Even an ordinary utility had gone out of prayer; you didn't need to pray in the Welfare State, remarked heavy-browed Crump, who, standing in the nave in the cathedral at Orleans had watched an Irish family light candles in silent respect, their faces luminous with what he thought must be an inner ecstasy, but a few minutes later, outside, their querulous voices as they bought ice-cream pulled down the mask of their piety, jarring on his nerves, making him want to clench his teeth. He looked out of the window. The

Volkswagen was parked some distance from the Irish family, Frieda leaning against a shut door, looking at the cathedral.

– Modern architecture hasn't the excuse of piety, she said. Nowadays it's the glorification of the state as with Brasília, or it's industries showing off.

– Or foreign embassies.

The bell rang; there was also the sound of books being shut and, through the thin walls, desk-lids banging in the adjoining classrooms.

– The nature of God, he said unlocking the car, was determined by the nature of the society which first decided to believe that he existed. The trouble is, he went on, driving away, wondering where they would be just before sunset, for he did not set himself a destination, merely took a room at a hotel in the town they happened to be near at about sunset, that society has changed and God, by definition of all the absolutes he was endowed with at his coronation, has had to remain absolutely constant. Redefinitions would compromise him. And that's what's killed him. Neither democracy nor communism can sustain him; we've no alternative but to be Goneril and Regan to his Lear. Tell me, my daughters . . . ha! All right, you may go, he said to the sixth-formers, don't forget the essay.

It had been a useless lesson, he thought, locking the room and carrying the keys like a jailor as he walked down the corridor. All the other classrooms were as inactive as extinct volcanoes, having already spewed out the lava of children desperate to escape their confines and to pour out into the valley of the playground, and he could see them there, green blazers splashing in wild motion. But they were a good group, the four sixth-formers, and if they replied sharply, this was because there was a tacit compact between them and Crump that an exchange of witty abuse was permissible when both or one of the parties felt disinclined to go through the routine of methodical textual analysis; and this was important, thought Crump, for he did not want literature to become a solemn altar but to remain an entertaining pursuit, a starting point for the wider discussion of all that appertained to existence. To hell with the age, he would say, this changing age, they can stuff it up their computers, there's personal strength to be derived from doing the most useless thing, reading a poem. They responded to that, excitedly. Once, Crump had invited them to his house and opened two bottles of a good wine for them and he thought that ideally that's how it should be, they should meet in pleasant circumstances, read their papers to one another and talk about what they had been reading. A dialogue, literature, that's all. The academics were only amusing themselves and what they produced was, on the whole, worthless. It was Nevers that they reached at sunset, he remembered when walking down the steps; a dull town where they had eaten a dull dinner, though in France even that kind of dinner was not without taste; he had ordered only half a bottle of wine and had had to order another half in the middle of the main course. It was a dull restaurant, too, which was probably why he had not ordered a whole bottle in the first place, juke box and no customers at nine o'clock. He had regretted the two half-bottles, for two halves invariably cost more than one whole. But then, paying the bill, he discovered that the waitress had forgotten about the first half-bottle by the time they finished the meal and had charged only for one half-bottle. He had not pointed out the error, and he knew that he would later regret not having done so, feel a little guilty, for he regretted any overt moral failure, although for the moment, when paying the bill, he could rationalize the failure by saying to himself that he deserved the gratuity of a free half-bottle as compensation for the dullness of the place and of the meal, and that restaurants, in any case, grossly overcharged on wine. The little bits of guilt we carry like rucksacks of tinned food to feed upon in moods of self-martyrdom, the breast-beating we enjoy. He turned at the foot of the stairs towards a door in the corridor, a glass door, through which he could see a fourth-former – a boy called Suter whom everyone called Kama – walking in his direction, and he could tell that they would both reach the door simultaneously. They did, and Kama, reaching for the door-handle first, opened it towards himself and, looking at Crump, who stood immediately on the other side of the door, with displeasure, with censure at Crump's impoliteness in not stepping back to give him free passage, dodged past him, so that Crump had to hold a hand out to prevent the door from flattening his nose. How similar this bloody place is, he had remarked, sipping the wine, to that restaurant in Amsterdam where we had to wait forty minutes to be served, how similar to the tourist-menu places on the Costa del Sol, the window-panes looking out on to the playground were dirty, he remarked, walking down the corridor, and what will become of Europe when even France gives way to a generalized mass appeal? In respect of taste, democracy and equality have substituted freshly laundered cloth with sheets of plastic, and yet who wants the phoney obsequious bowing and genuflecting to a decadent aristocracy? Democracy has created a dilemma man has never experienced before: it has made life mercifully free and at the same time made it abysmally cheap, all calculations, whether they are for the marketing of a product or the transmission of entertainment or for the catering of food, being based on the lowest common denominator. Kola stood in front of the boys' notice-board and Crump said to him:

– In a sense, the general trend of our progress is commendable, but, in another, more significant sense, it is a disaster. Life has become a saunter through a supermarket and a package-tour of shallow emotions.

– Quite, said Kola. Heaven doth with us as we with torches do, not light them for themselves.

– Good, said Crump, very good, turning the corner towards the staff-room.

– The only pity is, Kola said after him, who believes in heaven?

Crump opened the door to the staff-room, remembering the occasion in his first year when he had knocked on the door and had walked away before returning to enter and thinking at the time that he would remember the incident every time he approached the door in the future, such is the tyranny of associations in the mind. We'll show anything in public, he thought, except our embarrassment. He walked into the room where his colleagues were already sipping their tea. He hung his keys on the key-board, noticing the pile of papers left on the locker by Mr Davies, went to the sink where on the draining-board there was a pot of tea, several cartons of milk and a few red or green Melaware mugs – all the yellow and blue ones had already been taken – chose a green one, poured himself some tea, there already being a little milk at the bottom of the mug, took his mug to the table where there was a bowl of sugar, the fine sugar containing lumps of yellow where the wet teaspoon had hardened the sugar crystals, carefully spooned out a heap of sugar, avoiding the yellow lumps the sight of which for some reason produced an irritation in his throat and it would have made him sick if he knew that his tea contained one of these lumps, stirred it, sat in an easy chair, thought of the eight-armed Hindu god at a urinal and wondered which hand he would use to pull up his dhoti with, sipped his tea, put the mug down on the floor, took out his packet of Gold Leaf cigarettes, lit one with his Dunhill lighter, flicked the lighter shut, put away both the packet and the lighter into the left pocket of his jacket, took a long puff, inhaled deeply, thought of cancer just when his lungs were joyously inflated with smoke, and exhaled with a tremendous sense of relief. Five minutes left of a ten-minute break. I didn't see any almond trees in Brittany, she said. What trees had they seen in Brittany? he wondered. Sweet chestnuts in the square at Quimper, he remembered, pines at the hilltop in Morgat, he remembered, and there must have been oaks, there must have been beeches, but almond trees he had not seen, did not remember seeing, who remembered most things obsessively, repeatedly – as if the little bits of coloured paper in one's vision would somehow paste themselves into one indubitably meaningful and revelatory image!

Little bits of coloured paper are, pansophist Crump knew,

little bits of coloured paper; and that's all.

– Nor are there any vineyards in Brittany, she could insist; and nor did I see any fig trees.

That's not what I meant, but he did not say it, realizing that it would be the obvious and the obviously futile thing to say, I am not Prufrock nor was meant to be, he could add to himself, but said instead: The particular nature of topography is of immediate interest only to one's senses.

– That's pompous balls, she said. To some people the particular nature of the topography is their living.

– An earthy remark, if I may say so, he said, taking another sip of his tea, another puff of his cigarette, but I'm talking of our experience.

– And, besides, the weather is more certain here, she said.

– You're right, of course, he was compelled to admit, another three minutes and back to the room for one more combat with sabre-wielding Tamurlaine Sutton, but added to save something of the truth which he thought was contained in his original statement, but our pleasure, our delight is of the same degree.

– No qualifications, Mr Crump, she said. Please don't take me for one of your fifth-formers and expect to get away with any old rubbish that comes to your mind. Brittany is Brittany and Provence is Provence, and please don't kid yourself that you're spouting high metaphysics when in fact you're talking plain shit.

She could be quite uncompromising and it was no use saying You haven't followed what I've been trying to say, for that, at best, was the subterfuge of the inarticulate. Though he enjoyed that, her abuse, not wanting the wool of abstraction to insulate his intellect against precise perception. He was, after all, an Anglo-Saxon even if he was in France and liked France more than any country he had experienced. His right hand brought the cigarette to his lips again, his left hand firmly held the wood-rim steering-wheel, his right foot pressed hard down, and the long cherry-red sloping bonnet in front of him shot southwards towards Madrid. But the cigarette had to be stubbed out in the glass ashtray though, had he leisure, he could have smoked it for a while longer, and he had to rise, for the bell was ringing; still, it was that much less cigarette-smoke he had inhaled, hoping that the divine agency which marketed cancer among human lungs had taken notice. What a way to be remembered, poor old Davies, by a pile of papers which no one bothered to pick up and consign to the bin, he thought as he reached for his keys, and walking to the door, seeing his colleagues still sipping their tea, paused, and said aloud before leaving the room:

– To us, gentlemen, the boys should be like components on the Rolls-Royce assembly-line.

The next morning, he moaned in the pre-waking reluctance ever again to emerge from sleep, while the words she uttered had entered into and been rejected by his consciousness, as if there were a wall there from which even radio signals must bounce back, while, having his head against the pillow, he saw, only partly saw, for vision, too, rejected all but the vivid darkness of sleep, the profile of her face, a line of light running down from forehead to chin, a brightness in her eyes and perhaps she was saying, as she had said yesterday, We're late getting up again. It's a super day, she was saying, and we've missed half of it.

– What time is it? he muttered, hoping she would say six o'clock, so that he could go back to sleep for a while longer, but knowing that that must be impossible, otherwise she would not have said We're late getting up.

– Almost ten, she said, jumping out of bed.

Her nakedness provided the shock his eyesight needed to see things clearly. He observed her dispassionately. Excellent, he thought, to swell a progress, to start a scene or two, and wondered if that was a quotation but, if it was, did not bother his brain to search for its source. He watched her brush her teeth, looking with pleasure at the tight smooth skin of her back and, seeing her breasts hang out and wobble as she leaned forward, brushing her teeth, thought what absurd things breasts were, something women needed to support, a weapon in the sex war with which to make men mad, to allure, to entice, to thwart, to frustrate, to tease with or to offer as cushions of comfort, but in the end a burden, burdensome withered old dugs in the end. She gulped some water and spat it out into the basin. She placed her brush in the empty glass beside the basin and turned to pick up her underwear which was on a chair next to a window. She wore a pair of shorts and a blouse over the underwear, not buttoning up the blouse but simply tying a knot just above her navel.

– Aren't you going to get up? she asked.

– What are we going to do today?

– Get some breakfast first of all. There isn't any fresh bread, and there won't be any left in the village even if you did care to go and enquire. It'll have to be rusks.

She went out of the room, taking firm, decisive steps, looking busy, efficient. He still lay in bed, gazing through the window at the blue sky, and began to sing softly:

You have the wheat,
I'll have the husk;
You have the bread,
I'll have the rusk.

A feeble rhyme, he told himself; it wasn't worth getting out of bed if the performance of his mental faculties was to be at that level. In the candlelit room, waiters came and went in silence. She sat in her white satin Biba dress, a great bow at the neck, leaning towards him. They had eaten escargots and trout cooked in Pernod and poire belle Hélène, they had drunk a bottle of Montrachet. Now, sipping liqueur and smoking a luxury-length Dunhill, she talked of her long week-end in Albufeira – Just to get some sun, darling; this wet summer's depressing. He smoked his Upmann and sipped his cognac, nodding sympathetically. There was so much to talk about, to reveal! Of course, she was saying, I wouldn't go *there* for a holiday, a longish week-end is just about enough. For a holiday, anything north of Casablanca is absolutely out, darling. Leaving the restaurant, they drove away in his silver-grey E-Type, cruising gently at sixty through the London streets on which there was not a single vehicle, breathing in the pleasant mixture of her Primitif and his Fabergé Brut. They listened to a Mozart sonata on his Blue Spot while reclining in warm togetherness on a Heal's leather sofa in his mews cottage, he fondling the bow on her blouse and she passing the soft tips of her fingers across his cleanly shaven chin. Some years later, when they were married, she jumped out of bed one morning, brushed her teeth, put on some clothes, talked urgently of making breakfast, saying There isn't any fresh bread, it'll have to be rusks, and went out of the room, taking firm, decisive steps, looking busy, efficient, while he still lay in bed, gazing through the window at the blue sky and singing softly:

Oh what a life, what a life,
our dreams are awfully phoney.
We mirror the ads in the glossy mags
and think all the time of money.

That's worse than feeble, he told himself, but it'll have to do. He rose gently, wishing no violence to his muscles, and walked to the window. He looked down on a valley, remarked on the severely geometric pattern of fruit trees in an orchard, and turned to the basin to brush his teeth. He put on a pair of Levis and a black poloneck, combed his hair, and walked to the kitchen where on a table beside the stove Frieda had just served the breakfast.

– This brain of mine, he declared rhetorically, Hunts not the trail of policy, and sat down.

– Oh, speak of that, that do I long to hear, she said, knowing his game.

– Ah confusion, confusion, he said.

– You haven't shaved, she said. What were you doing all this time?

– O Heart, he began.

– What?

– I can't remember that one. I seem to know it. I begin it. I get stuck.

– You're all tricks, she said.

– A game, he said.

– What are we going to do today?

– I asked you that and you never replied.

– You know damn well what we're going to do today.

– Then why do you ask.

– Oh, Mike!

– All right, don't say it. I'll pull myself together.

– You know very well that we agreed last night that we'd drive to Arles today. And possibly also to Nîmes. The Roman towns.

– Ah, yes.

– Ah, yes!

– I'm sorry, he said, and sang in an effort to make her merry:

Today we shall
drive to Arles
unless we seem
to prefer Nîmes.

– Hurry up, she said, rising.

He finished his coffee, lit a cigarette, inhaled with satisfaction, thinking of cancer, and walked out to the small terrace. What are you up to today, then (he addressed the populace, shaking his fist like Castro), my dear Gaullists? For some reason, at that point, he remembered seeing a fourteen – at least he thought so, she could have been thirteen or fifteen – year-old girl in Paris buying a copy of *Elle* on her way home from school – at least he thought so, for what he took to be a school uniform could easily have been a product of *haute couture* or a special dress to satisfy a special client's special perversity, who knows what doesn't go on in Paris. Your future, he went on with his address, is in plumbing, my friends. The more advanced a civilization, the more refuse it generates; and the more sophisticated it is in disposing of the refuse the more civilized is its advance. So, look to your drains, Frenchmen. For that's the way the croissant crumbles, mes amis. He finished the cigarette, and went to the toilet. He heard Frieda singing to herself while he sat in the lavatory. She was still in the kitchen when he began to shave. He concentrated on the lather and the razor, not wanting to meet his own eyes in the mirror. He finished shaving and sat down on a chair by the window. He looked out on the orchard and on a mountain peak in the distance.

Frieda came in from the kitchen. He remarked on the way she had not buttoned up her blouse but merely tied the two front ends in a knot just above her navel. He had seen her do so when he lingered in bed and watched her dress and he had looked at her during breakfast; but it was only now that he remarked on the casual way she had dressed.

– It makes me penisthetic, he said.

– Is that one of your kids' words? she asked going away to the bathroom.

A note of irritation in her voice, he thought, turning to look down at the valley and at the fruit trees. An erotic possibility, no doubt, sex under the fruit trees; but he felt convinced that such a possibility was probably more satisfying as an imaginative concept than as an actual performance. Though there was no privacy there, under the fruit trees. Another Crump, say, at another window would see them. The earth was gritty, he could see, and the ground sloped. It would be pleasanter on Hampstead Heath after sunset on a July evening, especially if the afternoon had been warm. Or in the darkness of the ferns of Putney Heath. She was singing in the bathroom. He could not hear her words clearly. Good, he thought, let her voice lose its irritation. But she said on coming out of the bathroom:

– You still there!

– I'm ready, he said gently. Just waiting for you.

– For goodness' sake, Mike, we're on a holiday.

– What do you want me to do, run down a beach, laughing, and make a good picture for the travel agency catalogue?

– I've wet my hair, she said.

They drove away from Venasque.

– I don't know how you can live with that, he said, driving. The human mind abhors mysteries. Gaps in knowledge. Things out of place. Hence, we can't put a thriller down. What could have become of her? Could she have been kidnapped? Apparently not. For she was ill, or seemed to be ill. A kind of illness which does not appear to have been organic. A worry was it that she suffered from? A passion. Could there have been a lover?

– A thriller or a romance. I cannot say which. One makes up one's own story. We ponder hypotheses, that's all. Afterwards, it was ordinary. Mysterious, intriguing, yes, but nevertheless ordinary like everything else in life.

– Hardly!

– Well, in the sense that one has to go on living. There's never a choice, is there?

– Ah!

– Of course, I would like to know. There's a street in Berlin I'd like to visit. On the other side of the Wall.

– This is Europe, he said, looking at the asphalt. Here we go Volkscruising, he added, noting that he had been driving steadily at fifty-five miles an hour on the empty, poorly surfaced road and pointlessly remembering from the car's handbook that fifty-five was a speed at which he could obtain the best petrol consumption from the car.

– I wish we had gone via Madrid, she said. A great big city to get lost in. This empty road makes one so self-aware; it becomes oppressive to hear one's own breathing.

– I know. That's a better road, too, but crowded. Remember the time we went to Madrid?

– We did not go *to* Madrid.

– Yes, I know, we only drove through it. Twice. We were going south. But we lost our way in Madrid and were too irritated to want to stop, to want to look. Perhaps we could have liked the city, perhaps; if we had seen what, going in circles, the way lost, we did not see. But irritation, that's what I remember mostly of Madrid and a red stone building with palm trees; it looked cool, the building. But then we had to go round what must have been a football stadium. Oh, it was endless, all that going in circles. But returning, it was straightforward, we were so relieved that we didn't have to go in circles, we just drove right through the city without stopping and realized that we could have stopped. Had we stopped, had we stayed, spent time. Maybe, maybe.

– Those are cork trees, she said.

He observed that the road signs had been poorly maintained.

– I suppose there must be a fortune, she added, in eucalyptus, there are whole plantations of them.

– South of Madrid it's all olives. Vineyards, too, of course. Should we go and look at Seville?

– No, she said. No churches today. I want to jump into the sea. A warm sea. I've still got goosepimples from Brittany.

A ferry took them from Spain to Portugal. Here you are, he pointed out, between two shores, a fine old romantic situation. In the mouth of a river, the policed no man's waters, a foreign land on either side. What you can say or do there you can't over there on the other side.

They drove away from Venasque.

When they were driving out of Avignon, she asked: What are we going to see in Arles? I've forgotten to bring the Michelin.

– We're going to see Rome, he said.

– Rome?

– Yes, Rome, the power of.

– We see symbols, she said. A romance fills our lives.

– Fills?

– No, don't laugh.

– You were talking of your mother, he said.

– We're the fools of this age.

– What traffic, he said, and sang softly:

Give to me the road I love
and you in the Aston beside me;
a wood-rim wheel, black leather gloves
and four-litre power inside me.

– That's all they've done, that's all they still do, she said, conquer one another in turn.

– For various reasons, of course.

– For honour.

– Wealth.

– Aggrandizement.

– Territorial disputes.

– Purity of the race.

– Commercial claims.

– Prestige.

– Distraction from internal strife.

– Over-armament.

– Ideology.

– Revolution.

– The usual shit in fact, he said. Let's not go to Arles. To hell with Rome. What's the use of looking at an amphitheatre?

– But there's Van Gogh, she said. And, in any case, we'll soon be there.

– And in any case I can't do a three-point turn on the Nationale 570. Not history, then, but art. Journeys which begin, he thought, and then have to be completed.

He remarked how strange it was – and what a banal thing to say it was, he told himself – that the mouth of a river made so much difference. The architecture changed, the plantations were no longer just cork and eucalyptus. Geography remained constant across the river, at least the earth was coloured the same. Ah, but language changed, and, said Crump in a moment of dianoetic intensity, although we all see the same thing, the words we use make us look differently, that's all, language is what draws lines. Therefore, all human beings are not equal, not until they speak the same language.

–Ah, sea, she said, seeing a glimpse of the ocean when they crossed the bridge into Portimão.

They lay beside the shell-encrusted rocks on the firm sand of Praia da Rocha. The other people who lay on the beach were Germans, French, English, Belgians, Dutch, Italians, Scandinavians, Swiss, Austrians. The ice-cream vendors called out in Portuguese but could tell the price in any language the customers spoke. There was the sound of the sea mostly, the splash of waves against rocks, but when voices carried they spoke a foreign tongue. The majority of the people lay in silent obeisance to the sun. Girls stretched their legs out, heaved their bikini bosoms up and shut their eyes in inward ecstasy; or they turned and lay on their stomachs, undoing the strap of their bikini tops to tan also the white bra-line across their bronzed backs. The winter's full-colour ads, the jet-line commercials which had begun a week after Christmas, the waiting at travel agencies, the adman's image of couples holding hands and running down a deserted palm-tree-fringed beach, white-jacketed waiters serving iced daiquiris or Martinis to bosom-bubbling youth, the tedium of hanging around airports to catch the cheap night excursion, the entire business of exhorting society to shed its exhaustion of fifty weeks of work in a fortnight of Fun found its apotheosis here in each body which lay with its eyes shut behind the fashionable oversize sun-glasses. Crump felt restless. He could not lie for long with his legs stretched out and his arms held slightly away from his body, the palms open to the sun, without feeling that his mind had regressed a stage further towards becoming moronic, and rose every few minutes to throw himself into the water and to pursue at least some activity although the repeated exercise of swimming was becoming a little monotonous.

He heard a dog bark and a female voice say *Viens, Cola.* Presently he saw the owners both of the bark, an undistinguished terrier, and the female voice, a woman in her early twenties of well-proportioned body but no remarkable beauty.

A man with the kind of haircut immediately recognizable as French accompanied them. They put down their towels some ten yards away from Crump and sat down. The dog ran on.

– *Viens, Cola,* the woman called, and the man too cried out with more emphasis on the first word, *Viens, Cola.*

The man rose and ran after the dog. The woman called *Viens, Cola.* The man ran back with the dog in his arms, laughing at the dog, giving it soft, loving mock punches on the head. He placed the dog near his towel. The dog barked and ran to the edge of the sea. The woman's eyes were on the dog all the time. And again she called: *Viens, Cola.* The dog ran back to her. She stroked it. The dog ran away. *Viens, Cola,* she called. The man stood up and ran to the sea, diving when he was thigh deep in the water. Pulling himself up on his toes, he turned to look at the dog, and called, *Viens, Cola.* The woman rose, calling, *Viens, Cola,* and ran towards the sea. The dog ran back to her and then ran with her. She splashed her way into the water; the dog halted at the sea's edge. She turned round, called repeatedly, *Viens, Cola.* The man ran out, calling, *Viens, Cola,* picked up the dog and walked towards where the woman was. He took the dog to her. She laughed, stroking the dog's head. The man threw the dog into the water. The dog swam out, barking, his brown coat going a shade darker. The couple watched the dog shake itself on the sand, both calling simultaneously and alternately, *Viens, Cola.* They came out, dried themselves and lay on their towels, but with their elbows on the sand and their heads lifted, watching the dog all the time. When the dog went more than a dozen yards away from them, they called, *Viens, Cola.* The man rose and, producing a ball, began to play with the dog. The woman's eyes were a mixture of admiration and affection while she watched the man and the dog play. When the game ended, they collected their towels and began to walk away. When they were out of sight, Crump could still hear her call, *Viens, Cola.*

Crump imagined her in the Bois de Boulogne, calling *Viens, Cola.* Crump imagined her in her flat in Paris, turning from the washing-up on hearing the man return from taking the dog out for an after-dinner walk, calling, *Viens, Cola.* Crump wondered whether she ever talked to the man, whether *Viens, Cola* were the only words they spoke. Christ, what is it people live for?

Crump watched also the flat-stomached nubile goddesses come and go, their *ambre solaire* skin and the fashionable white lipstick (the mouth held slightly open, showing the glint of perfect teeth) giving their demeanour a savagery which provoked violent emotions and notions of a fantastic and cruel sexuality in the beholder.

And there were the walking pages from magazines which showed on their covers the cock-raising cleavage of a tantalizingly casually worn blouse, magazines which pretended to interpret a culture in a language whose terminology was a matter of fashion and in a philosophy which congratulated itself on its smartness of expression and the irrefutability of its logic, the fundamental premise of which, that money was the only good which achieved the virtues of pleasure, could be denied only by an idiot.

Crump felt increasingly like an idiot.

– This is Europe, he said, for something to say.

Frieda, lying on the sand, shifted a foot.

– We build up a civilization, he said in case her slight movement suggested she was listening. We create a culture. And what is there at the end of it? An industry provoking mass masturbation. I'm going to jump in the sea, he added.

They drove away from Venasque.

– Remember, she said, we drove from Portimão to Monchique one day? The road went straight across a dry plain and then began to spiral up the mountains. There was a spa on the way. The road forked and one arm of the fork suddenly ducked under cork trees and led to the spa. There had been signs on the road announcing the spa, inviting one to it. But we missed the road and had to look out for it when we were returning from Monchique, saying we must visit the spa. There was a hotel there, there were cafés. But the place was empty. Waiters, café proprietors stood in doorways or sat in the shade, waiting, silently watching. As if they didn't expect anyone. Were surprised to see us. And we parked the car and followed the directions to the fountains. We climbed and climbed. It was wearying. We never reached the fountains. We decided to have a drink when we came back to the car. We went into a café. It was dirty, the beer was tepid. We put a coin in the juke box. The man smiled, glad that we were enjoying ourselves. But we were only killing silence. The man stood smiling. Across the street, we could see other cafés, their waiters standing, waiting for the tourists to come. Mike, are you listening?

– That keeps returning to me, he said. We were returning from Venasque, we were on the ferry from Boulogne. It was a day of poor visibility. We were standing on the deck, looking out for England, when we saw him sitting on a bench. His head was one mass of bandages, holes for eyes, gaps for mouth and nose. His right leg was in plaster. He sat there on the deck, perhaps he wanted to glimpse England too before we reached Dover, or perhaps it was merely that he could breathe more easily there, on the deck. A woman sat with him. She looked sad. And we constructed a drama. We made up his story. *Total sur les routes du monde*. She did not speak, sitting there; he did not move. And in such situations, we asked, when a peculiar disposition of chances very nearly kills us, are we saved or destroyed? Utterly?

– What's left of Europe, you kept asking.

– A tourist, balled-up bandages for a head.

They drove away from Venasque.

– Going to Roussillon, he said, we drove through the Forêt de Murs and up on the Plateau de Vaucluse. It seemed a remote wilderness, so near Venasque. There were oaks, oaks, a dense forest of them, and then the arid plateau. And you saw them, you pointed them out, the little stone houses, and you turned the pages of the Michelin in your lap and said they were called *bòris*. They looked like primitive dwellings, like caves in the open air. We stopped to look at one. But we didn't enter one. You were afraid, you said, it reminded you of something in Africa and you didn't want to see it.

– But there was another, she said, though it turned out to be a little ruin and not a *bòri.* It had a door on which there was a message. Will return on Saturday, it said. We entered and found ourselves in a room without a roof to it. There was a shirt hanging from a line. There was a pair of boots. A corner was black from fires being lit there. A hammock was slung across between two walls. There was a guitar. And a cockerel strutted about, keeping an eye on us. And you said someone's chosen to live like this.

– A tourist among ruins.

They drove away from Venasque.

He parked the car in Marx-Engels Platz. As he was locking the car, a boy ran up to him and asked him if he had any cigarettes to sell. Surprised at the boy's use of an English phrase, he said (his mind conjuring up a concealed infinitesimally tiny camera in the boy's shirt button take his picture and imagining a whole network of espionage going into ruthless operation), Sorry, I can only speak to Number One.

– Oh, Mike, do be careful, she said, as they walked towards the cathedral. We don't want to land ourselves before the authorities. It'd be no use trying to convince them you were joking.

– You've been seeing too many spy films, he said.

– It's grim, to say the least, she said when they entered the cathedral.

– Ah, humiliated art thou, he said, standing in a corner while she walked towards some disfigured statuary, what's become of all the gold they flattered your vanity with? Among all god's creatures, thou, God, are the vainest. Of some thou demandest the fairest virgins, of some the slaughter of sheep; of some offerings of fruit, of some thy image in gold; of some thou expectest genocide and of some unremitting misery in thy name. Old hoaxer! King in the land of prestidigitation, robbed of all the old tricks, art thou? Ah, but what's become of us now that you're handcuffed, put away, not even made a public spectacle of, not even abused and spat upon, just put away? We've taken away thy images from the bedside tables and put alarm clocks there. We've taken down thy icons from the walls and sent them for auction at the art galleries. Dost hear? The whine and buzz and stutter and clatter of motorized bicycles, the workers are going home. Now thou reachest thy real state, true invisibility.

– Praying? she asked, returning to him.

– Devoutly, he said.

– It's all dust and ashes, she said. It catches at my throat.

Perhaps she had meant some emotion, he wondered afterwards when he needed to look for meanings in trifles.

– They're going to have dances and things for the Liverpool opening, he said, and laughed, his throat tickled by mockery.

She failed to grasp his irony, for she was trying to decipher the script on a tombstone beneath a statue of some soldier.

– What honour, O Berliners! he mocked, recalling the uneasy piety with which visitors shuffled through the Kaiser-Wilhelm-Gedächtniskirche. Heavy eyelids lifted and were weighted down again while the bejewelled ladies, all powder and rouge, moist scarlet lips held open, sighed, their eyes thrilling to the terror of what he said, their bosoms suffering the oppression of the strongly incensed airlessness.

– Old fraud! Sulking in corners, confined to that most solitary cell of all, oblivion, feeding on dust and the cruel shafts of sunlight. Dost hear? Here are your creditors, the demolition workers. They'll raze you to dust, plant lawns and flower-beds on your site, the corporation gardens will flower; or, if they can't be bothered with urban niceties, they'll simply put up a hoarding and a poster of bosom and smiling lips will distract the passing eye from the ugliness of your collapse. Mean old poker-faced fraud, dost hear? A piece of antiquity. A subject for lectures, conducted tours, colour slides. Ruin upon ruin.

– You look like the devil, she said returning to him, grinning like that.

But she frowned then, her eyes falling on a piece of a

statue, a nose and a mouth, that lay on the ground. She picked it up and walked away to place it on a bench.

– Our father who art. *Father?* Ha! Tell me my daughters which of you shall we say doth love us most? Unreasonable old fool! There's only one place for you. Out on the heath under the bad weather of your own making. Or try being one of us and see how far your damned omnipotence takes you. Walk down the street, watch the seventeen-year-old girls go past in their short skirts and low necklines, and see what it does for your vanity, old man. Sit in a plane and watch an engine catch fire at twenty thousand feet. Oh, but this is nothing, a pettiness, that's all. We've programmed omniscience into computers; the smart young public relations men have taken over. Poor old sod, thou art redundant now. Thou art truly and mightily screwed.

– Have you seen everything? she asked, returning to him.

– Yes, he said.

– There's the museum to see, she said, taking his arm as they left the cathedral, the doomed Dom.

A light rain was falling outside: the tail-end of a heavy shower which had descended upon East Berlin while they were in the cathedral. But they had to hurry anyway, for they had five minutes in which to see the museum before it closed for the day. They could have come another time to see the museum but knew that they would not come here another time. They need not have bothered at all, knowing that looking at a museum in five minutes was like suggesting that they reserve only five minutes of their married life for making love. But somehow the idea was daring, it was an affront directed at themselves, at their own belief in the slow, laborious, years-at-the-anvil methods of art; and there was a thrill in that, in compressing a lifetime's knowledge into five minutes of experience. The galleries were empty. Perhaps no one ever came here – how could they tell? – in this world of workers and productivity bonuses, of holidays to take by the seaside. The pictures seemed to have become blurred without beholders to observe definitions in them. Perhaps people came here on Sundays – how could they tell? – or during a lunch break to look at a painting or a statue for the enjoyment of looking or to be informed about some point in history or to keep away from the cold for a few minutes, or to see what they wanted to see, who knew why anyone did anything? They ran through gallery after gallery, her heels echoing from the stone floor. They saw centuries of art in one fleeting glance, a crazy montage, that's what it is, he cried, running. They ran down the steps of the hall and halted at the exit; for it was raining heavily again, a new shower had commenced. They waited a moment to find their breath and to determine the shortest cut to their car. Two old ladies, who had finished working at the museum for the day, were walking away, stepping into puddles as though circumnavigation were impossible, sharing an umbrella.

– Quite right, he said, driving away. What's the point of going in circles? You spend a whole life doing that and it leads nowhere.

– What else shall we see?

– Time we had a drink, he said.

– We can drink in the theatre, she said. Let's just have a coffee somewhere.

He drove in what he thought and hoped was the right direction, but a no entry sign confounded his mental compass, obliging him to take a turning he had not anticipated, and for five minutes he drove in what he was convinced was the opposite direction.

– This is other people's rush hour, he said, a traffic jam that's got nothing to do with us.

They observed the faces in other cars, silently watching them. A bus crawling along their left was full of people standing in the gangway, crowding in the seated passengers; those who sat by the windows looked down at the Volks-couple in the alien city.

– We just happen to be here, that's all.

People walking on the pavement turned to look at them, too; and the cyclists and the motor-cyclists, overtaking through the narrow gaps on both sides of the car.

– And tomorrow when they go home from work again some might remember they saw a strange couple in their midst, some might remember that they saw something which they can't remember, and some might think that perhaps they thought, but of course how can that be possible, it's so easy, they'll think, to imagine things.

– We won't be here, that's all.

– That's all, he said, finally extricating the car from the traffic jam and finding the right direction.

They left the car in Bertold Brecht Platz in anticipation of the theatre-time parking problem, and walked towards a restaurant they had noticed earlier on Friedrichstrasse. They saw a building in the distance, a small prefabricated structure, the large area of glass in its walls revealing its brightly lit interior and attracting them to it. Nearing it, they discovered that it was a police and customs checkpoint for passengers taking the train to West Berlin.

– Some old people were crying, she said when they had sat down in the crowded restaurant.

– It's Easter, remember, and the permission they give Berliners to visit for a week they might never again. A farewell can be a funeral.

– Please don't mention that, she said and added, changing the subject: It's been a happy journey so far.

– I know, he said.

– Perhaps they're tired after a day's work, she said after a pause, looking over his shoulder and remarking at the dumb crowd around them in the restaurant. Possibly it's no different in Lyons corner houses at six o'clock.

– I know, he said. You'd like to think their grim faces are a sign of the repressive régime. But I shouldn't mention that either!

– I know, she said, her eyes shifting in nervous observation, we're too glib in the West. We equate freedom with jollity.

– We've made a balls-up of it all, he said, the East and the West.

Perhaps he noticed, but certainly remembered afterwards, that a suddenly obscene phraseology which, although she did not censure it and in fact sometimes used herself, invariably drew a glance from her was on this occasion lost as she continued to look around her.

She went to the ladies, leaving him to have another cup of coffee. He hoped the play would be absorbing, for he needed distraction from the feeling of sickness in his stomach. Foul, he said to himself, a wretched foulness.

– Not cancer, I hope, he heard Stobbs say.

– You're a right old devil, Stobbs, he said, with those huge eyes of yours behind the thick lenses and that malicious grin.

But she returned quickly enough from the ladies to stop him from worrying about what he should do if she were kidnapped and made a hostage to facilitate the return of some petty Soviet spy. They walked slowly to the Berliner Ensemble.

At the theatre, watching the Picasso dove on the curtain, he was impatient for the play to begin. *Die Tage Der Commune*, he already knew, would be all the words he would remember. The rest would be a magnificent trick; the actors would speak a language, give its nuances deliberate emphasis which they would have perfected after days of rehearsal, they would declaim or be lyrical, use the rhetoric of anger or the pause of despair, but words, words would resound, and he, not understanding one of them, would see what other element there could be to make the performance sensible to him. The dove flew up, and lo! A feast, a spectacle, what colour, what animation! But he was confounded. The Parisian aristocrats were leaving. No one spoke on the railway platform. The lady with her furs and her poodle, and the engine hissing steam; and the porters who should have been deferential, sycophantic, were insolent, cocky. The train to salvation was rearing to go, a guard's whistle was blowing. At Friedrichstrasse station, an hour ago, a similarly silent spectacle, people departing, old people weeping; and now back almost a hundred years. Again the departures, again the silent expression of a peculiar misery. Oh Europe! Refugees, refugees. Somewhere the crowd was barking. In the Paris of the Commune, in Moscow, in London, in Berlin, in Rome, in Madrid, at some time, now or in the past, in football stadiums or in public squares where the well-groomed politicians addressed rallies or where soldiers appeared in armoured cars, at some time, now or in the future, in newspaper columns, on radio and television. Somewhere the crowd was barking. The silent killers were afoot.

Crossing at Checkpoint Charlie, the brilliant vulgarity of Western democracy's shop-window hit them with all its colour from cinemas, neonlit cafeterias, the advertisements which flashed on and off, the tail-lights of cars which had suddenly multiplied by thousands, the illuminated buildings, the *son et lumière* of life. Serenely revolving above it all was the blue three-pointed star, symbol of Mercedes Benz, high on the building at the end of Kurfürstendamm.

They went into a bar. He ordered Dortmunder beer.

– It's intoxicating to return, he said. One feels at home away from all that terrifying austerity. Those dark buildings.

As if he could convince her now! But he was surprised when she said: It was so peaceful in Venasque.

– I wanted you, he said, in the orchard.

– We shouldn't have come, she said, it frightens me.

That was something he could not forget, her expression of fear, but he said, as if chanting a memorized verse: I wanted you on Raguenès-Plage.

– Finistère! Have another beer if you like.

– Everywhere, he said. Even that flat, withered old woman's chest of a country, Holland. That cold beach in Bluemendaal. We come and we go.

– Will you sing me a song? she asked.

– Later, later, he said. Drink up.

– You have another if you like, she said.

– We should stick to Brittany, he said. It's gentler. Or am I forgetting?

– No, don't ask that, she said, that's not part of the game. And went on herself: But I missed the sea at Venasque.

Though it was hot enough!

– To remind you of Johannesburg? he mocked.

– No, she said. I think South Africa's a mistake. For me, that is. Was a mistake. Really, this is where I come from. Yes, I think I'll have another beer, too.

– Tomorrow Charlottenburg in the morning, he said, and Grunewald in the afternoon.

– South Africa was an artificiality, she said. A kind of speculation on the stock exchange. A dead loss in the end.

– And after that, he said, if the weather doesn't improve, we'll drive south. Am I playing well, Frieda?

– Yes, yes, she said hastily as if not wanting to break a spell. It could have been anywhere else, she went on. The United States, Australia, Brazil, the Argentine; it could have been England. Poor old England, the sanctuary for Europeans who've had to pack their bags in a hurry.

– Frieda, he said, Frieda Crump, was Lewis, was Lowes.

– Was Lowenstein, she said. That's why he changed the name twice.

– If I remember what I'd forgotten, then I won't think to remember what I'd forgotten before I remembered the other, later thing I'd forgotten.

– That's why, she said. No, I don't want another drink, but you go ahead.

– I wished, he said, the wind had not been so fierce at Armação de Péra.

– That, she asked, the beach had been better at Estepona?

– We always went south, he said. Until now. This harshness, this withdrawal of the north.

– I shall always miss Venasque, she said. Those still cypress trees. And Brittany for its windy passions.

– Brittany!

– There's no hope, then, she said. That blue star is the top of this world. What's the point of trying to reach higher?

– The Tibetans might have an answer, he said irrelevantly.

– Christ, I'm sleepy, she said.

– It's been a long day, he said, driving away to their hotel.

He was grateful to fall into bed, having thrown his clothes on the floor. She seemed already asleep. She had not bothered to spend the routine quarter of an hour in front of the mirror with her creams and finally her hair-brush before undressing, but had sleepily stripped herself and had gone to bed. He switched off the light beside the bed, stroked her buttocks for she was turned away from him, and himself turning, so that their buttocks rested against each other, prepared for the nightly oblivion to overtake his consciousness. He felt her hand touch his thigh and reach for his groin – an act, he thought, of a somnabulist, but full of incipient excitement nevertheless; so that he turned a little towards her to make it easier for her to reach him if, indeed, she were attempting to do so. He was deliciously surprised, and where he had been beginning to throb limply the blood precipitately ran its natural course and stiffened his muscles in readiness for whatever feat was expected of them. She had turned a little herself, so that it seemed discourteous for his hands to remain unemployed. Soon, his body was like a factory in full production, working overtime to meet an export order. Mouth, hands, feet, every point where contact was possible, manoeuvred into action.

At the final moment, he was aware that neither of them had taken any precaution, and that produced an after-thrill. He turned away finally to sleep. She slept embracing his back and in moments of half-waking he was conscious of her knees between his legs, her breasts clammy against his back, and a sweaty smell which was somehow intoxicating. At some time during that night, much later, very early in the morning, long before it was time to wake up, he again half-awoke and felt that her weight against his back was too much, or that at least he needed to shift his position now that he was aware of a certain discomfort. He shuffled a little. She moved back somewhat, so that he was free to lie flat on his back. A moment later, she again drew nearer to him and, finding him turned, kissed him on the mouth and in the wildness of sleep (or so it seemed to him later) shifted herself on him, and, pulling herself up, offered to his gaping mouth that strange oxygen of her breasts on which he would rather suffocate than wish for so futile a thing as air. He was fully awake again, alive.

The consequent exhaustion was all the greater. When morning came, he wished it had never come.

For he moaned in the pre-waking reluctance ever again to emerge from consciousness, aware in the half-consciousness of a higher ecstasy than his previous sexual experience had ever possessed him of, and he did not want to hear whatever she might be saying, some sudden urgency, some remark about the day's touring and how late it already was. He would have preferred to have remained there for ever in a state of unconsciousness, only half-waking now and then to be drawn into the savagery she had suddenly invented as though in her sleep she had sunk into a glorious barbarism. If she spoke, if she called out in her busy morning voice, it would be a barbed wire over which he must tear his flesh. But she did not speak. After a while, he began to realize, only dimly, that there was no sound in the room. Perhaps, he thought, he had woken before she did for once. He stretched out his hand. But she was not in bed. He looked through reluctantly opening eyes. But she was not in the room.

Imagining things, eh Crump? he said to himself, realizing how much of what was on his mind could be a fiction. Dressing, he packed his suitcase in readiness for checking out of the hotel, and went down to breakfast. He ate some bread and butter, ignoring the little dish of jam the waitress had brought, absently noticing that it was apricot jam, but why should there be any significance in that, he said, and lit a cigarette.

There was a queue of people outside the toilet. They will stick these toilets at the end of passages, he remarked to himself, irritated at having to wait for people to evacuate their bowels, brush their teeth, shave even, when all he wanted to do was to relieve his bladder, willing to defer the other activities to a more leisurely opportunity. Finally, it was his turn, and, having waited so long, he decided to take his time even though there was no question of his bowels moving in such oppressively crowded circumstances. He just sat there on the toilet seat with his trousers on, thinking that he had seen someone doing that, sitting on a toilet seat with his trousers on. He stood up, looked at himself in the mirror, agreed with his own image that his own mind need not have anything to do with the person called Crump who could well be a fiction in another mind which now observed from a detached point of view this figure standing in a toilet, facing a mirror, and said without speaking:

O Heart: this is a dream I had, or not a dream.

The words which had come to him and which his mind had uttered without his speaking were a quotation, a line from a poem by the American poet Stanley Kunitz, and not a statement which he expressed or could have expressed had he been speaking publicly or privately, which he was not, unless he was a critic delivering a lecture or writing a paper, which he was not. Just then the little room he was in seemed to give way under him, and, holding on to the door-handle, he stopped himself from being knocked against the little aluminium basin. Still, it was a relief to have got that out of his system, that line which had bothered him from time to time, and he left the toilet with the same feeling of satisfaction as when he had successfully evacuated his congested bowels. He walked down the passage, noticing that the stewardesses had packed away all the breakfast things, and that the sign had come on asking people to fasten their seat belts and not to smoke. The plane was descending, it seemed, in a series of bumps through a thick mass of cloud, and what hopes he had had of an aerial view of Manhattan were dissipated. He hoped there was better weather in Berlin, and remembered: For look, it's an extreme situation, demanding commitment. But we live with compromise, rusted with cosiness.

And: Don't even tell me when the time comes that it has come.

– And how do you feel about it? he asked. Are you still as

resolved?

– I don't know, she said. I don't know. Sometimes I laugh at myself, asking how can it be possible.

– Games, he said, suppose there were no games?

– But that's not possible, she said. Take one game away, another takes its place. For example, that we're here.

– And your mother?

– She had her reasons no doubt. I shall have to find out. If ever we go to Berlin.

– Here we are in Brittany, doing nothing.

– Do we do anything anywhere?

– Futility, he said, utter bloody futility.

– Oh, for God's sake, Mike! I can't bear your pessimism, your hopelessly negative point of view.

– What can I do? What can *you* do? The best human beings can possibly do is to have children and I'm cynical about that, too, if you want to know.

– Don't I know it!

–Look, he said. All action is futile, there being no choice. Therefore, inaction is not futile. How about that then, a simple deduction simply arrived at by applying the principle of opposites.

– You might as well sleep away your three score years and ten.

– Ever your eyes were as a lizard's quick, he said.

– What do you mean by that?

– Nothing. A quotation. Someone else's words, that's all.

– Bloody wonderful, she said, bitterly.

– If that can't matter, why should anything else?

She turned her gaze to the sea, repeating: Why should anything else?

– And I remembered that other line, by the way.

She did not turn back to look at him, made no gesture which could have been interpreted as interest in what he was saying.

– O Heart: this is a dream I had, or not a dream.

– What about it? she said, sharply, still looking away.

– Nothing, I just remembered. That's all.

– Talk, she said, looking down at her lap, her hand stroking the sand, too much talk. Delusions, that state of being drugged.

– All that could have happened, he said, and this could have been a reconciliation. Or this could have been the moment when we decided. . . .

– No, she said, stop! I don't want hypotheses.

– Right, then, he said, getting up. Action!

And he sprinted away from her. She watched him run down the half-mile length of the beach. Her hand, which had been involuntarily plucking at the sand, touched a hard object, a shell, she noticed. She inspected it, wiping the sand off it. It was a Great Scallop shell, about six inches wide. She rose and ran to the sea in order to wash it. Bending down to dip the shell in the water, she saw him on the far end of the beach, climbing up some rocks. She walked back to her towel with the washed shell and just before she sat down, she glanced in the direction of the point of rocks at the end of the beach but could not see him there. The bloody fool, she said to herself, probably gone and killed himself. She lay back on her towel, stretched her legs out and shut her eyes, glad that she was sheltered against the wind and that the sun was positively hot.

And what were the trees which bordered the road to St Rémy? His driver's view of them had recorded no detail in his memory except the trunks which were painted white at the base, and the bright Provençal sun through the trees cast successive shadows, leaving zebra stripes of light on the tarmac, to blur the image which should otherwise have remained clear. Kola still stood where he had left him, by the boys' notice-board.

– You ought to be warned, Kola, he said, that impiety has made a feast of thee.

– Oh, that's good, said Kola, that's very good.

Not far from them, one small boy was saying to another, 'Ere, if this is me armpit, what's this, then? Your bleedin' crotch, the other replied. No, you fat spas, that's me cockpit!

– As long as we know what we're talking about, remarked Crump to Kola, walking on, which can't be said of most people.

St Rémy had been a village to stop at for a drink and to drive on, to drive on, that curse, for the destination then was the old Roman town of Arles. The door to one of the classrooms had WOG carved on it, reminding Crump of the Indian teacher who had spent a term at the school and in whose honour the word had been carved there, reminding him, too, of the only conversation he had had with him: My prahblem is, three-piece-suited Mr Chandrasekhar (the staff had called him Mr Cha, and the boys, knowing this, had nicknamed him Mr Cuppa) had said, I can't understand vhat the chillrun are saying, and vhat's verse, they can't understand vhat it is that I am trying my very best to impart to them, and Crump had given what he now considered a predictable Englishman's reply, a jolly kind of non-statement, That's the universal problem, isn't it? and they had laughed, briefly, pointlessly. It was also Van Gogh's city; it would never be Crump's city, Arles. What made you come to Europe in the first place? he asked Frieda beside Van Gogh's famous bridge, and where he himself would have paused to search for an interesting answer, a psychologically portentous one, say, bleeding Crump, he told himself now, an insignificant turdle in the bog of ideas, all she said was, It was the fashion, as though Europe were a kind of hemline with which South African girls had to concern themselves to remain smart. Two boys were walking in front of him.

– Do you know what the cannibal said to his wife? one of the boys asked.

– Wha'? demanded the other.

– I could eat yer.

– That's spas!

And even this precaution of leaving the staff-room promptly had not succeeded, for the classes had already been coming in and Jim Sutton and his mates were already crowding his locked door when he reached it. He noticed that Sutton looked sulky, introspective, his arms folded across his chest, his eyes gazing at the floor, a mood with which Crump was not unfamiliar. He could ask them to line up in twos. He could refuse to let them enter the room unless they stood quietly in an ordered line. It would take them ten minutes to achieve such order. He could harangue them for wasting their own time. Or he could say at the end of the ten minutes when they were reasonably quiet, You've wasted ten minutes of the lesson, you've wasted ten minutes of my time; it will be fair for me to waste ten minutes of your time, and, therefore, I'm going to keep you behind after four o'clock, and if there's any more disturbance I'll just add on the wasted time: so, it's up to you when you go home tonight.

– I'm goin' now, mate, is one answer he would receive, as he had received in the past, or other cries:

– I've got a job to get to at five past.

I've got to go to the dentist, look 'ere's me card. (A few boys habitually carried a dentist's appointment card.)

– I'm not bleedin' stayin'.

Instead of trying any such scheme to obtain order, he made straight for the door, his face lost in deliberate distraction, gently parted the boys in his way, aimed for the keyhole with his key only to discover that some idiot had stuffed chewing-gum into the keyhole; luckily, he was able to push the chewing-gum through the hole – a hasty, unprofessional job, whoever had done it – so that it fell on the other side of the door. Throwing the door open, he marched urgently in, saying Come on, come on, there's a lot to do, and tried not to pay any attention to the comment

– Where you goin' to do it, then?

made by some wit behind him, nor to the guffaws of laughter, and realized that he had stepped on the chewing-gum which had now become stuck to the sole of his right shoe. He scraped it off against the leg of a desk in the front row and saw the boys jamming themselves in the doorway like a herd of sheep at the narrow entrance to a pen. That, too, he ignored, knowing that they expected him to go to the door in order to separate them and consequently to become absorbed by the mass himself. A push from those on the rear led to three boys at the front to be thrown in while two in the middle of the rush collapsed on the floor; this excited those on the rear to pretend that they were being pushed and they, too, fell together in a heap. There were cries, screams, laughter, and in the general noise language served no purpose other than the utterance of expletives. Crump continued to disregard the class, but noticed not without some surprise that Jim Sutton had nothing to do with the prevailing chaos, for he was sitting quietly at a desk. Maybe he had been caned during break or suffered from stomach-ache; it could, of course, be camouflage, an attempt presently to ambush Crump. He remembered Sutton's sinister threat in the playground. Crump sat down in his chair, saying To hell with you, which no one heard, opened a textbook, and began to look at it without reading it, his back metaphorically turned to the boisterous hooliganism which prevailed in the classroom. Or there had been the window to look out of, sitting in the first-floor bedroom of the small stone house in Venasque, down at the valley, and was it peach trees in the sloping orchard beside the vegetable garden with its portions of beetroot, tomatoes and lettuce, a salad-bowl cultivation, or was it cherry trees, his memory did not consider the precise fruit the trees bore as relevant, for he had been looking at a view and not attempting to make a naturalist's catalogue of what he saw, at any rate it was the proportion of the branches to the trunks which had elicited an aesthetic gasp and that is why the memory was one of form and not of content. Frieda was in the bathroom, under the shower. She had been in the kitchen earlier and, finishing whatever chore occupied her there, had come to the bedroom where he sat on the chair beside the bed, looking out, had come in shorts and a blouse which she had not buttoned up but tied in a knot just above her navel. It makes me penisthetic, he had remarked, looking at her, and she had said, Is that one of your kids' words?

She was singing in the bathroom. He looked down at the valley and thought of sex under the fruit trees. An erotic possibility, no doubt; but probably more satisfying as an imaginative concept than as an actual performance even if seclusion were possible in so open a space. The earth was gritty, the ground sloped. It would be pleasanter on Hampstead Heath after sunset on a July evening, especially if the afternoon had been warm. Or in the darkness of the ferns of Putney Heath. After the first sensual excitement of seeing her in the orange skirt and discovering that she wore nothing under it, even the thrill which came from a feeling of being daring, lying there under the pine tree in the forest off the route nationale, had not diminished the ultimate sense of disappointment: sex as an art form or as a personalized ritual needed a bedroom; under trees or on a beach it became urgent and animalistic and, to one participating in it with a view only to achieving subtle and refined degrees of pleasure and not procreation, a bore. The difference was one between having a meal at the Tour d'Argent and eating a sandwich; though, he expected, looking at that landscape, that in certain circumstances a sandwich could be an exciting novelty to some people, including himself. A cypress tree stood half-way up the hill across the valley like a punished boy, gloomy of aspect. That was nonsense, he realized, seeing that two different images had telescoped in his brain, for his eye, at the window in Venasque, seeing the cypress tree in the distance, had momentarily become confused with his immediate vision which saw the entire class, and not just one boy, standing up in total silence. There was a third image, one his mind had already begun to transmit to succeed the image of the cypress tree, and that, he realized, as he stood up, too, seeing that the class had stood up because the headmaster was in the room, was of a naked girl, not anyone he knew, just a naked female form with all those attributes perfect which are most prized by men whose thoughts are on sex. The headmaster was standing in front of the blackboard, silently glowering at the class, and Crump, seeing him in that censuring attitude, thought of his father, to whom, he remarked to himself, he had not given much thought recently, and tried in that moment to think when he had last given thought to him, but could not immediately remember, for the impact of successive present sensations, coming as they did, to a brain which was overworking itself with its own unprompted and random re-creation of past sensations, was overcrowding his mind, but, he thought, still in that same moment as when he was thinking when it was that he had last thought of his father, he should at least remember when he last saw his mother, even though thinking of one's father and seeing one's mother were two different things, and now, having pushed his chair back and having begun to take a step towards the headmaster, saying, Good afternoon, sir, he remembered that his mother was in hospital, which he did not require to remember for had anyone in the middle of a conversation about something else suddenly asked him, Crump, where is your mother? he would at once and without taking the slightest time to think have replied, In hospital.

– The last lesson is the most trying, the headmaster said, smiling weakly, reminding Crump of a similar smile on the faces of the heads of families in countless Hollywood films, lying in their death-beds, the family around them, even the faithful old dog, smiling weakly, giving the impression of a virtuous life virtuously completed, saying to the youngest son, Look after your mother, son, and, turning their heads against the bulging white pillows, dying, accompanied by violins.

The headmaster went out, stepping softly. Another hush-puppy man, Crump noticed while the headmaster quietly shut the door behind him, leaving Crump both with a certain order in the class as well as the incipient sounds of renewed chaos. A hush puppier, a hush papa, a hush Papist, a hush puppet, a hush poppet, words beget words; and that's something else.

– Now, listen, he said to the class, but mouths were already opening in mockery, jaws dropping in feigned disbelief, sounds of dogs baying, cows lowing, and winter winds blowing across moors were beginning to fill the classroom, that will do, you can be damned well ashamed at attracting the attention of the rest of the school and if you don't bloody well shut up, I'll make your backsides blue – bloody Andrews, with his Sir's burned a hole in me arse, what did he want? – with caning before you get home to your loving mums.

Abuse, slightly obscenely worded, worked sometimes, and it did now and the voice which cried *Sie-dist!* was embarrassed into silence when it was not joined by a chorus.

– Sit down and get your comprehension books out.

They sat down as one body like a well-drilled troop, and brought out their books from their desks. Crump set the work, explained what it was all about, uttered a few cautionary sentences to anyone who dared disturb the lesson, and began patrolling the aisles between the rows of desks. They worked in absolute silence, but to what purpose, Crump asked, knowing the futility of the kind of comprehension exercise which was usually set to B streams, for the work did not enlarge their understanding of language in any sense other than the chance learning of an occasional new word. It was for him to arouse their curiosity and interest, he knew, to win their absorption, but he gave too much of his energy to the A streams and especially to the fifth- and sixth-form literature classes (excuses, excuses!) to have more than an old-fashioned competence to offer to the intellectually less bright and that, too, only when these unfortunates were willing to give him a chance. Even the informal talking, the lengthy monologues which Stobbs enjoyed so much and which he himself considered an important part of his teaching exhausted him. Poor father, he felt compelled to think of him, Herbert Crump, tobacconist, confectioner and newsagent, whose signboard had been supplied by Player's cigarettes and stationery by *The Times*, for whom life was a balancing of accounts and business a matter of putting up a printed sign in the shop:

PLEASE DO NOT ASK FOR CREDIT

He had given up interest in Crump when Crump worked as a delivery boy for him at the age of twelve and, instead of delivering the papers in the shortest possible time, Crump not only got some of the addresses wrong but could never resist looking at the papers and frequently spent fifteen to twenty minutes standing at a street corner reading a paper. It had been no use inculcating upon Crump's mind rudimentary notions of a business sense just as it had been impossible to make him understand when he was not yet ten that simply because there were heaps of sweets in the shop did not mean that he could eat as many of them as he liked. And then, at the age of thirteen, to impress a classmate who boasted of mysterious sexual secrets, Crump had stolen a health magazine which contained photographs of nudists and which his father kept beneath a pile of *Exchange & Mart*, bringing them out for display during the hours that Crump was away at school, and old Crump, discovering the theft, was so torn between embarrassment and righteousness that he could not bring himself to scold Crump for fear of having to discuss nudity with his son, and simply kept quiet and began to resent Crump's presence in the shop. Crump's subsequently becoming a teacher alienated the two from each other still more, the old man pitying Crump for not having the knack (which he could so easily have taught him) for making money, and the son pitying the father for having nothing more interesting to do with his life than to be making money and that, too, in the petty pinch-penny ways of shopkeeping.

Crump walked up and down the aisles, looking down on the bowed heads, and was about to give some thought to his mother when the cry

PLAYMATES!

shrieked through the room. When it did, he was again at the

front of the class and for the moment his back was turned to the boys. The cry swung him round as though it were a body blow. He saw that Jim Sutton had sprung up to his feet, holding a magazine above his head, the pages turned to what looked like, and in fact was, the centre spread, and there on the centre spread was a picture in full colour of a nude. Sutton turned full circle three or four times, the nude's blonde hair seemed to whirl through the air, a lipsticked mouth smiled invitingly round the classroom, admitting each pair of eyes to an instant fantasy, white teeth flashed, and two inflated breasts brushed the mouths of all the boys, drawing their applause, cheers, cries of delight, and the urgent sexual rhythm of stamping feet. Crump could not very well confiscate the magazine, for an attempt to do so would bring shouts of What you goin' to do with 'er, eh pervert? Goin' to toss off, are yer? What'll yer muvver say? So he said coldly:

– Get out.

– No, I won't, Sutton cried back, and, hanging his head low, called: Elephant! Which was like a signal to the rest of the class to give out a yell of delight.

– Get out before I come and throw you out.

– Toss 'im out, cried a chorus, violently jubilant at its own capacity for sexual punning.

– Look, you miserable little coward, get out before I come for you.

– Show's your guts if you've got any, demanded Sutton, sitting down and leaning back in his chair, hands clasped behind his neck. He gave a maniacal laugh. The rest of the class became silent, but the eyes of all the boys were ablaze with the expectation of violence. No, I won't feed their love of violence, Crump said to himself although the blood was loud at his temples and there was a sensation in his arms which had involuntarily tautened his muscles, saying aloud:

– All right, stay behind after four o'clock.

– Chicken! called Sutton triumphantly, laughing again.

– Crump's a chicken, takin' a lickin', chanted a chorus.

– All right, began Crump as a prelude to attempting to

drag Sutton out, remembering that whenever he had tried to do so in the past Sutton had slipped out of his chair, run around the room knocking desks over and had run out of the class, all right, Crump said, you miserable little bastard, for that's what you are, aren't you? A *bastard.* Aren't you?

That produced an immediate and, Crump thought, a horrible silence, and he regretted the accusation, truthful though it was, he regretted the emphasis of the repetition. Sutton was still leaning back, hands behind his neck, still grinning maliciously when Crump spoke those words; a moment after Crump had spoken them, Sutton jerked himself forward, pushed his desk away angrily until it banged into the chair of the boy sitting in front of him, rose, kicked his chair out of the way, marched down the aisle, walked out of the class, banging the door behind him so loudly that the wall seemed to shake.

Make the best of a balls-up, thought Crump, and said to the class, I don't want any more disturbance until four o'clock.

He sat down at his desk, reflecting how easy it was to become cruel. He did not know how he could prevent being one more of the many representatives of authority against whom Sutton instinctively rebelled; he and every other teacher who took Sutton, together with the wardens of the succession of Homes which had been Sutton's home, the psychiatrist to whom Sutton was sent once a week, and the probation officer were all contributing to Sutton's eventually becoming a criminal although all of them were individually really trying to help him. Crump had taken Sutton into his room during a free period on four or five occasions and had attempted to talk to him, allowing him to say freely whatever he wanted. But even Crump's earliest attempts had been too late. Sutton, like some other delinquents Crump had encountered, had acquired a technique of talking in a manner which a psychiatrist, especially a non-psychiatrist like Crump who, in an amateurish way, thought he could cope with simple psychological problems, would find both meaningful and interesting. It was never easy to discover when a confession was not being invented. For all Crump knew, Sutton's apparent sincerity during these conversations could well have been a perverted cynicism. Finding that the conversations – in which Sutton faltered for words, muttered *I don't know* frequently, described his life at the Home, kept repeating *I don't care* – made no difference to Sutton's explosiveness in class, Crump had abandoned them; for he seemed to be giving special treatment to Sutton and receiving ever more refined degrees of aggression in return. It had already been too late when Sutton came to the school at the age of eleven; he was in his teens now; it was too late, too late.

– Here's something of interest to the social historians of England in the mid-nineteen-sixties, said a colleague in the staff-room, unfolding a local newspaper and adjusting his National Health glasses. Two news items, he declared, the first headlined ALLEGED ROBBERY WITH VIOLENCE. Six youths, it says, were committed for trial at the Old Bailey by the magistrates, on Monday, charged with robbery and violence. They are: John Butterworth, 17, electrician of Romney Road; James Crighton, 17, electrician, of Slade Avenue; Leonard Edwards, 19, travel clerk, of Lichfield Street; Bernard Rice . . . etcetera. These four are, gentlemen, I need hardly remind you, for some of you must have poignant memories of them if not a few scars (and Crump thought of Crighton deliberately pouring boiling water over his own right hand in the science lab so that he would not need to work; remembered how Butterworth once threatened a teacher with a steel-studded leather belt), all former stars of our B and C streams. The second news item is in the very next column, call it an extraordinary coincidence if you like, and is headlined HE DENIES SMOKING CANNABIS. The magistrates, it says here, dismissed a charge of possessing drugs against Richard Rice, 19, unemployed of Ashley Terrace, on Friday. Police had alleged that a matchbox containing cannabis resin was found near a park bench where Rice had been sitting at Romney Green on October 7th. But Rice denied dropping the matchbox and told the court, quote, I have never smoked cannabis and I have never seen it before. The matchbox was not mine. I have a lighter. Unquote.

There was some cynical laughter in the staff-room while another teacher commented, I can just hear him saying that in court, I have a ligh'er. But the teacher reading from the newspaper went on: The really interesting point is this: on a previous page – and he turned to the relevant previous page, licking his thumb before flicking the page over – there's a headline right across the page, and he held the page for everyone to see the bold black type:

NEW EDUCATION PLAN TO COST £659,000

– Is it worth it, I ask you, all we equip them for is robbery and violence and drug-taking and it isn't our fault they're not any better.

– Come, come, cried another member of staff, the point surely ought to be that that much money isn't *enough*. And Richard Rice was not found guilty, by the way.

– You know as well as I do, said the first teacher who had made up his mind during the Second World War that he knew what human nature was really like, what Dick Rice was like; he'd get away with bloody murder.

– I'm not so sure, you know, said the other. After all, the police have been known to plant these things on boys. Remember Hagan and the money left beside milk bottles? And, in any case, I don't see why you're so ironical about the new educational plan when you know very well that the Rices and the Crightons are a tiny minority, an infinitesimal fraction in an otherwise splendid school.

– You and your misguided socialism, Mr Bowen! said the first teacher, thus abusing both socialism and Mr Bowen and considering his statement a sufficient justification of his own sanctimonious righteousness.

Another teacher said some days later that he had seen Bernard Rice, adding: Bernie thinks he and his mates have a perfect defence for their Old Bailey trial to which they're looking forward to as if it were a soccer match. They're going to say that the man they attacked is a queer, that he tried to solicit one of them and that they came to their friend's defence.

– Which reminds me, said Mr Bowen, of the favourite trick of boys like Bernie Rice. One of them hangs about a public lavatory, waits to be picked up by a queer, and when he is the others pounce on the queer, beat him up and rob him.

– That, said the other teacher, is exactly what they did this time, and they'll get away with it because the country's laws are more tolerant of criminals than of queers.

– Well, what do you expect kids to do nowadays? Watch the box all evening?

The class was working silently with five minutes to go to four o'clock while Crump thought of the various boys who had once been his pupils and were criminals now. Short of taking them into his own house as lodgers and giving them parental love, there was nothing he could do to prevent them from becoming criminals. Talking to them, reasoning with them, as he had tried to do with Jim Sutton, was only a game for them, a manifestation that delinquency brought the recognition and special regard which dull conformity would deny them. In a sense, they had a point, for, remembering the boys who had become criminals, he realized that he seldom remembered as individuals the hundreds who conformed and were taught by him and left school to pursue glittering careers on factory floors, shop counters, post offices, banks, the Metropolitan Police and London Transport. A hand went up.

– What is it, Rogers?

– Can I be excused, sir?

– Use your common sense, Rogers. It's four minutes to four when you'll be excused for seventeen hours in any case.

Rogers made a face, shifted in his chair, and continued, or pretended, to work. A moment later, during which Crump's consciousness encompassed the thirty bowed heads in front of him, the grey wall of the classroom on which he had pinned up posters from numerous airlines and UP UP AND

AWAY TWA caught his eye and the line *Let me take you away* from some song sang in his ear, November gloom outside the windows on his right, a fragment of a conversation with Frieda when, coming out of the shower, she had said, I thought we were going to Arles this morning, and he, rising from a reverie in which he had been indulging while sitting beside the window, looking down on fruit trees, Yes, of course, I'm ready, and she, Oh, for goodness' sake, Mike, we're on a holiday, and the reflection that The civilizing process, as exemplified by Europe, must by definition (if it's to be defined in terms of personal security and comfort) ultimately defeat its own end – Hilary Michael, you'll have to be more bloody precise than that, but let that suffice for the moment (for there's so much that must suffice for the moment, be kept pending, as if there'll be secretarial assistance one day to deal with all these matters) – someone then, after that moment, obviously, or at least very probably, Rogers, farted.

The tension following Sutton's marching out of the room was finally relieved, the thirty heads looked up again, and a cry went up, and in the general noise some voices were heard to say: Juicy, Succulent. You've got the art, boy, It was them smelly pilchards, and two boys burst into one of the latest bits of nonsense which go through schools like epidemics: If the farter could barter a horse for the tartar, the Queen would make him a Knight of the Garter.

Let it go, Crump thought, smiled himself and said, Rogers, you'll find some toilet paper in the second cupboard on the left, a remark which drew applause from the class, whereupon Crump put up a hand and said, Right, put your books away and go.

Half a minute later the classroom was empty, but the desks and chairs were knocked all over the place. He leaned back in his chair, shutting his eyes, for the day and the working week were over. I will rise and go now, he began to quote, but remained in his chair, for there was, he remarked to the empty room, looking at the smiling Japanese Air Lines hostess in her kimono, no reason why words must match action or thought be one of the two parallel lines of which the other was experience, adding aloud, And I shall have some peace there. There were bits of paper, piles of exercise books and a register to clear from his desk. He looked at one small piece of paper on which was Mrs Payne's note to him for her son's absence: Sir, it began in a black biro of the cheapest quality, or perhaps it was merely running out of ink, for the cheapest biros wrote excellently, but the ink ran irregularly giving the impression that the words had been written by a trembling hand:

Owing to David's tummy trouble Wednesday
which hope has cleared now, without further
absence from school.

Yours Truly
C. Payne. (Mrs.)

He looked at another note which was written on half a page torn out of an exercise book.

Dear M[r] Crump,
Im so sorry Alan has not got his book this
morning only Iv put it up some were and I
just cant think were Iv put it for the moment
Im so sorry Ill give it to Alan just as soon
has I can find it, hoping you will
understand Yours sincerely

K. Berry

He folded the two notes neatly and put them in his pocket to add to his collection of twentieth-century artifacts, specimens which provided evidence, for what it was worth, of inadequacy, shortcoming, inability to cope, failure. High-powered Europe was riding in technological splendour while the Mrs Paynes and the Mrs Berrys were without a vocabulary or the literacy with which to express simple statements clearly. There were the hard-headed, emancipated, pill-swallowing career-women: the twenty-year-old model turned fashion designer photographed at Heathrow just before flying to New York on an export drive; the firm, bossy, thin-lipped women who ran employment agencies, modelling agencies, literary agencies; those creatures of cosmetics, false eyelashes and wigs who jetted their way across continents to model fashion clothes against an exotic setting, a minaret in Morocco, say, or a sunset on the edge of the Sahara or a cactus in Arizona; the petite public-relations women, using more bosom and smiling lips than work; the journalists with the with-it phrases; Courrèges-accoutred, driving powerful sports-cars, enacting the contemporary, heavily symbolistic ritual of success. And there were the Mrs Paynes who either could not afford another cheap biro or whose hand trembled when they tried to write the words of a language they didn't wholly understand. He ought to live in a country whose language he did not speak, did not understand, for then he would not realize how poor in imagination some of its worthiest citizens were. Then all would be a spectacle, a futile mime, and he just a passive beholder, who remembered now These things, these things were here and but the beholder wanting, but he was here, and what else could there be, eh Crump?

As it was, he held Puck's opinion of mortals. And he himself, he knew, unless someone heard him speak (of which he himself could never be sure) or read words written about him (and if he read them himself he would not necessarily be led to believe that he was reading about himself), was nothing more than a shape in space, often as non-existent as Puck.

He rose finally, his desk more or less tidy, and left the room. He was surprised to see Jim Sutton, whom he had expected to be walking, cigarette in hand, down the street by now, standing outside the room. He had been crying.

– I'm sorry, Jim, he said, finding, quite irrationally, he thought, for Sutton was a right old bastard in every sense of the word in spite of all the sympathy one is supposed to have for problem children, a sensation of sharpness behind his own eyes, go home now and try to accept the world's kindness and try and do something for it instead of attempting to smash it up.

Sutton walked away quietly in front of him, and the way his head jerked as he walked he seemed to be sobbing anew. Why had he stayed behind, Crump wondered, to show me that he had been crying? The poor sod, a failure; another specimen which would remain folded in the leaves of his brain. Crump walked down the empty corridors, for the school had been abandoned as speedily as a building on fire. He walked to his Volkswagen in the car park. He drove away. He took a circuitous way home instead of the shortest route, so that he could drive ten miles or so on the M4 and the Great West Road. On the motorway he drove as fast as the Volkswagen could go, finding the sensation of speed have the same relaxing effect on his mind as a gin and tonic with lots of ice after a wearying day.

There were hypotheses, he thought, continuations, the disjointed memories, a narrative only arbitrarily presumed to possess a chronology, a life. For instance. And that, too, was true, he thought, smiling to himself.

Once again she appeared before Holzminden, and wondered who Holzminden was. A Superintendent of Police, a Deputy Superintendent? Chief of a secret service? Head of an espionage organization? An officer in one of the armed forces? A petty bureaucrat? All she knew was that he was called Holzminden. She did not know his first name and sometimes, when alone in her room, she wondered what it might be. Johann, possibly; or Günter. It seemed out of place, irrelevant to their dialogue, to tell him, when appearing before him, that she would like to know what his first name was: because, not knowing it, she spent time thinking about it, giving him names and trying to imagine how his personality altered with each new name. So much of her perception depended on what she might discover to be the truth. To know him simply as Holzminden in itself defined his personality, setting a limit to her rational appraisal of it and yet teasing her imagination into attempting further definitions.

He had himself given that name only, he had said *My name is Holzminden*, smiling, the thin moustache above the thin lips. That is all she knew, a name, an arrangement of certain letters in the alphabet. And that, too, was chance. He could easily have been called Uffenheim, say, or Eissendorf, she pondered, thinking that so much of her time was spent on reflections which were essentially petty. She had lost count of the number of times she had appeared before him, five or six or ten, it was difficult to remember, each occasion was so like the previous one.

My name is Holzminden. I am here to establish the truth. Please stick to the facts. Do not confuse your statements with philosophy.

And yet he tried to be charming, would offer a cigarette, or apologize that he smoked so much in her presence. He would even rise and bow when she was shown in, a short, stocky man with a large head, the blond hair cut short exposing a wide pink area above the ears. The velvet curtain was always drawn across the window behind him, so that she could never look out and let her attention wander to some spire or dome or some tall building which might help her to establish her whereabouts in the city. All she saw was Holzminden, smiling behind his huge desk, a file in front of him. Certainly, he had poise and was prepared to maintain a welcome dignity in their conversations. It was not at all an interrogation, his voice was so soft, he was so willing to suffer her loosely assembled thoughts. His patience was like that of an artist's, his approach a kind of fastidious craftsmanship. There was no compulsion at all; an obligation, yes; a voice which sometimes insisted on being heard, yes, but not even a suggestion of force, not even a bare bulb.

She hoped that the present mode of her physical confinement would not be indefinitely prolonged. Sometimes she wished for another person than Holzminden to interview her, for she would welcome intellectual variety. But she saw no one else in the building the long corridors of which were invariably deserted, and the only people she observed were the anonymous silent nonentities who acted as guards and orderlies. There were other rooms where surely other Holzmindens sat, but no door had opened while she was being conducted down a corridor. The thick carpet sucked away any sound of footsteps, and when she was alone in her room, she never heard anyone. It was more like a grand hotel. At the end of each conversation, Holzminden suggested that they defer some unresolved question, and only once had she been on the point of asking what the conclusion was which he was hoping to arrive at. But she had not done so, feeling convinced that too much was still unresolved. To ask what would *happen* next was quite out of the question. What worried her, however, was that she was losing sense of time, and, thinking of the number of times she had seen Holzminden and not being able to state the exact number of times she had done so, that she had indeed lost sense of time. She could not have told, had she been asked, whether it was spring or autumn outside. She hoped that, losing sense of time, she would not lose other faculties, and her greatest fear was that the quality of her answers to Holzminden might deteriorate, that her own possession of her past might be taken away from her, that her mind, being compelled to release so many of its memories, might become confused. Alone, she would concentrate on some images, determined to keep them clearly in her vision even though she knew she looked at a blank wall which was painted a light grey. Physically, she considered herself fit although she lacked exercise. The woman doctor who had come to inspect her, taking away samples of her blood and urine, had advised her to keep up some elementary training even if it was only hopping frantically in her room; but no amount of exercise she could take substituted the normal movements of an averagely active body. Sometimes, she would combine both physical and mental activity, remember events and images while standing erect in the middle of the room, breathing in a deliberate rhythm, raising her stiffened arms and gradually lowering them.

Driving away from the theatre before the play finished, for

they feared the frontier might close at midnight, she had not been able to reconcile in her mind the need she felt to leave a city to which she intended to return. Perhaps it was for his sake that she wanted to secure, if only for one night, the safety of the neon-lit, chromium-plated city which was watched over by a three-pointed blue star. There had been no doubt then in her mind. And was she doubting now, she wondered, remarking on the time when she did not doubt? The worst time was the summer when they drove back to England, having ceased to play the game of pursuing ideas as though they were twisting streets and alleys in some foreign city which might lead them to some point of discovery. At least the game had been entertaining. They could sustain seriousness until the teasing idea lost all plausibility. That drive back had seemed unreal, they were going as fast as the car could go and yet each had the impression that they had come to a stop. His posture at the wheel had remained stiff, and she, looking out to see what there was in the landscape which could command her attention, had seen only a fleeting blur. On the ferry, he sat in the bar, drinking, while she stood on the deck, the wind drawing a wetness from her eyes, so that all she saw was the blue haze of an immense emptiness. *We have lost*, she had said to the wind. The house was cold in Shepherd's Bush in the damp summer they returned to; continuing to live together, she realized, was the new game they were playing, and their surface normality was like an uneasy peace. There was a fortnight left of the summer holiday and it was almost by mutual arrangement that they took turns in spending the day out. If it was fine, she went to Holland Park and lay on the grass where many young mothers, some in bikinis, sunbathed while their children ran into the adventure playground and played pretending games. During dull weather, she visited the West End, spending whole afternoons in Selfridges or Fenwicks, observing, she thought, the very heart of Western civilization. One night he said gently: *Let us discuss the situation unemotionally and without hysterics*. The discussion was amicable, she remembered, they kissed each other at the end of it almost as if they had been reconciled after a separation resulting from an unfortunate misunderstanding. They were in agreement.

Her room in the basement of the building was not uncomfortable, and if it was locked at all it was she who locked it from the inside; as far as she could see, she could walk out of it at any time. Perhaps she would be halted at some stage if she were to walk out, she did not know, not having attempted to escape. But, then, escape was the wrong word, for she was not a prisoner. She was just there for the time being and perhaps soon the time would come when she would leave. She was prepared to listen to Holzminden. She was willing to answer his questions as best she could. She was sorry for his sake that she could not make her answers more precise, but then she could not decide what the nature was of the precision which he demanded. And thinking of that she worried about the generality of her answers to her own questions, she was afraid of the vagueness of her own thinking. When she looked at the wall again, concentrating her thoughts, all that came to her mind were images which lacked focus: movement predominated, a long road with cars and lorries, the repetitive image of going under bridges on the autobahn, of overtaking and being overtaken. Isolated frozen images would sometimes stop the vague, silent motion in her head. A worker putting a *For Sale* sign outside the house. The waiting at the ferry terminal where he bought a picture postcard. And then the long road, not the autobahn at first, that came much later, but the long steeply cambered road which went south. Brittany, Provence, then across the Pyrenees, south, south, a relentless flight or a desperate search, neither could have said which. Perhaps he was proving a point, perhaps she needed evidence. They reached the Mediterranean, then the Atlantic. She shook her head. *No, no.* At which his eyes brightened, at which he smiled without comment. She could still love him, her feelings at least were still constant. Only the thought that ten years, twenty or thirty years. *Oh what's the use,* she had said, *when you reduce all expressions to futility.* How many months was it, seven, eight, nine, what is this blur, she said, in my mind? We take language with which we preserve, even ennoble ourselves, we take language, look for new terms for old definitions, take note of nuances, search for interpretations, for the clear, unambiguous meaning, and in the end the words destroy us. *No,* she said at Easter, *let's go to Berlin, I don't want any more of your Europe which will reject us in any case when we run out of money.*

There were distractions, if she needed them, during the first week which she spent in a little hotel near the station. But she did not wish to be a tourist among the ruins of the city she had come to, preferring to let her instincts assert themselves. There was also the anxiety of declaring her intentions, establishing her identity. Attachments, she knew, would grow in the course of events. While she had been determined that the conditions of her existence would be positive, otherwise she might as well submit to the slow strangulation which she was attempting to escape from, she suffered moments of despair when she wished there were someone to guide her. She was not sure of the procedure she had to follow. The matter was not one in which she could consult a precedent. Whatever she attempted was a tentative hypothesis which, she could only hope, would lead to a meaningful discovery. She did not speak the language and could not ask for directions of any passer-by. Whether it was a stubborn hatred of what she had been or an excitement deriving from the feeling that renewal was possible that she felt on coming, her immediate emotion was one of intense nervousness.

She did not encounter any raised eyebrows or a guarded hostility at the police station. She asked to see someone who spoke English. She was taken to Inspector Dreyer, a fat-cheeked man with pale blue eyes. He listened to her with no more interest, she thought, than he might have shown had she come to lodge a complaint against a neighbour who had the radio on too loud. She had rehearsed her story well, giving an intellectual depth to her reasons and a touch of drama to her final revelation, but Dreyer seemed to her to be unimpressed, even bored. At the end of her statement, he said: Do you play hockey?

– Why, yes, she said. Well, at least I did as a schoolgirl, she added hastily, trying at the same time to suppress a slight anger at the impudence and the irrelevance of Dreyer's question.

– Then you should enjoy watching a good hockey match, he said. Our team is one of the best in Europe.

– But, she said.

– No, no, he said, putting out a hand, suggesting that he was too busy to go into details. It will be no bother at all. If you wait in the hall, one of my men will bring you all the information in a few minutes. It's going to be an excellent match. You really must come.

She walked out of Dreyer's office, trying not to let the nerves of her anger twitch visibly. Out of his sight, she found herself biting her lower lip and thinking that a joke was one thing she had not expected and asking herself next what was it that she had expected. Seriousness, she said to herself, that's all. By the time she reached the hall, however, it occurred to her that perhaps Dreyer had not been joking; perhaps some chance, the playing of the hockey match that afternoon, or some subsequent afternoon – he had mentioned no details – his personal preference for a larger arena than the confines of an office for continuing the kind of dialogue she had begun, some chance, then, or some notion that he had of which she possessed no clue, had made him decide that she should go and see the hockey match. What made her angry, she thought, was the peremptoriness with which he had made the suggestion, his tone indicating to her that what she considered to be a serious proposal was to him a contemptible frivolity deserving an equally frivolous counter-proposal from him. While she stood in the hall, looking at the portrait of the bearded leader of the country, she debated whether she should take Dreyer's suggestion seriously or walk away and think of another approach, so that the few moments of her indecision made the choice for her. For presently a uniformed youth came and gave her a sealed envelope.

She did not open the envelope until she was back at the hotel. On the way she had to cross a square at one end of which was a theatre. She wondered whether she had done the right thing. They had driven away in the dark of the dimly lit streets. Had she mistaken the lack here of the commercial ostentation of the night life of the city across the barbed-wire for an intellectual seriousness? She could not tell, having, in any case, reasons of her own not to do with theoretical speculation. What she had drilled in her mind had been ideas, however, not practicalities, but, still, if she had expected any drama it was certainly not of a farcical nature. In moments when she dreaded what would happen next, the worst she had imagined had been physical pain. Now she realized that ridicule was a sharper instrument than anything with which her body could be tortured.

The envelope contained the name of a stadium and a ticket. The match was to be on the following Saturday afternoon, which was three days away. The casual way in which she had been received struck her as absurd. Perhaps she ought to go to another police station and hope to be received by a man who took his duties seriously; perhaps she should visit the Ministry of Justice; perhaps she should commit some petty crime and be charged for it. For so far, in this state of stern laws and a dedicated ideology, no one seemed to know or care if she existed, and the one person she had confessed her intentions to had done no more than to invite her to a hockey match. She felt humiliated, hurt, feelings which were not assuaged by the notion that the hockey match might be a cover for some other game. The emptiness of waiting gave her a keen sense of the futility of all things. She hated to admit that, for he was always mocking the aspirations of her commitment by positing futility as the final human condition beyond which there was nothing but despair and self-annihilation, until she had cried out *No, no.* Her defiance seemed pitiable now, her positivism a word which a lonely sailor might invoke under a storm in the Pacific.

At least it was a fine afternoon on the Saturday. She had looked at her map so often that she knew the way to the stadium by heart. It was two miles away to the north of the city and, having nothing to do, she decided to walk to it. Still, she arrived more than an hour early. The car park beside the stadium was deserted. She walked towards what appeared to her to be the main entrance and found that the gates were unlocked. She went in and, walking across an open space, reached the entrance to the public stand. There was no one in attendance and there was nothing to impede her from going in. There were covered stands on the four sides of the pitch which was immaculately marked out, the corner flags hanging limply from their poles. The stands were completely empty. She walked to the pitch, carefully stepping over the white side-line. The closely cut grass was soft and pleasurable to walk on after the two miles of paving-stones. She walked to the centre of the pitch. She looked around at the stands. At the centre of a public stadium, she was alone, unobserved. It seemed to symbolize her presence in the city. She began to laugh, softly at first and then loudly and hysterically until she choked and doubling over fell to the ground. She pressed a palm to the grass, found it dry, and decided to lie back on it, for the sun was warm. She shut her eyes to the sun. She fell asleep.

When she awoke, she felt a hand clasping her arm, shaking it, and saw a uniformed official bending over her. She heard a murmur and realized it was from the crowd which now partially filled the public stands. She stood up and began to walk away, the official following her. The crowd applauded, and she also heard laughter. Compulsively, she stopped and raised her arms up to the crowd, which expressed its delight with a roar and renewed applause. She bowed and walked hurriedly towards the main stand. Here, she produced her ticket for the official to examine and was shown to her seat. People observed her with a certain merriment in their eyes and she hoped that if she blushed they would have the charity to attribute the colour to her having been in the sun. An empty seat next to hers was taken by Dreyer a few minutes before the match commenced. He greeted her with a smile, but immediately fixed his attention on the players. He had been right in predicting that the quality of the match would be good, for she was soon absorbed in it.

– Well, and are you enjoying it? Dreyer asked at half-time.

– Yes, very much, she said, but tell me why. . . .

– Have you observed how clever Esslin is at inside-right for the state team?

– Which one is he? she felt compelled to ask.

– Ah, I must point him out when they resume.

– What I'm wondering. . . .

– The future seems most promising. We shall qualify from our zone. But forgive me, are you not thirsty?

– No, thank you, she said to whatever he was about to propose, realizing that he was not going to answer any question of hers.

– Then you will please excuse me? he asked.

– Yes, of course.

Rising, he bowed, and walked away. Presently, the match was resumed, but Dreyer did not return. From time to time, she looked in the direction in which he had gone, but saw no one. The game again absorbed her and she concentrated on trying to determine which player might be Esslin. Just when the referee was blowing his whistle for full-time and the crowd was applauding loudly the satisfactory conclusion of a good match, a voice next to her said: My name is Holzminden. She was a little startled, for Dreyer's seat remained unoccupied during the second half of the match. Turning to the other side, she saw a stocky man sitting next to her. When he saw that he had caught her attention, he repeated, My name is Holzminden. You will come with me.

– But Inspector Dreyer, she began, suddenly frightened.

– I know, Holzminden said. He has told me everything. You will come with me. I have studied your file. You are my problem.

She went with him, rather pleased now at committing herself to a mysterious course and no longer frightened. The notion that there was a file about her was rather reassuring. An awareness of the slight apprehension she felt added a thrill to whatever adventure she was embarking on. In his way, she thought, Dreyer had been efficient and she mentally apologized to him for the abuse she had expressed at him when brooding over the vexatious thoughts during the previous three days.

– There's nothing mysterious, Holzminden said when they were seated in the chauffeur-driven car, no cloak-and-dagger stuff, I assure you.

– Why couldn't Dreyer have sent me to your office? she asked.

– Why is it, he said smiling, that one demands explanations for something which is only very slightly unconventional?

– Well there must be a reason.

– Oh, reasons are always very simple when you arrive at them. A mystery is much more absorbing. One can always brood over it while filing down one's finger-nails.

– You make it even more mysterious by saying that. No, thank you, she added, declining his offer of a cigarette.

– I was out of town, he said. Dreyer knew I was going to be at the hockey match, for I'd sent him two tickets, inviting him and his wife. You see, I'm an old hockey player and one of my present jobs is to advise on team selection. I rather enjoy doing it. It was an excellent idea of Dreyer's to bring you along.

– Why didn't he introduce you? she asked, not believing one word of his explanation. And why did he go away at half-time?

– He probably had a call from his office and had to leave in haste. Police officers, like doctors, never have any peace. As for the introduction, much as I would have enjoyed conversing with you, I thought I should concentrate on the hockey, for, after all, it is my duty to do so, having a report to prepare on my opinion of the players.

She did not press him for a more plausible explanation, realizing that he was not going to alter his story. The car turned into a wide avenue and came to a stop in front of a building the exterior of which was black with two centuries of dirt and also from wartime air-raids. She was taken to the basement where she was shown into a small room.

– I hope you will be comfortable here, Holzminden said. As I stated, you are my problem. It is unfortunate, but it is so. And you must remain here until I have solved it. The problem, that is. What luggage you have at the hotel we shall look after until then. Of course, we know everything about you. We knew before you went to Dreyer. We are quite competent at alerting ourselves. But, although we know everything, we will, of course, expect to find out everything from you. We are prepared to assume nothing. You will, I trust, find us hospitable and sympathetic.

She accepted his statements without any misgiving, for he was not without charm and surely could not intend anything but justice to determine the course of his decisions. Time, she thought, was meaningless in her present state of suspense between two worlds, her rejection of one and her waiting to be accepted by the other. But as time passed and as each of her interviews ended inconclusively, requiring a resumption on another day, she began to worry about Time. She had too much of the actual hours and minutes, but of that quality of existence which Time alone makes meaningful, she had none at all.

– You were talking of your mother, Holzminden said. What was her maiden name?

– I've told you, she said. I've told you all I know.

– Forgive me, but you didn't tell me what you know. You've only told me what you think might have happened. Fact and supposition are two different things. I hardly need to point that out to you. The name you've mentioned already, I agree. That's only a starting-point. I'm sorry, but each time we have to start at the same point. It's a drill my experience compels me to pursue. You'll reach a stage one day, perhaps today, when you will lose your conscious control over your answers and begin to tell the truth. Not that I am suggesting that you're not telling the truth. I simply do not know as yet. Repetition is my procedure for knowing. So, her name?

– Sybil Hoepfner. Sybil Karen Hoepfner.

– Where was she born?

– All I know is that her family came from Munich. Maybe she was born there.

Holzminden lit a cigarette, inhaled deeply, and looked at the file in front of him. His eyes seemed to glance over a whole sheet. He turned it over and scanned two more pages.

– All right, he said. I'm sorry that this is too tedious for you. We agree that you know nothing positive about your mother. She was just a mother to you, not a police file which you memorized.

– Yes, yes, she said, expressing her agreement a little too excitedly.

– You said about her that she enjoyed the social life in Johannesburg which was available to women of her status, being married to an eminent businessman. That she did so until her mysterious illness. What do you want us to deduce from that?

– I don't know what you can possibly deduce from that, she said, watching him inhale deeply. For me, it expresses a kind of disillusionment. But this can't be a fact. It's merely a thought *after* the event. I wish I had evidence to give you which suggested reasons why she could have wanted to abandon her life in Johannesburg.

– But even if you could produce such evidence, it would not be a proof that she chose to come here, would it? You don't know if she had any money on her when she disappeared. It's a long way from Johannesburg to Cairo let alone any destination in Europe.

– I'm not so naïve as to imagine that you don't have agents in South Africa. Oh, but this is so much beside the point.

– What is the point, then?

– Simply that I think that she's here. *If* she were fed up with the society she found in Johannesburg, then she could not have wanted to go, say, to London or New York where her society would be materially the same; and nor could she have gone into a primitive part of Africa for that would not offer any scope to her abilities. *If* she wanted to give up the New World, she must have wanted to return to the Old World, not just any place in the Old World but somewhere in the Old World where her sympathies lay. *If* she wanted to give up a system, it must have been to embrace a new system. *If* she felt strongly enough to want to abandon her husband and children for the sake of an idea, then she must have possessed a very strong intellect which could not under any circumstances continue to accept the idea as lived out by the lives of the people around her and the idea which she wanted to live out herself must have been a very compelling one. *If* I am right in my assumptions about her character and her intellect, then there is only one place she could have gone to. Here. She came here.

– Just as you have?

– Yes. Just as I have.

– Tell me, did you ever discuss the notion of coming here with your husband?

– Yes and no. We played games.

– I'm sorry, Holzminden said, stubbing out his cigarette. I don't understand. What do you mean played games?

– It's difficult to explain, she said. It was a verbal game. People play games. We're playing a game now, question and answer. It's something to do against boredom, isn't it?

– I see. Though of course I don't, he added, smiling. You realize my difficulty is how to establish that you are being honest. That your reasons for wanting to come here are genuine and sincere. It's not just a passing fancy, an experiment in which you briefly want to take part. If you're bored by your way of life, please don't expect to come here for entertainment. There are other serious considerations.

– Espionage?

– Espionage, he said. We can't rule that out, living in the kind of city that we do.

– I know, she said. I am guilty of every accusation you can level at me until I can refute each one of the accusations. I am all the personalities you suggest I am until I can assert my own personality. Is that it?

– You are so co-operative.

– But how can I prove anything, sitting here, talking to you?

– Tell me more, he said. As far as I can see, you are a beautiful young lady; perhaps a little confused in the head, but, still, very charming. But, for all I know, you could be one of a thousand things. You might or might not have anything to do with espionage. You might or might not be a murderer on the run. How do I know what you are not? Therefore. Tell me as much as you can about yourself.

– I've said so much already!

– Listen. Let me put something to you very bluntly. Forgive the rudeness, but perhaps it will make the position clear. You are not doing us a favour by coming here. Unlike the West, we're not interested in the publicity that can be created by someone defecting to our side. We don't run society on gossip columns. Your press glamorizes defections to the West and suggests that anyone who happens to come along is offered political asylum. I can assure you that that is not the case.

– But I haven't come to do you a favour! I've come for myself. I've come to surrender myself to an idea.

– It's the Jewish blood in you, he said. You want to suffer. Too content in the West, bored with the satisfaction of all your expectations, you want to come here where you think your soul might have a chance of getting bruised. You're bored, too, with the lack of drama, especially with the lack of tragedy. I can tell you that life isn't very different here. Obviously, there are certain actions which the West so ingeniously calls liberties which are not permitted here and certain actions here which we maintain as basic human rights which the West does not allow. And obviously our concepts of society are different. We all know that. But in its essentials, as it concerns the actual daily living of the people, there is no difference at all. Certainly, you could say that our people do not have certain commercial choices and certainly we could say that your people are not given choices but inescapable alternatives aimed at exploiting them. These are fine points of ideology. They affect attitudes, making people happy or unhappy in a superficial manner. They do not affect the actual living which goes on for the simple reason that it must go on because man has no choice in the matter. You think you're making a grand gesture to your soul, rejecting the surface brilliance beneath which are the desperate currents of boredom and emptiness, you think what you might discover here is a little old-fashioned struggle, a little suffering to make you feel your life is worth while, even noble. Am I right in saying that before you came here you thought of Israel and rejected it because a Zionist ideology is an anachronism in the secular consumer-goods-orientated modern world which the West is so proud to have achieved?

– I've never been a practising Jew. The idea of being a Jew has never occurred to me.

– But your choice of words. You said a moment ago that you'd come to *surrender*. As if we could offer you a martyrdom off the peg!

– No, no, she said. I've come to live usefully. Not to suffer. Not to see what my soul looks like when it's thrown in the gutter.

– Did you get a divorce before coming?

– No.

– You are, you say, twenty-eight. You make a break in your life, you close a book to begin a new one. You make a choice which you think is going to be irrevocable. And how do you do it? As though you've come on a fortnight's package tour!

– What motive could I have which I have not already stated?

– How should I know? As I see it, you could be very

sincere and therefore incredibly naïve. Or, you are very, very clever and have ingeniously evaded every question that I have asked. Your mother, your own life, everything could be an invention, and you could be living out another identity for some reason.

– That's not true.

– But you can't deny the possibility?

– I can't, of course I can't. Just as today could be yesterday or tomorrow. Philosophical doubt can go on for ever. I suppose the thrill of being a spy is that your own identity can be suspended temporarily. Everything about your real identity becomes false, for your job, your bank account, your family are all an illusion especially created to camouflage the identity you've been asked to adopt.

– Careful, you might be describing yourself.

– Indeed, I might, she said. I could even be taking your philosophical doubt one step further.

– One thing is quite clear, Holzminden said. You are so obviously not a spy that you could possibly, and probably, be one.

– That's a great help!

– All right. Suppose we agreed to grant you asylum. What would you do?

– Ask you to help me get a job.

– What could you do? You didn't even bother to learn German before coming here.

– I spoke German as a child.

– But you've forgotten since.

– It would be easy to learn. It must be there in my unconscious mind.

– Why haven't you learned it already?

– Really, I think this is a very tiny problem. In fact, my ignorance of German ought to suggest to you how eager I was to come that I could not wait to learn the language.

– On the contrary, it suggests to me that you have taken a sudden, wilful decision which you might later regret.

– You doubt everything.

– I try to see as much as I can.

– Well, what do you propose? she asked, a slight note of exasperation in her voice.

Instead of answering her question, Holzminden asked: Do you know that you are pregnant?

– How did you know?

– The medical report. And this I find interesting. You were married for five years or so and had no children.

– What are you suggesting?

– You tell me.

– I wanted a child.

– But not during the last four years?

– No.

– A time came when you decided you wanted a child, right?

– Yes.

– When you had made up your mind about coming here?

– Yes.

– You're like the alcoholic who decides to celebrate his decision to give up liquor by opening a new bottle.

– No, that's not true, she said.

– No? You wanted to bring a little souvenir with you, perhaps? How can you give up when you create new associations of what you're trying to give up?

– What will you do with me? she asked, suddenly tired of his questions.

– I still don't know enough to decide what I will recommend. But I can tell you what the alternatives are. You can be allowed to return to the West. In that case, you'll simply have to pretend that you came here as a tourist and have had a good holiday. Or we can imprison you indefinitely on a number of charges ranging from espionage to wilfully deceiving our police control at the frontier. Or we can offer you asylum, in which case you'll be given some arduous post in a remote part of the Republic. If it's suffering you're after, there'll be plenty of it.

– I want to be in Berlin!

– There you are, making your materialist demands already!

– If I can't be in Berlin, I'd rather go back.

– You're no longer free to do that. We decide your next move.

– No, she cried, no.

Five years of that life, and all she remembered was the long road and the trees. *Those are cork trees, eucalyptus those.* The forest of silver birches cut back for the autobahn from Hanover. The poplars in France. And oaks, oaks. The Europe she had tried to come to terms with was a light grey wall in a small basement room. She had perhaps been too innocent in her expectation that a positively made choice would attract a positive response. Idealistic fantasies, she admitted, never consulted an advocate like Holzminden who could suggest that there was an underlying foolishness to such thought. She ought to have invented Holzminden, she ought to have carried out the repetitive dialogue with him until either there was no need to meet him or if she did meet him then the dialogue would have had the advantage of prior rehearsal. Again she wondered who Holzminden was, this image in her mind, as she looked at the grey wall, of a fair-haired genial man with a thin moustache who smoked too much. He was too charming to be true to one's notion of such interrogators. It was almost as if she had invented him, or remembering someone seen in a film, and, lying in Holland Park beside a chestnut tree, were imagining what must have happened to her mother if certain speculations in her mind were possibly true. It is easy, she reflected ruefully, to retreat in space; but not in time. And, she said, the most difficult feat of all is to remain in the same place and in psychologically the same time without needing surrogates to live the lives for us which we can't. In such a situation, we accept the notion that we could possibly be going mad.

– In *any* situation! added Crump with unnecessary emphasis.

I will, like a true drunkard, utter all to thee. That was written somewhere; someone had uttered the promise to utter. Crump, pen poised over the register, a Sheaffer Imperial II, containing blue-black ink with which he must inscribe noughts to record the faces not seen tried to ignore the words which were beseeching his attention, tried to swish them away as though they were mosquitoes at his ear. He did not call out the names when marking the register and wait for cries of Yes, sir, or Present, sir, but simply glanced up to see who was not there; this was a procedure which had become established, for it was quicker, not requiring him to order the class to maintain silence; they talked on about the football match they had seen on the telly or about the film they had gone to or the girl they had taken out on Saturday night. The usual, in fact, he said, though they were all talking and not listening to him, all except Green who was copying Cowie's maths homework at a pace guaranteed to ensure that he, Green, would learn nothing even from copying.

– Kola and Brown, he called, who is the third behind you? When I look up there are only you two but when I look down at the register I am conscious that I have seen another.

– You're bonkers, sir.

– Never mind, Brown, but tell me, Kola, how can one ever see anything without the sum of all one's experience and learning, and I'm very learned I'll have you know . . .

– Ha!

– . . . qualifying one's perception?

– You mean like being perpetually drunk, sir?

– Your figure of speech is not inappropriate, Crump said, turning to the register, remembering again the words which had come to his mind: I will, like a true drunkard, utter all to thee. Had he spoken them in the pub the night before, or did they come from someone's writing? It was too early in the morning, he decided, saying to himself, Feeble excuse that, Crumpmate, not prepared, however, to entertain the possibility that confusions were beginning to enter into his thinking, that the flowing sediment of immediate experience and the volcanic lava of memory were combining to petrify his mind into an igneous rock, glittering – hardly! well, at least possessing a dull sheen – but dead. If anywhere, it would be in the Works, he could look them up; perhaps, later, not now with chores to do, absences to record, former absentees to interrogate, dinner money to collect; not now, not now; later perhaps he would remember and not need to look up the Works. There was too much on his mind now. Having marked the register, he counted the days to go to the end of term, twenty-three, not counting the week-ends, of course, when it would be morning in late March, some spring excitement in the air, he hoped, and the Volkswagen parked on the quayside at Dover, the ferry coming in from France to take him to some destination he had not yet determined.

– Childe Roland to the dark tower came, he said.

– Yes, dad, cried Chapman.

– Dinner money's going up next term, he announced, and I suggest that to get used to the idea of paying half-a-crown extra you start bringing it from next week and paying it to me.

– Boo! they cried, Spas! and one muttered: I'm not havin' no bleedin' dinners.

– Why, you modellin' for Oxfam? someone quickly asked and received the answer, I ain't Twiggy!

And that led to a rapid exchange of Pinworth wit:

– What's wrong with Twiggy?

– Two things.

– Oh belt up, Spas!

Cooper came up with his dinner money and Crump, noting down the receipt of five shillings, asked him, Do you like school dinners, Cooper?

– No, Cooper said.

– How would you like them improved? Crump asked. Now let's be democratic about this, what would you like? Shall we say a rump steak on Mondays to start with instead of the messy brown stew you're invariably offered?

– Come off it, you can't get much for five bob, can yer? Cooper said.

– Why complain, then?

– I ain't complainin', you asked if I liked them and I said I don't. That ain't complainin', that's jussa plain fack, ain't it?

– Why not complain, then?

– Blimey, I got to be satisfied with what I gets, don't I? For five bob, I mean!

When Cowper came up with his money, Crump asked: Did you have a good week-end, Cowper?

– Not bad.

– What did you do?

– Not much.

– What did you have for breakfast?

– Not enough.

– Do you like girls, Cowper?

– Not 'arf!

– You'd better lose some weight, then, hadn't you?

– 'E don't 'arf ask some stupid questions, Cowper told his friend Chapman.

– His wife must drive him nuts, Chapman suggested, searching, as always, for a sexual explanation.

An icy morning outside was beginning to develop a pale blue in its sky. What a month, February, Crump thought, nasty, British and short; the grass gone coarse, all substance vanished. In all probability they had a better meal at the school, for their mums very likely relied more on frozen food than did the school's catering staff.

– I can just imagine, he told Watson who had come up with his five shillings, your Sunday dinner. Heinz cream of tomato soup, Bird's Eye steaklet, Ross peas, Dine instant mash potatoes, Swel quick dried onions and Bird's Instant Whip. And in five years' time you'll be complaining to your wife that she doesn't cook like your mum used to.

– What you on about now? Watson asked, paying his money and going, a look both of bafflement and concern on his face.

Crump added the money he had collected, checked the entries in the dinner register, asked Chapman – one way of getting rid of him for a few minutes – to take the money and the register down to the school secretary, and rose to address the class.

– You were all born, he said, speaking softly, for he knew that his first few sentences would not be heard whether they listened to him or not, in 1952. Except four of you who were born late in 1951.

– Silence ho! Caesar speaks, cried Murray whereupon his companions laughed.

– Murray, the day you were born, 10 April 1952, I remember very clearly that I was rowing on the Serpentine. It was a typical foul-and-fair April afternoon, gusty winds, the sky now a stunning blue and now swollen with black clouds. There was one hell of a thunderstorm later and I rather suspect that your entry into this world coincided with the lightning and thunderclap which at 3.23 p.m. tore open an oak on Hampstead Heath, and consequently you still go about wondering what the devil has hit you.

– 'E's a bit soft in the 'ead, Watson said.

– Precisely, Crump agreed, wondering why he had not let them amuse themselves with gossip for the remaining ten minutes of the Monday morning registration period and why, instead, he had risen to speak to them. Like a true drunkard. He had their attention now and was obliged to continue, thinking, Hell, there must be a reason to it all.

– As for you, Watson, you were born during the Lord's test match. It was the Indians that year, I remember; Godfrey Evans almost scored a hundred before lunch, but the match is remembered principally for Vinoo Mankad's great innings – he was bowled in the end by Jim Laker, trying to sweep, but how Laker suffered before that success! Cuts, sweeps, pulls, drives – and for his, Mankad's, marathon spell of bowling.

Christ, the things one remembers for no apparent reason at all, the conversations one begins, the debates one enters for no reason, no damned reason at all, it just happens, that's all, Crump told himself, pausing for a moment between sentences, and remembering in that pause that it was the

Australians under Hassett a year later and that he had read somewhere that when the groundsman asked Hassett on one morning during the Lord's test which roller he'd like to be used on the pitch Hassett, poker-faced, had said: A spiked one.

And there was Hazare's sour-faced innings of forty-nine and Peter May and Hutton, and that was the summer Freddy Trueman, the shock of black hair bouncing on his head, the right sleeve which he rolled up each time he walked back to his mark (Christ, the bits of information, for no reason, the images the mind hoards, for no damned reason at all, and there was someone in a *New Statesman* competition who suggested that Truman be presented with shirts with half-sleeves), 184 Mankad scored before being bowled, sweeping.

– What about it? Watson asked. I hate cricket.

– Nothing at all, Crump said, I was merely identifying your birth with a great moment in sporting history, and if you expect any meaning in that it may well be that you are not worthy of that moment.

He did not hear Watson's rejoinder which made the boys near him laugh, for he was satisfying to himself his own compulsion to utter the quotation, Lord, I am not worthy.

– And, incidentally, you might well ask why Peter May stopped playing for England ten years before England could have even thought of finding a successor to him. Indeed, the historians of Great Britain ought to take the premature retirement of May, Doggart, Subba Row, Dexter and even Sheppard as a peculiar sympton of what was happening to the country in the sixties.

– Cricket is for pansies!

– It is typical of the working-class English mind to dismiss any tough intellectual pursuit like playing cricket or writing poetry as soft.

Three boys at the back of the class, who had been whispering to one another and scribbling on a sheet of paper on the desk of the one in the middle, smiled at one another, nodded, and sang out loudly:

I was born one morning when rain stopped play
My mama she said I was made of clay
My old man he said I was a useless lump
And it's rough being taught by a mug called Crump.

The class applauded. Many cried: More, more!

– Well, Crump said, and the class listened to see if he could match its own wit, the year in which most of you were born has as distinctive a flavour to me as the taste of roasted chestnuts. If 1952 is clear in my mind, how much clearer must the following years be! In other words, as far as the social history of England is concerned, there is nothing which has not been assimilated by my senses, weighed by my intellect, which is considerable I'll have you know, and permanently lodged in my consciousness. Therefore, every event, be it Stirling Moss's victory in a Vanwall in the British Grand Prix at Aintree, 1956, I think, at any rate the first British Grand Prix win by a British driver in a British car since the war, which I witnessed, or the rise of the betting shops, or the phoney patriotism which turned the Union Jack into a selling pattern for paper-bags, or the pop explosion which changed a staid, contemplative culture into a garish, extroverted one, every event which may or may not to some extent have deformed your characters, personalities, sensibility, in short, your moral outlook, is known to me more vividly and intimately than you can imagine.

– Peepin' Tom Crump! someone cried.

–You're quite right, Crump said, the perceptive man is in one respect a Peeping Tom. As indeed God must be, for omnipresence must have its temptations. I know more than a social historian for, apart from the social environment which has made you what you are, I know also the family history of each one of you: whose father comes home drunk, who suffered from pneumonia at the age of six, whose elder brothers keep him under their shadow, whose shopkeeping parents make him stand at the counter all Saturday. I know what causes the tensions, hatred, disturbances, inadequacies, a general carelessness, dispiritedness, unwillingness within you. And having known you yourselves for five years, having observed you grow physically or mentally or remain stunted in one or the other respect, or both, I have the power to reveal to you your absolute nakedness.

Chapman returned from his errand just when Crump was uttering the last sentence and his eyes brightened at the mention of absolute nakedness.

– What's this, then, he muttered, talking of sex behind my back?

– And like a doctor, Crump went on, who diagnoses an illness and then prescribes a cure, I have the power to show you your worthlessness and then help to make you worthy. Lord, I am not worthy, he added to himself as compulsively as a Catholic crossing himself on passing a church. That is, if you want any help; that is, if you care to come down from the heights of self-conceit and care to realize that you need help. You are fractions of a sum which adds to the total of one, a perfect unity, in a sense, in my mind. You exist because I choose to see you.

Here Kola interpolated: Are you a god? Would you create me new?

– Very good, Kola, very good indeed, and you may well remember the line from the fourth act, too, Kola, remember it? And here we wander in illusions.

God, he said to himself, gold-gloried in Ouro Preto (what do I not know, O God!) what madness is coming over me? What illusions am I wandering in now?

– Ah, but man, Kola began, but was stopped by Watson who said, Stop fizzin', Coke! 'Ere, sir, what you goin' to do to us?

– That's a good example, Kola, of the vulgar always stopping the mouths of the wise. We're ruled by the mass, by a beautiful democracy, don't expect your voice to be heard.

Kola smiled as if he had been admitted to some exclusive order.

– When's he going to strip us, then? asked Chapman.

– You, Chapman, are a slum in a new town, a hoarding on a beautiful landscape, a whooping cough in the Festival Hall during a Mozart sonata, you, Chapman, are a walking offence to all the aesthetic principles ever expounded by man.

– What's he on about now? Chapman asked the boy next to him, adding: The bleeding spastic.

– Somefin' about an anna sphetic.

– He needs putting to sleep, Chapman, who would rather speak any old nonsense than remain quiet, said.

– They ought to look at you, Crump said to Chapman and his friend, when politicians talk of the great future of this country. They ought to consult you when they get over-sentimental about democracy.

He did not listen to Chapman's rejoinder, thinking it would be all too predictable anyway, but turned away from the class, sat down in his chair, sorry that his talk should have degenerated to pettiness, the word reminding him of a line, And I have something to expiate, and, he thought, that in a sense this was his condition, petty, he who had accepted, long accepted that all the grandeur he could ever attain to would be false. The several vanities of the pilgrims, he said to himself, realizing that he said that because his eye had caught a volume of Chaucer, one of the Tales. He picked up the volume with some pleasure, thinking, At least there is this, there is something after all. It was a scholarly edition which he used with the sixth form, containing twice as many pages of notes as of text, but it annoyed Crump to see that one whole page had no more on it than the words

For my daughter CATHERINE

What a presumption, he thought, what damned cheek, a bloody editor dedicating one of Chaucer's works to his daughter as if his introduction, notes and glossary possessed a uniqueness which excelled that of the poem. And there were the editors of anthologies who did even less than this scholar, assemblers of other people's poems who simply put them together in some spurious order with such sections as Seasons, Moods, Portraits, etcetera, did not even provide notes and then had the damn nerve to dedicate the book: To My Wife. The shit that goes on in this world. Vanity, that great turdle which mankind assiduously uses as a daily cosmetic. But the poem soothed him, some lines he had marked and annotated in the margin (perhaps, he thought now, he ought to dedicate the margin to someone) calmed him down.

> For thogh we slepe, or wake, or rome, or ride,
> Ay fleeth the time; it nil no man abide.

There, he said to the horn-rimmed-spectacled assembly, smiling to himself, is all English literature in one galloping couplet; the rest has been elaboration of circumstance, change of social scene, complexity of situation, sophistication of technique, changes in vocabulary, subtler definitions, but personal testaments to the same old truth. But Professor Carmichael, sitting across the walnut table from him in the seminar at the conference of European scholars in an East European city, politely disagreed, saying, Professor Crump is no doubt hoping to provoke a controversy by postulating what looks on the surface to be a naïve generalization.

– Nothing of the sort, said Crump to Murray who had come up and asked to be excused. First thing on Monday morning, really!

– I've got an upset stomach, sir, Murray said, backing away and leaving the room.

Chaos begins again, reflected Crump, hearing the bell which ended the Monday morning registration period, come confusion to my thoughts, for that is all it is, that is all there is.

– Right, chaps, he told his fifth form, time you went to your maths and again fell into the illusion that tabulation and formulae is what it all is, go and feel elevated with the notion that you're learning something really useful, something which will help you in your glittering careers, shopkeeping or laying down carpets.

– What a form teacher, Watson said, jerking his head, bleedin' joker.

– Crump's all right, Chapman said to Watson, going out, good for a laugh anyway.

Crump's all right, Crump said to himself, looking out at the frail beech tree.

The forest of silver birches had been cut back, leaving deserted land between the autobahn and the forest. In the distance was a wooden tower, the hut at the top of the stilts looking like an old Prussian helmet. A policeman sat in the hut, invisible to the motorist, looking out of the narrow slit of the window through a pair of binoculars. Crump wondered if he would be shot at if he stopped the car and walked out to have a pee.

No language at the frontier. Just eyes that watched. And forms and rubber-stamps. The long army coats with the bold buttons. The man with the little mirror attached to the end of a long stick, thrusting the stick under the car and looking for strange reflections. Silence. Eyes. Queues of cars with silent faces, fixed eyes. Engines dead. Forms. A finger pointing to a dotted line. Signatures. Crump wondered whether the officers would give verbal instructions if he spoke their language or whether they considered language unnecessary since they had absolute power. That is what it is, he said in the closed car, deriving some comfort from words spoken aloud, how it will be when the human soul is finally crushed, no one will understand you if you speak or shout or scream and they with their silent gestures will direct you from one hell to another. But he had to be quiet, had to follow another direction. The steel hut with the letter-box slit through which a soldier slipped in their passports for a final check. Against what? A list, a computer's memory?

Europe! One long stretch of road. But frontiers, checkpoints, the armed soldier of ideologies. A piece of silk torn into ribbons.

Dear, dear Frieda, he had written, I who have never been

south of Cadiz and know nothing of the tropics, can imagine, even on a frosty February evening in England, how your sky must go purple at sunset, how the fierce blue must withdraw, and the day's heat rise from the pavements, and your sleeveless arms (arms that are white and braceleted and bare, he recalled now, one level of memory superimposing itself upon another), but that is not what I meant to write. When you come, I will take you to Europe and perhaps I can show you what I mean to say. There's a subtler barbarism at work here. We like to think it isn't so. Much of the time we don't even see it. Because it's so refined, because, but come. There are places even in Europe where these words are meaningless.

– Can we come in, sir? a voice asked.

The third years were coming in, the smiling, cherubic faces of 3A. Once one of them had asked him the meaning of *wan*. Well, he had said, look at, and he himself had looked at each one of them to see if he could pick out a wan face, but there was not one which was not ruddy and full-cheeked, and he said, Well, at least I can explain the meaning of the welfare state.

– Good morning, good morning, good morning, he sang the line from the Beatles' song to them.

Some laughed, some clapped their hands to their ears to suggest that the sound offended their excellent taste in music, some gaped at their unpredictable teacher, and one who had entered last came up to him and said, What are we going to do today?

Crump sang to him: Good morning, good morning, good morning-uh!

– As long as we don't have to work, the boy said, going to his place.

– What would you like to do today? he asked, adding (for they were making enough noise getting to their places to hear him) you miserable little turds on a pig farm. All right, listen now. What about poetry, shall we read some poems (boys, waiting for the end)?

The class responded with an emphatic *No!*

– Oh, but they're lovely poems.

– Poetry's spastic, one cried, and another: Poetry's crap.

– All right, would you like to *write* a poem?

– *No!*

– All right, no need to be so passionately demonstrative, this isn't Downing Street. We'll go back to the usual routine, we'll pretend that we never had any imagination, we'll start the week with a composition. What've you got your hand up for, Clarke?

– Sir, can we read some poems instead?

– The thought of having to think hurts, does it? No, it'll have to be a composition, and none of the usual nonsense either. I'm sick and tired of hearing about your hobbies or how you spent your Christmas or how you would go about arranging a camping holiday with some friends of your own age or which country you would choose to emigrate to and why or what you think about blood sports or how much pocket money you think you should get and how you should spend it (there's always some lying hypocrite, isn't there, Bush, who writes: I save half my pocket money to buy mum a present) or how you spend a rainy afternoon or how you can help old-age pensioners or why you enjoy being a boy scout – shut up! he called to Reeves who had begun to say Jones does, and Crump knew would end with because he's a queer – or imagine that you're a journalist and write a report of a football match or a report on the launching of QE2, no, none of that. Today you'll write about yourselves, about what you are, what you think you ought to be, what other people mean to you, what England means to you, what Europe means to you, where it is all going, what it is all about, can you do that? Or at least try?

Damn well *try*?

A hand went up.

– Yes, Goodwin?

– Sir, can I write about being an air-pilot?

And another: Can I write about being a lighthouse-keeper?

Is that what they understood of what they meant to themselves? Write (God damn you) just write. And soon chatter, noise, argument, disputation filled the room.

– Look, get out your books and work, Crump called to the class.

No one heard him. He rose from his chair, stared silently at them for a moment and said: Stand up. They looked offended by the command, but stood up, some still chatting. Hands on your heads, he said. They put their hands on their heads, an action which always had the effect of shutting them up.

– Jones, I said hands on your heads to the class and I did not except you.

– Oh, I didn't hear, Jones said, putting his hands up.

Crump suppressed a sudden inclination to walk up to him and to slap him across the face, and noticed that another boy had put his foot up on a chair and was untying and then tying up a shoe-lace – a familiar ploy against the hands-on-the-heads offensive.

– Sir? Clarke called.

– Shut up, Clarke, I do not wish to hear your asinine question.

– Sir, why are we standing up?

– I said I didn't want to hear your question. And why is it that you're the only one who always protests innocence? No, don't answer that.

– It's unfair, Clarke said.

Crump ignored him and said to the class: I set a composition, I did not ask you to start acting like the stockbrokers you no doubt would love to become one day. Now sit down and work silently.

For a few moments chairs scraped the floor, desks were pulled, desk-lids opened and banged shut. A hand went up.

– Yes, Bush?

– Sir, I haven't got a pen.

– What do you expect me to do, Bush, ring up Strakers and ask them to deliver a Parker 61 by special messenger?

– That would be very nice, Bush said.

– Has anyone got a spare biro or something?

– I've got something, someone said, another boy laughed, and Jones put a hand up, saying, I've got a biro.

– There you are, Bush, Jones has a spare biro.

– I'm not lending it to Bush, Jones said, he stinks.

The class laughed, and Crump thought that he ought to have anticipated Jones's trick.

– Right, Jones, stand up. You knew I asked if anyone had a spare biro because Bush is without a pen. If you had no intention of lending it to him, then why the devil did you say you had one?

– I've got one, haven't I? Jones said.

– He's *got one*! the class exclaimed as though in disbelief.

– Oh, sit down, Jones, and get on with your composition.

Petty, he told himself, a pettiness.

– Bush, I suggest you stand up and remain standing.

– What've *I* done? Bush cried, astonished.

– You, Bush, have committed the cardinal crime of not bringing a pen to school. You, Bush, have taken two or three minutes of the class's time and provoked idiocy from Jones.

– What's that? muttered Jones.

– And you, Bush, have the presumption and the impertinence to say what've I done!

– I only forgot my pen, didn't I?

– Look, soon, very soon, I'll forget you're only a thirteen-year-old thick-headed peanut-brained squeamish little runt and be obliged to treat you like a baby with too much wind in its hiccoughing wind-pipe. So shut your piping little trade unionist's trouble-making mouth.

There was a moment's absorption in the exercise books. A hand went up.

– Yes, Phillips?

– Can I borrow a ruler, sir?

– And what in Euclid's name for, Phillips?

– To draw a line.

– You don't need to draw a line, we're not doing geometry.

– It's for my heading.

– Listen, Phillips, there's no point whatsoever in underlining a title, just carry on writing.

– Ay, ay, cap'n.

– Oh, switch off, Phillips, will yer, cried his companion.

Another hand went up.

– Yes, Britten?

– My pen's run out, sir.

– Well, go and fill it, you know where the ink is.

– Here, Britten, look what you've done, you spastic! cried the boy who sat next to him.

– What's up with you, then, spas?

– Sir, Britten nudged me, Nicholson said, holding up his exercise book to show a blot.

– That's it, Nicholson, don't be patient, don't be forgiving, don't for a moment think that it's not all that easy living with other people, but scream out at the first and the slightest provocation, shout out to the world how vilely it treats you, show your wounds while there's still blood about so that we may all weep for you.

Hurt, Nicholson ostentatiously tore out the page, rolled it into a ball, threw it on the floor, and began anew. Meanwhile Britten had filled up his pen and now came up to Crump and asked for blotting paper. Britten had ink all over his fingers, and ink-drops had fallen from the pen on to the floor while Britten walked from where the ink-well was to Crump's desk.

– Look at what you've done, Crump said, pointing to the ink on the floor, trying to remain calm.

– It's not my fault, is it? Britten said.

– I'm very sorry, said Crump, that modern technology is humiliated by your incompetence and hasn't produced a pen which won't leak, smudge or run out of ink, I'm even sorrier that I'm a very kind person who wishes no harm to poor little blue-eyed children and I really am awfully sorry that I'm summoning greater powers of restraint than has made religious fanatics into martyrs and not clouting you one round the earhole, but Britten, dear lad, be a jolly good boy, go to the toilet, wash your hands and your pen, and fetch a mop to clean up this mess. Will you be ever so sweet and do that?

– All right, said Britten, going, dripping more ink.

Crump watched him go. Just when Britten was walking out of the door, Crump shouted after him: And have a bath while you're there.

The class laughed.

– Quiet, he said, I'm not having any more nonsense.

Clarke put a hand up. Crump ignored it. Clarke kept his hand up in the air.

– That's a fine way to sit, Clarke, as though you were hanging on to a strap from the ceiling.

– I want to ask a question, sir.

– A question? I don't want a question. I hate questions. Who do you think I am, an oracle?

– Who's an oracle? Clarke asked.

– I can tell you that I am not one, Crump said. Therefore, I cannot answer any questions. So shut up.

Britten entered, carrying a mop and a bucket. Some laughed, some clapped, for Britten looked like a blundering fool coming on the stage in some facetious situation comedy, a window-cleaner, say, entering an impeccable drawing-room just when a most distinguished guest had been expected.

– Carry on quietly, Crump told the class, and to Britten: Just wipe away the ink, that's all, there's no need to make a drama out of it.

– Now what've I done? Britten asked.

Crump, deciding to anticipate the performance which would follow, rose, took the mop from Britten, wiped off the ink from the floor with one sweep of the mop, held the mop with both his hands and did a quick waltz, told the class to belt up when it laughed, gave the mop back to Britten and guided him out of the door, saying, Go back to the broom-cupboard where you belong.

Jones, who had been dreamily staring at the blackboard, suddenly spoke.

– I know, he said, it's a boat. Isn't it?

Everyone looked up. Some spoke, some laughed, one said, Jones is a queer, more laughed.

– And what may it be, Jones? Crump asked.

– The coracle you were talking about, Jones said. That's a boat, isn't it? In Ireland. I saw a programme on television about it.

– Thank you, Jones. You are quite right, for how can television ever be wrong? Carry on quietly.

What a class of idiots, he thought; but manageable; dim-witted non-thinkers whom he must somehow raise to the level of middle-class non-virtues; the non-people of tomorrow; and such non-parents they had too (I would really like Nigel to go into accountancy but do you think his arithmetic's strong enough? they asked annually on their Open Day visit to receive such crazy answers as: Oh, but I think Nigel is really gifted for the Law. I know he's only thirteen and it's a bit early to tell yet, but there are always clues which give a boy's aptitude away, and I certainly think it's Law for our Nigel). And there was nothing he could do to make these idiots better. With luck, one of them might see beyond the suburban hedge which enclosed him, but the majority would remain contented clerks.

Britten re-entered and walked to his place while Crump said to him: You'd better work with a pencil from now on.

– Here, Britten, look what you've done now! cried Nicholson.

– Wasn't my fault, Britten quickly protested.

– Sir, look.

– Shut up, Nicholson.

– It's unfair, Nicholson said.

– Indeed, it is, Crump said. Let that be a lesson to you. Life is pretty unfair much of the time.

– What a life! Jones muttered.

– Here, Phillips said to Finch, do you know how to make a Jewish omelette?

– How?

– First you borrow two eggs. . . .

– Spas!

– Your composition had better contain sharper and more original wit than that, Phillips.

One of these days he ought to teach them some poetry, he thought. How will you teach poetry? he remembered being asked in an interview for a teaching job once. I'm afraid there can be no answer to that, he had said, and a school governor's eyebrows had risen, a little too predictably, he had thought, going on to say, There are techniques which are assumed to be functional (saying to himself: what rot this interviewee's jargon) such as the employment (why not *use*?) of tape-recorders to bring out, say, the rhythm of a particular poem in order to reveal a special musical quality, in order, also, to stimulate interest in verbal patterns, and I shall be happy to experiment with these techniques. That had impressed them, the word experiment; give a scientific bias to any undertaking, and it becomes acceptable – languages now need laboratories; some universities offer poetry workshops; the mind is being denied its capacity for spontaneous ecstasy, for words are acquiring a utilitarian, money-making purpose. Once he had the job, he had, of course, refused to experiment, preferring merely to read a poem and to read it again. In his first probationary year, he had suddenly been visited by an inspector, a Miss Lacey, during a fifth-year literature lesson. They had been reading a narrative poem by Robert Frost when she entered, smiled at him, and quietly took a chair at the back of the room. They continued to read the poem. At the end of the reading, Crump said, for the poem had been tediously long and he had begun to be irritated by it: I don't know how you chaps feel, but I'm beginning to think that Frost is about the most over-praised American poet of the twentieth century. He is simple; all right, simplicity is a virtue, that's been drummed into us ever since literary criticism began – and I wonder now if simplicity has been made a virtue to make life easier for the literary critics who have to make a living by expounding literary virtues and who certainly, by the very reason of their having chosen to write about writing and not to create themselves, must possess minds of a lesser complexity than the writers. And, incidentally, this is a common phenomenon of our age, to praise the mediocre, the shallow and the third-rate, for by doing so the literary pundit can give the impression of having a superior knowledge than the artist, he can be seen to be taking an interest in art and at the same time to be discrediting it as a disreputable profession for surely you must hold in contempt something of which you applaud the lesser practitioners. But this is by the way, very much by the way. With Frost, I get the impression that he's simple because he's capable of being nothing else. He hasn't struggled through a mass of complexity to achieve this simplicity, he just does not know any other way. Sure, he wrote two or three marvellous poems, but how many hundreds must you plough through – and plough is appropriate here considering the New England farms he's forever going on about – to get to the two or three marvellous ones? And these narrative poems which you've been reading with a dullness they thoroughly deserve, they have moments of sharpness, but let's not kid ourselves that they're great literature, let's not lean over backwards to make the sort of allowances about time and place which, let me remind you, we never need to make with any of the great poets. Frankly, they're dull, naïve, sentimental and occasionally downright banal. The verse is mechanical, the rhyming is often sloppy, the style is monotonously repetitive: he uses the same form for a variety of subjects without introducing any kind of variety within the form. Somehow there's no necessity, no inevitability about just about every poem in *North of Boston.* And this one really is puerile when we consider what Browning did with the same form. And, to be absolutely honest, it leaves me with a deep feeling of boredom, and is precisely the kind of poem which makes people sneer at poetry. Now, let's hear what you've got to say. Do you agree; and if not, why not? Yes, Page.

While Page spoke, he felt that he had been carried away by his own dislike of the poem and had rather overdone the tirade against Frost. At the end of the lesson, Miss Lacey said that he tended to lecture above the heads of the children (by which he understood above *her* head, for the sixteen-year-olds he'd been talking to were by now quite familiar with his methods and knew, at least in a general way, what he'd been talking about), that he was carried away by his own knowledge of the subject (meaning that *her* knowledge was limited), that, frankly, she did not consider his teaching likely to make any impression on the children – she kept calling the teenagers children – nor did she expect his teaching to help them in passing examinations. Oh, well, Crump smiled at her and saw her walk away – very probably to the headmaster's office. Crump prepared in advance for her next visit – a kind of emergency programme to be put into action as soon as she again entered his room. He obtained gramophone records on which radio actors read an anthology of verse in the special, nauseating way actors have of reading poetry; he taped two boys reading some verses. When she came, he said to the class, which happened to be 3A: We have been reading and enjoying poetry this term – which was at least half a lie, but the boys, he had noticed, were always prepared to be on their best behaviour and to be co-operative whenever there was a visitor present. Today I want you to examine the mechanics of poetry, I want to introduce the idea of rhythm to you, for that is the most fundamental mechanical thing to a poem, it's a kind of simple arithmetic without which no mathematics would be possible (good to have an image from a solid subject like maths, he thought, deciding to tell them some other time that, of course, mathematics could exist without simple arithmetic). So, to begin with, I would like to do a little experiment.

He fetched the tape-recorder, the record-player and the records, and the printed volumes of the anthology, all of which had been stowed in his cupboard. First he asked Ford, the worst reader in the class, to read aloud Browning's 'How They Brought the Good News From Ghent to Aix'. It was a lamentable performance and they did not need to go past five or six stanzas. Next, he played the tape-recorder on which there were two slightly better versions of the same stanzas. Finally, he played the record. A few leading questions soon elicited from the class the information that the rhythm of the poem imitated the rhythm of horses galloping.

Miss Lacey, who had sat enraptured throughout the lesson, very probably regretting that such wonderful teaching aids had not existed when she was a freckly little red-haired girl at a grammar school, was suitably impressed. And thus Crump became a fully qualified teacher: by substituting his own personality and knowledge with a couple of machines, and by muttering under his breath the one word which summed up the situation: Balls.

The bell rang, intensifying the noise which had gradually been increasing while Crump sat brooding. Collect the books, will you, Jones, he said, looking out, noticing the net curtains on the windows of the semi-detached houses whose gardens came up to the bicycle shed. The problems of net-curtained civilization were not his, he considered, whose thoughts were a Persian wheel drawing more and more water from the same old well of European culture; but never the dear water, clear water (playful in all your streams, he felt obliged to complete the quotation which had begun itself) for which he thirsted, but that which contained the sediment of distraction, irrelevance and pettiness. Mainly pettiness. He could imagine them, these people with net curtains, why only these, even those who drew Heal's fabrics across their windows, wondering when to have their first child and, having had the first child, whether to have a second one – So that Christopher will have someone to grow up with – whether the second child should come within a year – But, darling, ought not we to *enjoy* Christopher first? – problems, problems, here we sit at what we still presume to be the centre of creation, debating pettiness after pettiness. They taxi from Heal's to Habitat, pausing at Harrods on the way, sampling fabrics, arguing over colour-schemes – Look, darling, I found just the right thing at Tatitat's – applauding the clumsier designs in furniture for the severe functionalism attributed to them by week-end columnists, remembering daily to live up to the image of themselves which they believe is the result of a good education, a liberal outlook and a gifted mind which thinks for itself when all that has happened is that they have been spending their Sunday mornings with the colour supplements. Are these net curtains to be forgiven then? Crump asked himself, remembering what he had thought earlier of his own mind, confusions, confusions, but the question, he said, speaking to the fifth formers, is like the one which asks whether an illiterate man is worse than one with a university degree when each possesses the same manic greed, selfishness, cupidity, both being victims of a mass culture the abominable quality of which they make worse by the very fact that they are victims of it and, in order to survive, must live with it and, by doing so, be contributors to the general degradation which makes them helpless victims. The way things are, trying to live, we cannot help killing ourselves. And the question of differences between people is a moral question, but our age has no time for moral questions, only those which can be expressed quantitatively, those which can be answered by a social survey: answer yes or no or don't know. Carry that line of enquiry to its logical conclusion, and you can only achieve an egalitarian society when all mankind has ceased to concern itself with moral values, which is another way of saying when independent thought has completely been replaced by obedience to governmental decrees and to advertising. And if you accept that, then there is this implication which you'll find both horrible and unacceptable: that egalitarianism is the most vicious thing invented by man.

To whom are you telling all this, eh Crump?

Ah, to hell with it, time to leave it all, what's it to me who've stood on the borders of madness, not mine, but a madness, leave it at that, leave it, time to go, he said, walking down the empty corridors, for the school had been abandoned as speedily as a building on fire. He walked to his Volkswagen in the car park. He drove away. He took a circuitous way home instead of the shortest route, so that he could drive ten miles or so on the M4 and the Great West Road. On the motorway he drove as fast as the Volkswagen could go, finding the sensation of speed have the same relaxing effect on his mind as a gin and tonic with lots of ice after a wearying day.

But, he went on, whether he had returned, he did not know, or whether he had not gone away at all, or whether it was another time and that time happened to be now, he did not know, but he went on. And what the hell does that imply but that we're kidding ourselves in thinking that democracy is the only tolerable system of running man's affairs? It isn't, is it? Just as the process of growth in the human body is one which leads only to death, so it seems that the process of our growing up from barbarians to creatures of civilization is also one which will ultimately destroy us. And isn't that what's happening to European man today? But don't think I'm making out a case for the other side, for I've looked at Spain and Portugal and wandered in the streets of East Berlin. Perhaps there's another way. We are, of course, supreme hypocrites when we scorn the propaganda techniques of the totalitarian states, implying that we, thank God, are free; forgetting, of course, that public relations is just a fancy name for a more insidious type of propaganda. Still, the more I see of Europe, the more I'm glad to return to England, grateful that we at least have acquired a capacity for lagging behind, of being incompetent, that we at least continue to blunder on in an amateurish way. Though I sometimes think that we ought to drop the pretences we live with, make a choice between capitalism as it's practised in America or socialism as the communist states practise it. Our compromise will kill us. Do I contradict myself? All right, then, I contradict myself. These words are not entirely mine either.

Crump sat brooding, a Paul Newman among schoolchildren, while the fifth-year group loitered in. Crump: a narrowed eye, a pouting lip. He shook himself in his chair, wondering whether the lesson in which he had been talking to the fifth formers had taken place at another time, or had just finished, or was about to begin.

– What bad news have you got for us today, sir? asked Stobbs, leering from behind his thick-lensed spectacles.

Crump glanced at him, lengthened his face, uttered a non-word and looked away.

– Oh dear, he's not well, said Stobbs. Do you feel foul today, sir?

– Rotten, said Crump, looking at him, plain rotten.

– Not cancer, I hope.

– Cancer, I suppose, said Crump. A malignant tumour. A vicious growth. A rapidly multiplying cell. A civil war within the state which appears outwardly stable and prosperous. A kind of Narcissistic cannibalism. A corruption. An explosion of commercials during a television programme. Soldiers' boots in the quiet streets. Rats in the sewers of a great healthy city. A virus in the clear air under the blue sky. Multiplying, growing, malignant. Rottenness, just plain rottenness.

– Where, asked Stobbs, the lungs?

– Everywhere, said Crump, everywhere.

– Wha' a life! muttered Barnes.

– Cor! said Chapman, look she's tickling herself.

White, sitting next to Chapman, giggled.

– Bring it here, Crump said, realizing that they were looking at a magazine.

White blushed, but Chapman said, It's adult reading, sir.

– Come on, Chapman, let's see what absorbs you. I may have been wrong about your intellect.

– You've asked for it, said Chapman, coming up and placing an *Observer* colour supplement on Crump's desk.

– The other one's juicier, said Murray.

– Bring it up, White.

White came up and placed a *Sunday Times* colour supplement on Crump's desk, and Chapman said apologetically, Well, you're always telling us to make a habit of reading the serious papers.

– Indeed, I am. Go and sit down.

Crump glanced at the two magazines and found what had

been amusing the two boys.

– All right, listen to this, he said, quoting:

> He then automatically draws the nipple into his mouth until his gums can grip the pigmented area around its base. He'll begin to suck strongly and rhythmically, his tongue massaging the stretched breast tissue and nipple against the roof of his mouth.*

– Cor, succulent! someone exclaimed.

– Precisely, said Crump. The article is, of course, about babies. And of course it makes itself out to be a sophisticated piece of analysis, full of profound psychological insights. Let's take a couple more quotations. First:

> As the child grows a few months older and co-ordinates eye and hand, he experiments on new objects. He licks, sucks, bites, strokes, pulls, and when the odds-on chances of texture, shape, smell and sound all add up to a *rattle* he will probably discard it for the moment for something fresh.

And another:

> The graph of an infant's attachment to his mother rises sharply in the second half of the first year, reaches a peak between one and four years and then begins to diminish gradually.

Now, I put it to you that nothing new, significant or important is said in these bits of revelation, nothing that any young mum won't be able to tell you. Common observation is here made to look like a scientific discovery by using such portentous words like *co-ordinates*, *experiments*, *texture*, *graph*. For Christ's sake, do we need a graph to tell us how a child's

* *Observer*, London, 13 October 1968.

attachment to its mother grows? Such language, friends, uses a jargon which is calculated to make you feel you're reading something serious, something which is valuable, something which will increase your knowledge, make you able to cope better with the Great Problems. At the same time it's an easy enough language for even a dim-witted idiot like Chapman to understand. The idiot is flattered into thinking that he's clever, and the clever are flattered by the feeling that their intelligence is capable of comprehending everything. But look at this picture.

– Juicy! cried someone while Crump held up the page for the class to see, showing a young, attractive mother, smiling from her holy nakedness.

– Precisely, said Crump. You make the point for me. A hazy, romantic colour picture, it's meant to give the baby's view of its mum. There can be nothing sweeter or more innocent than that. But what do *you* see? You see a breast. You see sex. Where nakedness in pornography is supposed to be filthy, precisely the same nakedness for a presumed scientific exposition is charming and healthy. I put it to you that this is no science, this is no advance, this is not even the useful information it pretends to be, a kind of know-your-baby guide. I put it to you that this is a disguised attempt at titillation and an attempt to win the gooey sympathy of women. And now what do we have in the respected *Sunday Times*? We have 'The Evolution of the Female Form',* god help us. Here we have Jayne Mansfield in a bikini, we have quote New Guinea girl with a swelling stomach and small bosom which (notice the pseudo-intellectualism) might have been painted by Van Eyck or Cranach unquote, we have eight actresses dressed up as Cleopatra, we have early nude photography (purely for historical reasons, of course!), we have women in corsets, we have two dozen nudes from painting, we have pin-ups including the famous calendar pose of Marilyn Monroe (which, surely, is in very bad taste consider-

* *Sunday Times*, London, 13 October 1968.

ing how sorry we're all supposed to have been feeling for her ever since she committed suicide). And who are the authors of the articles? They are artists, archaeologists, historians and physicians; in short, apparently a group of intellectuals who cannot possibly be frivolous, what they have to say must be of the utmost importance – at least that's the impression the paper would no doubt like to create in the minds of its readers (which, surely, is an inappropriate word; should they not be called *voyeurs*?) and the paper would no doubt easily defend itself against my type of accusation by suggesting that I must be a fool to think that such respected and eminent historians etcetera would take part in a scheme the object of which was to excite sexual fantasies in minds no more developed than those of schoolboys. But don't tell me that anyone having all these breasts bouncing in front of him is going to say, Here are some learned articles about the development, sorry, Evolution, of the female shape, sorry, Form, a most important and indispensable subject, which I simply must read in order to be better informed about life. No, it's all an excuse to titillate. And this isn't the first time either, this isn't a coincidence. They've had pieces before on some aspect of art, say, or the cinema, and when you look at them what you see is breasts, a kind of trade-mark of the nineteen sixties. And these two papers were once worthy institutions with what seemed an incorruptible courage. Over Suez, I remember, the *Observer* used the entire paper for opposing the Government, not caring to lose readers because the truth, as it saw it, was more important. Now they wouldn't dare to champion such truth for fear of losing the readers so dearly won by producing rubbish about babies, women, food, design, fashion, trends, cars. I am telling you this because you're the ones who are being conned by the adults of the world in which you're growing up. I myself don't give a damn what anyone publishes; what I do resent is the kind of subtle deceit which is being practised on me by this sort of publishing. If I want to see pictures of naked women, I'd rather see them in *Playboy* where I know I am being shown naked women because I, the reader, like looking at naked women. It serves them damn well right that they should have found their audience in two giggling, mentally less than average, adolescent nitwits of Pinworth School, White and Chapman.

The class was shocked into silence as Crump flung the two magazines to the back of the room with the last sentence of his speech. Even Chapman, suffering such direct abuse, sat open-mouthed.

– Confusion and chaos, Crump went on, a general rottenness. Take the arts. It used to be a basic principle that a work of art was one which endured, that survived the test of time. And, as an artist, you achieved that quality by working away for years at your craft. What you produced was well done, sometimes lastingly memorable. But suppose you were not good enough to achieve such a standard? Well, then, you blundered on, you tried to do your best. It was the survival of the fittest. Not nowadays, however, for nowadays if you're not good enough you simply change the rules, you make up a new philosophy of art, you go about saying that we're living in a culture whose products are disposable and therefore its art must also be disposable, you say Nothing is meant to last, you coin new slogans, you say, Fragmented art reflects the chaos we live in, you say Bad poetry is socially significant, you say Art must be an explosively instant product because Man might be blown up in an explosive instant. Everyone makes his own shoddy product and then fabricates a theory, using some fashionable catch-phrases, to justify the utter shoddiness of it. And no one has the decency to stop and think for a moment; instead, everyone joins in, a chorus begins to chant the praises of the most ephemeral construction, so much so that the honest artist who attempts to produce any work at all is discredited, laughed at. If you can't paint, then all you've got to do is not to try to learn painting but to go about saying that anything from a blank canvas to a framed sheet of glass is painting; if you can't write a poem, then for goodness' sake don't do so foolish a thing as try to find out what the hell poetry is all about but, instead, all you need to do is to go around saying that sneezing, coughing and any old assortment of words is a poem; and if it also contains a good sprinkling of four-letter words, then you can assume that it is also a tough, relevant, contemporary poem. If you can't win, you no longer have to join the other side, which is so much stronger than you, you simply say that the other side doesn't exist, or that reasons for its existence are no longer valid. If whatever your asinine proposal is has a commercial value, you'll be applauded and fêted by art dealers, publishers, editors and the public. If you go about naked, they'll compliment you on your fine new clothes. Each one to his own novelty. Continuity, what's that? Tradition, what's that? Seriousness, isn't that word out of the dictionary yet?

– What's he talking about? Murray asked Holroyd who shrugged his shoulders.

– Nature, said Crump, changing course on being interrupted, has ways of fructifying itself, of. . . .

– Sir, what's that word? asked Chapman. Fructifying.

– Don't you know, Chapman? Tell him Barnes.

– Wha'?

– The meaning of to fructify.

Barnes, looking down at his desk, absorbed in some inner mood, muttered absently: Fructify know.

Even Crump laughed. Stobbs, looking at his watch and perhaps concluding that there was still time for work to be set if the interruption put an end to the flow of nonsense from Crump which he did not need to listen to, said: What's wrong with giving people what they want?

–You've asked me that before, Stobbs, said Crump, and I know you have an eye on your watch and are worried if I might do something so rash as to set work at any moment. But I'll answer your question which bases its premises on a commercial vocabulary, supply and demand you'd call it, I suppose. Well, Galileo and Newton and Alexander Fleming and Einstein did not have to see the way they did. People in their respective times did not clamour for the discoveries these scientists had to offer. After the discovery has become public, one wonders how life was at all tolerable before it. Nor would you have a literature or an art of any importance if all the compulsion to produce them came not from inside the writer or the artist, from his feelings, from his way of seeing things, but from public demand. The public is loath to change; it's very conservative at heart. Every age has needed, sooner or later, to defy this conservatism, to throw a brick through the windowpanes of complacency in the suburban terraces and the country villas. Except ours, which shocks itself not with intellectual discovery but with variations on the theme of sensational novelty, which keeps its net curtains clean and receives nothing more serious through the post than invitations to take advantage of discount houses, not to mention the heaps of coupons with five pence off for some detergent. Of course, it suits big business, small business too, to have you literate enough to be earning sufficient money to buy consumer goods, to be just about getting the message of the ads, and not so well educated that you begin to think. It suits politicians, too, for they too are selling an image, a product, though I can tell you that before they offer you anything they make damn sure by consulting opinion polls that that's precisely what you want. Why else do you think there's this general disillusionment with politicians? Because not one of them dares any more to exercise his vision, his imagination, his concern for mankind because the opinion polls indicate that he'd get more votes if he, too, offered five pence off to the people. We don't have leaders anymore, we have damned detergent coupons ruling us.

– But. . . .

– Yes, yes, of course, I'm exaggerating wildly, but that's the only way of kicking you towards the truth of the matter. I know there's some humanity left, but this is the way things are going and are bound to go now that we've committed ourselves irrevocably to the principle of the consumer society. Everyone's out to sell you a product. Don't you realize that you're being taken for a ride by the whole bleeding set-up? Everyone is in the racket of trying to make a damn fool of the next person. Even those self-styled pundits, who in the few minutes they have to spare to themselves between making a television appearance and writing a newspaper column and crossing the Atlantic to give a series of lectures (probably a witty oh-so-delightful series called The Decline of Great Britain) flatter themselves into thinking that they're the country's intellectuals, are in the racket. They will talk, for example, of the finer points of what they've themselves labelled the Pop Culture. Of course, they'll say, it produces a lot of rubbish but, dear fellow, the contents of our dustbins can be as meaningful as an illuminated text from medieval times. They will lean backwards and take pleasure in praising a nauseatingly bad pop song because, dear fellow, it's an interesting phenomenon. They'll applaud the most tenth-rate poet or artist because, dear fellow, he's of social significance. And so it goes, fructifying itself, as Barnes would say, from the disc jockeys, that most fawning, most hypocritical species of salesmen of the mass culture, to the industrial and political bosses.

– Sir, why are you telling us this?

– I don't know, Murray. I suppose it's a form of masochism. For I know that most of you have not been listening at all, or only half-listening. And I know that even if you have understood and fully sympathized with what I've had to say you'll go on as before, you too will end up by being exploited without realizing it, for you'll be conditioned to saying to yourselves what a good time you're having and what it's like to live in a free and culturally exciting country where people really are equal and where people are so enlightened and discerning that they've thrown out the stuffy old-fashioned culture and embraced a swinging with-it trendy one. It frightens me. I, as a teacher, must consider myself a failure if I cannot teach you to ask questions. I know that you do not see this as my job. Neither do your parents. Nor does anyone in the educational hierarchy. Realize this: a machine which is so perfect that it needs no attention, fuelling itself, servicing itself, so perfect that it can perform the job for which it was created with absolute precision and for ever, such a machine will not attract one's interest; it will become dull; it will be taken for granted, so much so that one would forget that it existed. I would have failed utterly if you became like that.

Forget it, Crump, he told himself, your ranting, even if it had the attention of all Europe, will make no difference. Humanity's dead, its components are canned for instant consumption whenever the smart TV producer needs to shed a few public tears for its demise.

He walked out of his room and through the empty corridors, for the school appeared to have been abandoned as speedily as a building on fire. He walked to his Volkswagen in the car park. He drove away. He took a circuitous way home instead of the shortest route, so that he could drive ten miles or so on the M4 and the Great West Road.

No sooner they recede than they approach again, like giant breakers, the wintry Atlantic raging, the borders of madness.

This and much more, he remembered from somewhere, much more than twice all this. And there was that other line, ah yes, Let's choose executors and talk of wills. Uttering it all, like a drunkard. On the shore, beside the sea which broke in splinters, the menacing breakers rising.

Ah, forget it, forget it.

And deciding to forget it he drove away to a party in Tite Street. The Hirschfelds, Bruce and Brenda, had recently taken a basement flat there and were throwing a party before moving in. Although he had driven twice round Sloane Square to be respectably late, he was still one of the first to arrive. Walking through the dimly lit passage, he went through the open door of the flat which was even darker, the source of illumination being candles placed on window-sills and a few hurricane-lamps. It was also very cold, there being no heating. He could distinguish Bruce's voice coming from the large head on a mass of clothing, and presently, becoming used to the darkness, saw him clearly. He stood, cupping his hands round a candle-flame for a few minutes before going up to greet Bruce. He noticed that Bruce wore a bottle-green satin shirt with a long, curve-ended collar, a ruffled front, a very wide pale yellow tie with a green paisley pattern on it, a lime-green velvet suit the jacket of which flared out in a graceful arch at the back.

– How souper of you to come, Crumpey, he said. Meet Henri Laval. I must get Brenda to move on with the wretched drinks, she's taking an awful time organizing them.

Alone, Crump and Henri Laval faintly smiled at each other.

– Gorgeous people, Henri Laval said, bowed slightly and walked away.

Crump saw a couple standing in the middle of the room. She wore a very short silver crochet dress and silver boots up to her knees; her hair, a mass of curls, was early Hollywood. He had on a nylon fur waistcoat over a poloneck sweater and grubby jeans. They stood in silence, her head turned to the window through which she could probably see the feet of passers-by.

Crump walked in the direction of the hall, hoping to discover the toilet. Light from a hurricane-lamp fell on to the hall from one of the rooms and, peeping in, he discovered that it was the bathroom. He went in and shut the door and was about to lock it when a woman's voice said, It's early to be thinking of an assault, isn't it, darling?

With an immediate reflex action, and muttering an apology, he flung open the door.

– Oh, it's you, Crumptious! Uh, mumm, mumm.

The woman, wearing a kaftan, came up to him, reached up, brushed her cheek against his, barely touching it however, and made a kissing sound with her lips; she was Brenda Hirschfeld, he recognized, somehow also becoming aware that she wore no bra under the kaftan, an awareness that produced a retrospective thrill when she drew back.

– I thought this was the loo, he said, and I wanted a pee.

– This is the fridge, darling.

He saw that the bath was full of large chunks of ice and dozens of bottles of champagne.

– Are you keeping watch here? he asked.

– No, Sumptuous, I just came to fetch a couple of bottles and to see, she added jokingly, if I might not encounter an eligible young adulterer.

– That robe's gorgeous, he remarked in case she was not joking, reflecting that he ought at least to fulfil the male's function at a party of flattering the female and conscious that gorgeous was not an adjective he frequently used.

– Oh, you're a beastie, Pierrot, it's not a robe. A kaftan. Picked it up in a bazaar in Tunis. Last month, she added with emphasis.

– What, winter sports?

– I said Tunis, darling. Go on, do your doodah, and get back to the party. Mind you don't let a drop fall into the tub. We want to keep it chilled.

She went out and Crump locked the door after her, wondering why she had called him Pierrot. Several more people had arrived when he returned to the principal room a few minutes later. Bruce was carrying glasses of champagne on a tray. Crump took one. While he paused a moment to facilitate the transfer of the glass from the tray to Crump's hand, Bruce said: How did you get on with Monsieur Laval? Fine, said Crump, a gorgeous man. Bruce, looking elated, walked on.

Crump took a sip, lit a cigarette, exhaled and glanced at some of the new arrivals, concentrating on women. There was a girl all in white lace. Her blonde hair, held high above the neck, had three white lace roses pinned in it. Her lace dress, sleeveless and accentuating her slender figure, was given substance by ribbons and glittering sequins – even in that candlelight. Her white lace-patterned stockings and white satin shoes guaranteed that her figure stood out from head to toe in the poor light. A girl in a pink voile dress, which had pantaloons gathered in at the ankles, looked exotic, especially as she wore a turban-like periwig made of lilac-coloured paper flowers, which were echoed on her wrists in the form of bangles and her throat as a neck-clasp. Flower-power made sophisticated *à la Vogue*, thought Crump. A maiden with a Victorian look wore a plain black dress with a white organdie collar and matching cuffs, great blooming petals of white across her bosom and the forearms. There was another with the Regency look; her burgundy jacket was trimmed with ruched braid and tied with a tasselled bow. Crump could hardly see her skirt, which must have been very short, for her legs seemed all satin thighs and burgundy suede boots.

There was little conversation, little movement. People wandered in, took statuesque positions, and if a hand moved and a glass touched a lip it was as if in a mime. Then, from another room, with an explosive suddenness, came the noise of a band beginning to play, disturbing Crump's concentration as he feasted visually on the sexual delicacies before him. He had not expected Bruce and Brenda to hire a pop group for the occasion, but since hiring pop groups for parties was the current trend he was not surprised. Crump swallowed what remained of his champagne and went in search of more. There was a kitchen past the bathroom and he could distinguish some activity there, a shadow flickering on a wall, as he walked down the hall. The candle-light, or it could have been another hurricane-lamp, casting long shadows on the wall, suggested a couple in an embrace; perhaps the couple was not embracing and it was merely the way the shadows engaged each other on the wall, he thought, retreating nevertheless, not wanting to disturb any incipient passion this early in the party. He found the bathroom unoccupied, picked up a bottle from the bathtub, uncorked it gently and re-filled his glass. He drank it quickly and poured himself another glassful. With the bottle a quarter empty, he could carry it under his arm. He walked out and re-entered the principal room which echoed loudly with the drumming from the next room. There were few people there and no unattached girls. He walked to the room where the music was. Drums, double bass, guitar and vocalist, warming up to full volume in a room of which the longest dimension was its fifteen-foot length, seemed determined to bring down the walls of Tite Street if not Jericho. Tightly packed though the room was, many couples were dancing. Conversation was impossible. The bodies seemed released from the frigidity of silence;

movement was all now that the music compelled everyone in earshot to abdicate speech. The group was called the Jet Set, Crump saw from the writing on the drums. The four members of the Jet Set wore very slim trousers, tight at the thighs, and different coloured satin shirts, unbuttoned at the front, showing hairy chests. The hair of each was a mass of curls, but only the drummer sported a moustache, a droopy one in the Mexican style. The drummer was singing

She's a pattern on my mind
like art nouveau on wrapping paper

Crump saw the Regency girl standing a few bodies away from him, holding her glass which he observed was empty. He slipped past the bodies to her and poured her some champagne from his bottle. She smiled briefly at him, looked away in the direction of the vocalist who screamed

She's the universal archetypal blue-print of love

and ignored her full glass of champagne. Crump withdrew, attempting to return to the emptier room. But there was something attractive about

She's a pattern on my mind
a dust-jacket on the book of my life

which made him continue to look at the group and at the dancing couples. Yet the song was all wrong

My fibre-glass thoughts are moulded on her body

disconnected jottings shouted out except for the refrain, seeming to possess a theme, appearing to be clever and pretending to an originality of thought without, however, being able to give the inventive imagery a real direction. The dancing was a personal elaboration by each couple, a physical enaction of a similarly undirected inventiveness. But in the far corner a girl wearing a very low cut dress in Lotus Elan yellow was dancing by herself in the frantic, climactic quivering movement of a Hawaiian, her thighs and abdomen, breasts and shoulders convulsively moving in a blatantly sexual rhythm, her head thrown back, her eyes shut, her mouth open. The area in front of her seemed to clear itself, for the slower dancers there, suddenly aware of her frenzied dance and tremendous attractiveness, withdrew and became spectators. Gradually, all the dancers except her stood still. It became a performance. The drums beat louder, the guitar became urgent, for the group now played to her, began to offer the alcohol of their music to her speeding, maddened body. Crump, the blood drumming in him, withdrew to the other room which was completely empty now. There being no furniture, he went and sat in the corner farthest away from the music although distance within the limited space of the flat seemed to make no difference. He lit a cigarette and filled up his glass, attempting to decelerate the racing blood within him. He observed the floor, drinking, smoking. A great cheer went up in the other room. Crump imagined the girl had torn her dress down to her waist in the ecstasy of her motion, but the music had stopped and people were leaving the room so that soon he was obscured by people standing in front of him. There was little talk; mainly drinking and smoking. He rose, thinking that this was the moment when, had he been standing, he would now be wanting to sit down. He drank; he smoked.

– Ah, there you are, Crumpey, he heard Bruce say. He looked round and saw Bruce coming in his direction, guiding someone, holding him by the arm. Meet Henri Laval, Bruce said, left Laval with him and disappeared. Laval bowed. Crump bowed. They looked away from each other. Crump saw the girl in the yellow dress standing exhausted against a wall, a man next to her brushing his lips across her bare shoulder. He looked back at Laval and at that moment Laval looked back at him.

– Gorgeous people here, Laval said, bowed slightly, and walked away.

– It's empty again, Crump heard a woman's voice next to him. He turned to look and realized that the voice, belonging to the Regency girl, had addressed him. She was holding out her glass. He filled it up and discovered that his bottle was now nearly empty.

– I am Crump, he said, but at the very moment that he began his self-introduction, the music burst out again and she did not hear him. She went away to the music. Crump finished the rest of the champagne and went to the bathroom to fetch another bottle, deciding to have a pee while there. The latter resolution, however, was frustrated, for a man sat on the toilet seat, a girl in his lap, and the two were making the best of a difficult position by ingeniously employing their hands and lips. Crump exchanged his bottle, said to the couple, Ah, the flush of passion, and went out.

Dancing had commenced again and even the room which had earlier remained empty now contained an overflow of dancers. He saw that Brenda was dancing with a short, curly-headed man, not dancing so much as very slowly moving in a tight embrace. The girl in the Victorian dress stood alone by the wall. Crump went up to her, held up the bottle to her and asked if she would like a drink or to dance or both. She turned her beautiful but severely chaste-looking face to him and stared sadly at him. Her white-lipsticked lips did not move; her false eyelashes seemed still as a *Vogue* photograph.

– Your eyes are lovely, Crump essayed.

She continued to look with profound melancholy until he began to feel uncomfortable. Cornered, Crump felt aggressive, and in order to shock her out of her constant stare, said: Shall we make love? Still he did not seem to penetrate her mask. The aggression increasing in him the longer she stared, he said, raising his voice: What about it, soul-creature, shall we have a frolicky-fuck? Still she stared. He was about to abandon her when her hands sprang up, held him at the shoulders, pulled him to her; she kissed him briefly but viciously on the mouth, and violently pushed him back so that the bottle and the glass in his hands fell and crashed on the floor. She leaned back against the wall and, stooping, took a cigarette from a man who was sitting on the floor and whom Crump had noticed earlier. She took a drag of the cigarette, exhaled, arching her neck back, closing her eyes. Her manner and the strange aroma as she exhaled suggested that it was not tobacco that induced the look of entranced melancholy on her face.

No one paid any attention to the crashing bottle, the contents of which now flowed under the feet of the dancers. Looking around the room, Crump saw that everyone, surrendered to the anarchy of his own soul, was utterly self-absorbed, and noticed that Brenda and the curly-headed man had manœuvred to a corner of the room and that he was engaged in pressing her against the wall and that her long white arms encircled his back. He walked softly to the bathroom and, ignoring the shape on the toilet seat, went straight to the bathtub to pick out a bottle. A male voice said, What a gorgeous party, Monsiur Crumpey.

He realized that the shape on the toilet seat which he had, without looking, assumed to be that of the couple he had last seen there, was now that of Henri Laval. The bottle in his hand, he stood watching Laval who had a magazine in his lap. Crump gently eased the cork out of the bottle and, not having a glass, tried to drink straight from the bottle, but rushing foam overflowed from his mouth, ran down his neck and under the collar, and he had to jerk his head forward, coughing. When he recovered, he said, Not much light for reading here, is there?

– I must have a magazine, Laval said, when I'm sitting in the W.C.

Crump looked to see if Laval had his trousers down, but apparently did not. Maybe he shits in his pants, he thought.

– Do you read it? Laval asked, holding up the magazine to show the cover on which Crump could dimly recognize a bosomy girl dressed up like a rabbit.

– Only at the barber's, Crump said.

– Oh, but this is my study, Monsieur Crumpey.

Randy old bastard, Crump thought, but Laval went on, You may not have heard of me. I cannot say I blame you.

One can't keep up with everything that's going on. I have a small reputation here. But I have lived long with the English, years in the war at the B.B.C., and various visits since then, including three years at one of your excellent new universities, spreading, you might say, the gospel to the younger generation.

But Crump had remembered seeing an article somewhere attacking highbrow culture and, suddenly associating the name of Henri Laval with the article, realized that the man in the turdlating position in front of him was a well-known French philosopher who had won widespread notoriety by advocating that anti-art and the pop culture had been the greatest developments in the history of civilization. Before he could tell Laval that he knew of him, Laval commenced his lecture.

– All your serious art is a piece of *connery*. Forgive the French word, but it's most appropriate. Over and above the French meaning, there's the suggestion, when used in an English sentence, that someone's being conned. Now, if there's anything wrong with Western European culture, it's that its highbrow element is too pretentious, too self-perpetuating, too conceited to be of any value to the living European. It was all right, say, up to a hundred years ago when your educated class was a privileged minority, invariably a wealthy one. And the main trouble with your serious artists, poets and composers is that they continue to believe that they're serving the same minority. That is unpardonable. We're liberated now, emancipated; the democratic principles have gone beyond politics – which is probably why we don't need them *in* politics anymore. Now, unless you serve the majority, you are nothing; you are worse than nothing; you're anti-social, anti-democracy; you're subversive, corrupting; you restrain the forces of progress, you bring confusion to healthy thought. At your best you're obscure, at your worst you're inarticulate. You do not exist without those cultural middlemen, the critics, who are your link with the tiny hives of your public; you have no way of directly communicating with your public. By definition, you're old-fashioned, and, therefore, not of this age. Your failure simply is that you've been overtaken by a pop culture which has gone so far ahead that you continue to deceive yourself that you're alone on the road. And please don't flatter yourself into thinking that there are two cultures of which yours, of course, is the superior. No. Existence is a matter of being of some importance to others' point of view, and in this respect you don't have a body at all. You're not only inbred, but also parasitic, feeding on one another. You are worms under the great rock you call tradition. The slightest exposure to the sunlight of actuality kills you. The body of work which you like to think is culturally the heart of Europe is irrelevant to the present condition of the European. In any case, it was never the heart of Europe, for that's only a myth which you yourself are fond of reiterating. At best, it has been a little toe which Europe has from time to time found it necessary to examine in passing, in order, say, to pare an overgrown nail. The heart of Europe always has been commerce. Hence, a pop culture is everything that you can never be, a real, living, important phenomenon: because for the first time in European history cultural pursuit has assumed the stature of an industry and become part of the general commercial pursuit. You abuse judgements which are not arrived at after prolonged deliberation, failing to recognize that they're the only judgements we have the time for nowadays. All human activity is aimed at self-advancement; therefore, to be able to sell a product is one of the highest achievements man is capable of. Your serious art abhors the idea of selling, and is consequently decadent, introspective, self-pitying, and by setting up its own standards it further alienates itself from political and social reality. Life is not what you make it out to be. Life is aggressive selling. Life is political sophistry. Life is a continuous explosive chaos. Life is wife-swapping in suburbia while the teenage daughters masturbate in a hall watching their pop-idol on the stage. Life is an unending hysterical shriek. Life is a happening. Not your nice judgements, your fine balancings, your delicate delineations, your subtle psychological probings. Pop culture reflects the explosive chaos; it *becomes* the chaos;

consequently, it *is* life itself. One great big band. If the world were to go pop in another four minutes, it'll be your world which will collapse; for the pop artist, the world's going pop could well be the moment of supreme triumph. Well, Monsieur Crumpey, what do you say to that, eh?

Walking out with his bottle, Crump said: The next time you want to shit, why don't you first lock the door?

The hall was crowded with men leaning against women and the women leaning against the walls. Bruce seemed to have interlocked his tongue with the Regency girl's, his velvet lime-green jacket against her burgundy. The Jet Set was soaring in the higher realms of sound, revving at a volume which could be muffled only by deafness. The girl in yellow sat on the floor, leaning against the wall, and her low-cut dress would have presented a pleasing image had not the hand of a man sitting next to her come round her neck and planted itself in the cleavage there. The Victorian girl had passed out and lay flat on her back on the floor and a man lay at a right angle to her, his head on her bosom. Around them, dozens of couples still danced, each after its own fashion. Returning to the hall, he saw Brenda and the curly-headed short man come from the passage outside the flat and walk towards the kitchen. The back of Brenda's kaftan was soiled at the shoulder-blades and at the seat. The Regency girl seemed to have been abandoned by Bruce, for she stood alone. Crump went up to her and held the bottle up before her eyes.

– I've lost my glass, she said.

Crump swigged from his bottle, held the champagne in his mouth, stooped forward, kissed her and injected some of the champagne into her mouth.

– Thank you, she said. I know of a better way of making *you* drink.

Crump observed that her burgundy jacket was unfastened at the front, enabling him to conjecture the champagne fountains beneath the white satin shirt that she wore under the jacket.

– Where's Bruce? he asked.

– In there (she indicated the bathroom) with Georgina.

– He was doing all right with you a moment ago.

– I'm both his hors d'œuvre and dessert. Georgina is his main dish.

– And that's all right with you?

– One's first and final mouthfuls give the most pleasure.

– Unless one's overstuffed with the main course.

He saw Brenda come from the kitchen and go into the bathroom, and said to the Regency girl: Well, then, shall I give you another drink or are you going to insist that I drink from you?

– Yes, she said, ambiguously.

Just then he saw Brenda come out of the bathroom, holding a bottle in her hand. Seeing him, she said, Hello Voluptuous. Where's Frieda? I haven't seen her around.

– She had to be with her mother who's ill.

– Sorry, darling, she said, reaching up to brush her cheek against his in sympathy, making a kissing sound with her distant lips and murmuring, Mumm; so that Crump took an instinctive step towards her, and was again aware that she wore no bra under her kaftan. She withdrew and walked away to the kitchen. Crump retraced a step to be again with the Regency girl, but she was no longer there.

Outside it was raining. The leafless beech tree offered its branches as gutters for the rain. The descending jets were making a lower approach to Heathrow and were consequently louder. The washing-lines in the back gardens dripped. The roof of the bicycle shed threw a straight line across the asphalt below it, defining the extent of its protection, dividing the dry from the wet. The noise, the clamour for attention was from 3B.

Still, they seemed to have accepted the desirability of work, or at least were giving some attention to the task he had set, and if their noise never abated it could be that that was the natural environment in which they preferred to exist. He had begun to put into practice one of the axioms of teaching which he had arrived at early in his career, that he could only help the B stream children to make an educational advance if he first discovered what interested them and then set work accordingly. The old textbook exercises (rewrite the following three simple sentences as one compound sentence, beginning your sentence with a participial phrase) had failed; the new textbooks with their clear typography and large areas of visual interest were gimmicky (one suggested that the class be split into groups for a letter-writing exercise: first, one group should construct a real-looking letter-box of cardboard complete with EIIR and times of collection; the second group should write the letters and mail them in the box; a third group should collect, sort and distribute the letters which should have been addressed to a fourth group). If learning could be acquired only by playing games, then Crump preferred to invent his own. The present task was to construct a collage from advertisements cut out of colour supplements, building new persuasive messages from the copy of several advertisements. A fine piece of self-mockery, he thought. Cut out the words of the slogans, boys. Cut it all up. Bits of paper. That's all.

–I find it difficult to believe, he said aloud in case Bill Whiting cared to listen, and why should he not, he thought, if I must let my tongue despumate the thick mess of words in my brain, lick at the pores of a philosophy (mine!), if I must, if I must (such cannibalism among the grey cells!), then let him hear it too and make of it what he can, the poor sod, bemused and yet so superior in his detachment, listen, Bill, I find it difficult to believe that I have done, why done, for that presumes a prior wish to do and some concession to the notion that there is some continuity (five dramatic acts to a tragedy, say) in what has been done, been involved in, then, the actions that I think I have been involved in one way or another, willingly or unwillingly, with intense interest or reluctantly and with feelings of repugnance, or, put it in another way, Bill, write out each of the actions I have been involved in, write them all out on one sheet of paper, tear it up in tiny bits, fling the bits into the air, that is how it is, involvement, fragments, that's all it comes to, the bits fall here and there, someone's amused, maybe you, certainly not I, that's what it is, bits of paper when I think of these actions which I think are the ones I have been involved in, and I should certainly be interested were I to pick up one of these bits and read some statement there, curiosity, I suppose, like looking at someone else's correspondence even when it's no more than a letter to a mail-order firm, and I would go around looking for more bits, the universal habit of collecting and categorizing would assert itself and I'd go around looking for the bits to paste together to form the whole, to establish the pattern, to delineate some sort of unity and, having done so, cry out, It's all here! But what foolishness, what vanity.

He paused to see if there was any response from the curved, heavy-sack of a figure in the hammock, sunning himself in the nude with a tattered old straw hat covering his face.

– It's not, of course, he went on, although the weight in the hammock did not stir, a matter of belief, for belief is a word that wears ecclesiastical robes. Let us say knowledge, then, though you may well object that the word knowledge can also lead to confusion since philosophers use it in a special sense, relating it to existential propositions, whereas the common use of the word is to do with acquiring and storing up learning or information. You see, Bill, I'm trying hard not to be obscure, and my concern about the right choice of word, belief or knowledge or some other, is in itself a good example of my concern about trying to establish whether or not I played any part in the various dramas, confrontations, informal meetings, dialogues or whatever I think I was a leading or a minor participant in, and, tell me, Bill, how can you establish memories or facts or occurrences when it is so damned difficult to establish that you and I, only two of us of the millions in this world, find it hard to agree that we both understand the same thing by the words we use, how can we, Bill, when, simply when I'm trying to explain things to myself, am not sure, can never be sure, that the words which I'm using are the right ones? Am I succeeding in saying what I am trying to say or are the words urging upon me sentences which I ought not to be uttering? Answer that, Bill, and you'll be the wisest man on earth.

Still he discerned no movement in the hammock, and he said: As usual, for this is the condition which makes human discourse at all possible, let's take a short cut, let's agree that belief would be the word to use – approximations to truth, that's all we can achieve – let's agree that you understand what I mean when I say that I find it difficult to believe certain things about myself. So. Here's a nice bog for one to daggle through! Well, why not? A time comes when the brain becomes a mire, a dungheap, when a story must either end with the expected or the unexpected ending or be interrupted and its contents vilified. Continuations are possible, of course, in another context, elsewhere, elsewhere, not here. I should have been Hamlet. It would have been much easier. But. A dungheap. That's all.

Although the heavy sack did not move, a hand came up to push back the hat, and he took that to indicate that Bill was at least listening even if he refused to express a vocal interest.

– So. If it is to be a matter of belief, if I am to be asked to testify to the truth of any descriptive statement, one whose veracity could possibly be imagined (*imagined*, Bill, never, *never* established) by referring to accounts of independent witnesses, then I will be obliged, in all truth, to declare that the substance of all descriptive statements about the nature of which people can be in general agreement (such statements as that I wore a black poloneck and drove a Volkswagen) is often too trivial for one to care whether or not the statements convey a truth; and if it is demanded of me that I confess my intention in uttering descriptive statements of which the thing or the action described was experienced only by me without witnesses being present and to state whether I had indeed experienced it or whether that I merely thought that I experienced it, then I will be obliged, again in all truth, to declare that I have sometimes felt myself to be in the position of a spy who has had to adopt a fictitious identity and cannot, from time to time, help pondering on the other man who lies suspended as though deliberately maleficiated or reduced to a state of chronic catalepsy, thinking about whom is an act of the imagination and if the imagination posits states of being for this other man, then I cannot, during this suspended time while I am not this other man (and how else can one consider one's past self?) be responsible for what is supposedly true about him even when the statement about the supposed truth about him has been uttered by me; and, finally, if I am asked to state what degree of truth is to be ascribed to the abstract statements which my mind has attempted to convey, then I will be obliged, once more in all truth, to declare my sympathies to be congenerous with those philosophers who assert that all perceptions one records are indicative of nothing more than the particular language one has learned, the habits of speech that one has acquired within that language, and the extent of the vocabulary one can command within that language; nothing more. You hear that, Bill? Nothing more. Just nothing bloody more. Except delusions, except those storms of the mind that drag down the trees of memory, except that sleepiness which comes over the heart in moments of contentment, except those obsessions with categories, except those fantasies of having done ill or having done well. False, all false. What foolishness, what vanity.

To whom are you telling all this, Crump?

You hear me, Bill? You deserter, you fake, you hypocrite, you tramp on the edge of civilization! When there's a disease abroad, it's best to isolate yourself. Explanations! Why should I explain to you? I spent years talking to kids. I wanted to stop talking, that's all. I no longer wished to be, it's as simple as that, without undertaking any heroic self-mutilation. Just opting out, disappearing, that's all. You smirk. Why should I invent a romance to amuse you? Of course, there was a romance. Nothing extraordinary, just a love which I hoped would survive the usual erosions. You want me to elaborate, tell you the pattern and the colour of the curtains it took us so much time to choose? No. The usual erosions will have to do. The mind has forests it wanders through in dreams. We were sane, oh, utterly sane. And what do you do when you realize that beyond the forest is a valley and beyond the valley is a forest and beyond the forest is a valley and beyond the valley is a forest? Go on, try it for yourself, you've stood at the edge of the Sahara you say. A fine dropout you are, bloody tourist. Tricks with mirrors are tiresome. They may beguile a childish imagination. What do you do when you realize that at best all experience comes to you second-hand, a bargain you make with your tired senses, raiding the ever-impoverishing exchequer of language? It survived, isn't that enough, and it would have survived. The usual erosions. One learns to construct defences. The neat little moat of a deposit account. The dykes of decision – we shall do that next, or that. But for a romance to keep going you need a mansion beside a lake, occasional stormy weather, a grand piano and the tragic death of one of the lovers. You can smile, you damn cynic! All right, maybe I've achieved that psychologically, she going there and I coming here. But that's not even a fraction of the story. I'm not here to perpetuate a romance. She had reasons, whether they were piously political or vaguely atavistic, I neither know nor care. Damn it, of course I care. But what concern is it of yours? Faced with nothing but repetition, what nobler act could we commit? I'd recommend it to you if you were to go back after you've finished playing this game of being a dropout. The only satisfaction I have in telling you all this is the one I derive from the knowledge that I am telling you nothing at all. It is a source of great comfort to me that I can utter words without at the same time offering a guarantee that they represent a comprehensive truth. Go on, raise your thin eyebrows to the skies if you like. I was beginning to enjoy the universal silence of my existence until you came. Silence was essential. I'll have to get back to silence. For words remind me of the disease I wished to escape from. Given an audience, it's all too easy to become melodramatic, to start telling a story, to invent – and you wouldn't know, you bastard, as long as the words seemed convincing. You'll have to go. Or, alternatively, I'll have to go. It has been no escape, I can tell you. Not if by escape you mean a dreamy turning away from responsible action. It hasn't been a bloody holiday, I can tell you. For you it's a holiday all right, I can see that. Frankly, I wish you hadn't come. I'd never worked out how I'd survive. I didn't even think of it in advance. I'd thought, only vaguely, that once I was in the forest then somehow my instincts would take over, that my senses would develop an animalistic keenness. Nothing of the bloody sort. I itched for cigarettes. I dreamed of long roads and Aston Martins. Whisky, wine and champagne tore at my lips with the claws of their memory. Instead of developing sharper senses, I was at first blinded by hunger. You listening? You may believe, if you like, that this is the truth. Observe, you distortion, you rippling water into which I look, observe how allegories break down into the constituents of chaos. Images of feasts gave way to the man at the zoo who threw a chunk of raw meat at an encaged beast. What, foolishness, vanity? Stripped, all gone; or intensified, for extremities are so subtle sometimes that they assume each other's identity. I'd go mad thinking of fish and chips while the forest seemed to have nothing to offer but the bark of oak trees. I began to remember the TV commercials for dog foods as I bow-wowed my four-limbed way across the fern-floor of the forest. Try learning to crawl sometimes to be nearer the earth, to be nearer the earth's tit-bits, you scavenger, picking on my bones in this Provençal heat. It took five days of gradually increasing hysteria, of wretched self-pity (oh, woe, woe, woe is me! see the breast bruised, look, here, it's not sun-burn!), of lying at nights curled up among leaves I'd torn from the oak trees, shivering and sobbing, five days of fear as much as hunger when it was no use telling my mind that I'd be all right, that I'd die soon or that sudden lightning would split open an oak and reveal a magical, the most perfect, the most wholesome, the largest loaf of bread, it took five days before I began to see again. It took another two days before I ate anything. My first meal was a squirrel. First when I saw a squirrel I rushed at it. It was a clumsy, desperate act. The squirrel furiously ran up a tree and looked down at me amazedly for a moment and disappeared among the higher branches, leaving me more wretched than ever. I sought out more squirrels. I began to think up ways of trapping them. It took me two days to catch one. Having caught it, what could I do? I hadn't taken a knife with me. I held it firmly by the tail and smashed its head against a tree. I was both sick at what I was doing and elated at the thought of getting my teeth into some meat. The bleeding, horrible mess in my hands, it now occurred to me that I had no means of skinning it and no means of lighting a fire. That didn't bother me for more than a second, for I was already tearing at the bloody thing with my overgrown nails, with my ravenous teeth. It must have taken me no more than a minute to chew its feeble flesh. My hands were bloody, my mouth was bloody, my chin, my chest. I ran to a stream, I lay at the stream's edge, washing my hands and my face, scooping up water to drink. At first the water coloured a little. Then it cleared. Then I was clean. That's when I first tasted what I'd eaten. I began to be sick, horribly sick. A squirrel! scolded a voice inside me as I vomited more than I had swallowed. I tried not to look at what I was throwing up, for my imagination suggested a greater horror and there was a moment when I thought that I had swallowed whole the squirrel's eyes, like oysters. Afterwards, I felt that more than my stomach had been purged. For a time, I felt a sweet relief. As if I'd learned to survive. That I wouldn't be destroyed, that death, if it came soon, would be of my own choosing. And how blind I'd been! There was so much in the forest besides oaks, besides squirrels! You ought to try it for yourself sometime, without an initiation ceremony conducted under my priest-like observation. You feel so much freer once you know that you can choose your own death. Once you know that you've left that old disease behind, that isolation has worked, made you immune. At last. Whom am I telling all this? *You?* You lousy deserter, my companion, my brother! You want the lurid details when all I care to give you is a muddled philosophy. Europe is choking my gullet, its poison infects my blood. Isn't that enough? And you want me to crack open my skull and show you what's happened to my brain! Europe is dying and its peoples play games at being alive. That's all my knowledge has made me understand. What can I do with such knowledge but allow myself to become absorbed by the earth, what can I do but let the loose, damn earth suck at my blood? I've not come to save myself. This is no bloody martyrdom. It's just a refusal to muck in with the phoney hopes of common humanity. The choice before European man now is either to attempt to postpone being killed by his own poison or to withdraw from the noxious gases which he mistakes for the rarefied atmosphere of human progress and emancipation and, withdrawing, to choose his own death. The former choice demands that the hypocrisy be maintained that the future is limitless and that an intensified universal materialism is a laudable goal. The choice to withdraw may be seen to be the negativism of despair, though I would say that it is the only sane act available to man. And somewhere, here in the Forêt de Murs if you like, or on the banks of the Rhine, let them begin again if they want to. I'm not bloody interested. I just don't want to know.

– Experiments towards existence, she said, a touch of mockery in her voice; at least he thought so, for he said to himself that he could be imagining things.

– Or towards death, he said, answering her seriously nevertheless. Total darkness can suggest sharp outlines to the imagination. Possibilities become real, and then what do we not suffer?

– A story, for example? she asked, her tone still ambiguous.

– Yes, he said. If you can understand it. Or have patience with the conventions.

Though he doubted himself if there were solutions. Certainly, withdrawal was not. There's the inevitability of commitment, he thought, of wanting to see the day through whether the jungle was in the Amazon or in Shepherd's Bush. Hypotheses, certainly, speculations towards some end. The continuation of the game, that's all.

It was still dark in the forest, but the sun must have risen over the Plateau de Vaucluse. It was damp in the forest. The sun's heat, he had noticed in recent days, no longer penetrated the mass of oak-branches which had rapidly been losing leaves and, ironically, letting in much more light than in the summer. The sodden oak-leaves on the floor of the forest had begun their slow disintegration. The hunters must have set out before dawn, for he could hear the dogs barking distantly. There was a soft, muffled yelping. The air about him seemed to whimper. He began to hear a palpitation in the earth as though his ears listened to his own heart through a stethoscope. He rose, excited, imagining the hunters shoot a deer and the wounded deer, running madly as though it could leave its wound behind, as though it could outstrip its injury and become whole again, come to him and die exhausted at his feet, offering him its flesh. He could hear a murmur like that of wind caught in a tunnel, or the ocean heard through one's window while one lay in bed at night. The dogs were barking clearly and loudly now, but must still be far away, he thought, for sounds in the silence of the forest seemed much nearer than they were. He heard the report of a gun. It was followed by a dead silence. Then several guns fired in quick succession, and the dogs began to bark louder than before. He imagined that they had shot at grouse or wild duck. He looked up as if expecting a bird to fall dead through the leafless branches of the oaks. He heard a horn sound, its long note echoing as if across a valley. There was a shuffling of horses' hooves in the air as if the hunters were changing direction. He could clearly hear the thudding of the horses' hooves, and the dogs barking. More gun shots tore through the forest. He imagined a hare, running at a desperate speed, suddenly being hit in the side, being flung across sideways and coming to a dead halt. There must be something, he thought, if they were shooting so much already. He stood in the open space between two trees, turning towards the direction from which the sounds seemed to be coming. He remembered a hunting scene from some film, the hounds foaming at the mouth, the huntsmen at full gallop, their riding-boots firmly in the stirrups, the tails of their red coats being flung up, the huntsmen's firm-set jaws, their faces flushed, their unblinking eyes, but not here, not here. He heard more shots and the dogs' hysterical barking and hoped that the sound came not from the film but from beyond the trees there where the darkness was being washed away by the slow pouring in of grey light. He imagined a fox swift and soft as the rotating beam of a searchlight which swishes across the darkness. He decided then that this could be his chance, that the random lottery of flying bullets could win him a prize. The barking and galloping was so loud now that he thought the huntsmen must be passing very near to where he stood. He looked up at the sky through the branches. It was the pale blue of early morning, a cold blue. When he looked around him again, he thought that he saw a moving blur. Perhaps it was a trick, for he had been imagining so many things, and there had been occasions in the past when his excited mind had confused bushes with animal life. What visions did not hunger suggest? If only, he thought, ah, that would make it so much easier. A chance, a lottery, a lucky number. That long note on the horn again, and the guns firing. Suddenly the blur resolved itself into a well-focused image and he saw the pack of hounds. Only for a fraction of a moment, however. For the image was quickly obliterated from his mind as his hand involuntarily jerked up to clutch at the point below his heart from where blood had begun to gush out and in that very brief moment while he held his hand at his chest he thought that he saw the huntsmen in a great hall with oak beams and a stone floor raising their glasses of champagne to toast one another in congratulation of a successful hunt while over the fire in the middle of the room his own skewered body slowly rotated, his blood dripping and his flesh turning a crisp brown, and saying, Cannibals, bloody cannibals, he fell forward upon the thick layer of oak-leaves.

– Is that the way you see it? she asked, looking up at the almond tree.

– We're past our mutual absurdities, he said. Impossible these ideas, and any finality, even that of the grave, is only another hypothesis.

We turn back to our dying, he remembered from somewhere, rising from his chair; he walked up and down the aisles between the desks, glancing over shoulders, pausing now to compliment an effort and now to offer advice. It was futile to expect them to work in silence, for they seemed more absorbed the more they consulted one another. Walking up an aisle, he heard a boy ask another:

– Got a rubber?

– No, mate, I'm on the pill, the other answered.

He walked on in the crisp February air. Oaks and silver birches, solemnly stoical of demeanour, were still, their leafless branches hanging limply. He walked through the darker passages of the wood like a child, playing out a jungle fantasy in a London heath, remembering what a pupil once said to him – Sir, I reckon you 'ave fannessies – and remembering, too, another desperate statement: For love of God seems dying, while at the back of his mind was that other line he had tried to remember from time to time and recalled only now. Dear dead women, with such hair, too – what's become of all the gold used to hang and brush their bosoms? I feel chilly and grown old. Tonight His frost will fasten on this mud and us, tonight the convoluted channels of the brain will spill their dreams.

– I have gone the whole round of creation: I saw and I spoke, he told the four sixth formers, concluding the lesson. Spoken too bloody much, he added to himself, wondering if they would realize that he had ended with a quotation. Let them figure it out, and if they can't, what does it matter, eh, Crump, literature and life are one. Each borrows from the other. When he was alone again in his classroom, tidying up his desk, it occurred to him that perhaps he *was* Puck, an airy thing; for if his imagination could conceive of something that was neither tangible nor immediately perceptible, then his own substance could equally well be an intangible and not immediately perceptible conception in another mind.

God's, eh, Crump? he laughed at himself, remembering: One long stretch of road. But frontiers, checkpoints, the armed soldiery of ideologies. A piece of silk torn into ribbons. This and much more, much more than twice all this on the shore, the wintry Atlantic raging, the borders of madness beside the sea which broke in splinters, the menacing breakers rising.